PRAISE FOR *THE OBSESSION*

"Sutanto has crafted a page-turning work of suspense that questions the line between romantic 'research' and stalking in the age of the internet, analyzing the roles played by abuse, misogyny, racism, and violence in contemporary relationships."

—*Booklist*

"Set against a Northern California private school backdrop, the sensational plot is riddled with twists that come at a furious pace... A suspenseful page-turner."

—*Kirkus Reviews*

"This tense, quick-moving thriller is also a thought-provoking story about the different shapes of abuse. Fans of high drama fiction with a dark edge, like Karen McManus's *One of Us Is Lying* or Gretchen McNeil's *#MurderTrending*, will be hooked."

—*School Library Journal*

"[A] taut, twisty thriller... Readers who enjoy their psychological thrillers paired with a bit of vigilante justice will find Delilah's final scene especially satisfying."

—*Bulletin of the Center for Children's Books*

ALSO BY JESSE Q. SUTANTO

The Obsession

Dial A for Aunties

JESSE Q. SUTANTO

Copyright © 2022 by Jesse Q. Sutanto
Cover and internal design © 2022 by Sourcebooks
Cover design by Erin Shappell
Cover photo by Carlos Caetano/Arcangel Images
Internal design by Ashley Holstrom/Sourcebooks

Sourcebooks and the colophon are registered trademarks of Sourcebooks.

All rights reserved. No part of this book may be reproduced in any form or by any electronic or mechanical means including information storage and retrieval systems—except in the case of brief quotations embodied in critical articles or reviews—without permission in writing from its publisher, Sourcebooks.

The characters and events portrayed in this book are fictitious or are used fictitiously. Any similarity to real persons, living or dead, is purely coincidental and not intended by the author.

All brand names and product names used in this book are trademarks, registered trademarks, or trade names of their respective holders. Sourcebooks is not associated with any product or vendor in this book.

Published by Sourcebooks Fire, an imprint of Sourcebooks
P.O. Box 4410, Naperville, Illinois 60567-4410
(630) 961-3900
sourcebooks.com

The Library of Congress has Cataloging-in-Publication data on file.

Printed and bound in Canada.
MBP 10 9 8 7 6 5 4 3

To my Menagerie Family,
the ones who first read this
book ten years ago and have
believed in it ever since.

CHAPTER 1

The morning I'm about to leave for Draycott Academy, Ibu almost makes me miss orientation because she has to take exactly eight pictures of me in my navy-blue Draycott blazer for good luck.

Normally, I'm cool with my mom's superstitions, but this is basically the first day of the rest of my life and we're gonna be late, and they'll kick me out of Draycott, and then I won't be able to go to college, and then I'll have no future and basically spend the rest of my life licking avocado husks for lunch or whatever it is that boomers think young people should do to get by.

"May I remind you that you're not Chinese and that Dad never even believed in all this stuff?"

"Shush." She takes two more pictures, counting under her breath. "Last one. Bigger smile!" After the last click, she straightens up. "I need to send these to your gong-gong. You know he'll count, make sure I got the number eight somewhere in there."

My frustration bleeds out in a small sigh. Ibu is right. My late dad's dad is the exact sort of petty patriarch who would hold it against my mother if she didn't take the right number of pictures on such an important day. Not because he cares about me, grandkid number 1724386, but because he'd grab any excuse he can to prove to the family how my dad made the biggest mistake of his life by marrying my mother—a native Indonesian instead of a Chinese-Indonesian.

As soon as she's done, she moves with superspeed, grabbing things off the kitchen counter before rushing me out of the house like I'm the one holding things up. And then we're off on the three-hour drive to my new school.

Draycott Academy. School for the elite, as in kids who are most definitely not me. I swear, even my new uniform knows it's not meant for people like me; my navy-blue blazer keeps snagging on my ragged nails, and already I have a small stain on my plaid skirt. Maybe from OJ, maybe from the Javanese sugar syrup I covered my pancakes in this morning. It's like my entire outfit is rebelling against me.

Ever since I got the offer from Draycott, I've been having this nightmare of being greeted by an admin who looks like she was built by an AI. Basically someone who looks like Betsy DeVos. "I'm so sorry, Lia," AI Betsy would say, "but there's been a mistake with your scholarship. You see, this school is a jewelry box, and you are not a diamond." And then she'd flick me away like a piece of lint.

No matter how many times I try telling myself that I belong here, that they sought me out for track, telling me I was "the next Usain Bolt," I can't shake this feeling deep in my core that I'm all wrong for this place. That no matter how fast my legs are, they can never outrun my background.

The sight of Draycott Academy doesn't soothe my nerves. The place is gorgeous, tucked into the lush, green hills of Northern California. The sloping, red roof of the school peeks over the top of cypress trees as we drive down an aggressively manicured lawn. Then the line of trees ends, and suddenly we see Draycott in all its glory; a palace masquerading as a boarding school. My mouth goes dry at the sight of the main building. It's an eff you to the laid-back style of most Californian architecture. Tall, imposing, and so utterly extra.

Ibu slides into a parking spot, between a Jaguar and a Benz, and takes off her seat belt.

"Mom, what are you doing?" I say.

"I want to see this school. And call me Ibu. I don't like it when you pretend you're not Indo. And I need to take pictures for the family—"

"I'll send you pictures!" The thought of my mom going

into ridiculous, gravity-defying poses to get the perfect angle for her pictures is making me shrill.

"Oh, alright. You don't want me here, I get it."

"It's not like that." I mean, it sort of is.

Ibu smiles at me, but it's strained. "Got you a present."

"Really?"

She takes something out of her bag. It's an old pair of shoelaces. From my very first track shoes.

"Wow." It's like a punch straight to the heart. I can't believe she kept these tattered things all these years. "Bu—"

"I'm so proud of you." She tucks my hair behind my ear, her eyes filling with tears. "You got your kris?"

I pull out my pendant from under my shirt. The pendant is an actual metal kris the length of my pinkie. The curvy edges are sharp enough to cut someone, so it's always kept in a golden sheath. I've worn it ever since I was too little to know what a kris was. As with everything Ibu makes me do, it's for good luck.

"Just keep it on you at all times, okay? Don't tempt the fates. Now go before I change my mind and take eighty-eight pictures of you in this place."

I laugh through my tears and plant a kiss on each of her brown cheeks before getting out of the car. I take deep breaths as she drives away, then I turn back to look at my new school.

I've seen it online, but nothing prepares me for actually

being here. If this were a hotel, it's the kind that would have bellhops swanning around with top hats and white gloves. But here, instead of a bellhop, there's a pretty, Asian girl. She's wearing jeans and a light-pink sweater. Why isn't she wearing the school uniform?

Then it hits me. It's Saturday. We don't have to wear the school uniform today. Argh. Is there a tree I can change behind?

But too late; I've been spotted. The girl waves at me with a smile.

"Hi, Lia Set—ser—eye wan?"

"It's pronounced Set-ee-ah-one, but don't worry about it. Just Lia will do." My surname, Setiawan, has tripped up more people than the rogue step at my old school.

"Welcome! I'm Beth, your RA. I'll show you around and help you get settled in and everything. Oh, you look great in our uniform."

"Um, I should change out of it. I totally forgot it's Saturday."

"Don't worry about it. You could take off the blazer. You must be dying in it."

I am, in fact, dying in it. I wasn't expecting such warm weather. Damn you, climate change. But underneath the blazer, I'm wearing a Walmart shirt with a sad rhinoceros saying, "Extinction Sucks," and now I can't remember what possessed me to wear this shirt today, of all days.

"Oh, I'm fine. Don't worry about me!" I chirp, while sweat slowly trickles down my back.

"Okay, come on in, we can drop off your bags at reception. They'll send them over to your room."

The front doors sweep open. I step inside. And pause.

It's impossible not to stop and gape at the main hall. It's like something out of Harry Potter. The floor is a dark-chocolate wood draped with thick, intricate rugs that swallow people's footsteps. On the right is a large reception desk, inlaid with rich, green leather. The reception desk people are dressed in tailored black suits and speak in low voices, which makes them seem über-important.

"You okay?" Beth says.

I hurriedly close my mouth. Be. Cool. "Yeah." I walk after her and try to look like all of this is nothing special to me. There are about a half dozen other kids in here, checking in. None of them gives any of this a second glance—not the giant fireplace, not the chandelier, not the life-size paintings smiling benevolently down at us. Beth bypasses the line of students and gestures at someone. A second later, a bellboy appears—complete with hat and white gloves—and whisks away my bags before I can say a thing.

"Ready to go?"

Beth opens the French doors with a flourish, leading me out onto a huge quad. There is so much rolling greenery, dotted with students just enjoying the morning. I remember reading in my welcome booklet that the school grounds are about two hundred acres. I didn't know, then, how big that is. Now I do. It is hella big.

As we walk, I study my new schoolmates from the corner of my eye. Need to get a feel for the place, figure out how to fit in. Or at least how to not stick out so much. None of them, I realize with a sinking feeling, are wearing their school blazer. A few are wearing T-shirts, so I take off my blazer and stuff it into my backpack.

"Oh my god, I love your shirt!" Beth says. "What is that, Prada?"

Is she being sarcastic? I honestly can't tell. "Um."

"Aiya, I'm just kidding. That's obviously Kenzo, isn't it? I adore their spring line, but my mom wouldn't let me get any until after I decluttered. She really got into Marie Kondo's show and hired her to declutter our house—"

"Wait, your mom hired. Uh. Marie Kondo? As in the Marie Kondo from Netflix?" I say.

Beth stares at me. "Yeah. Why?"

Does she honestly not see how crazy pants that is? "No reason. Yeah, everyone I know hired her too," I joke.

She nods, completely serious. "Same. Anyway, Marie said I needed to go through all my stuff one by one, and I tried, I really did, but that would've taken me the entire summer, and then I'd have to go through my second closet, and then my third, and..."

How many closets does she have?!

Beth doesn't even get the chance to finish her list of closets before a shriek, raw and desperate, pierces the air.

"What the hell's that?" Beth says, but I'm already running, instinct taking over my entire body. The screaming is still going on, an animalistic cry that's an almost-physical yank. Beth struggles to keep up with me, but there's no chance of catching up; my legs are the sole reason I'm here, after all.

I'm one of the first to get there, and I have no idea what to do.

It's another Asian girl. It strikes me for a fleeting second that there are a lot more Asians in this school than I thought there would be. She's gorgeous, like K-pop-level beautiful. And she's kicking and screaming like a wild animal. Two campus policemen are literally hauling her out of the building.

The sight makes me feel sick. It's wrong, seeing this beautiful girl being dragged away like that. My entire being is revolting against it. I take a step forward, not sure what I'm about to do, and another campus cop appears, out of nowhere, and says, "Stay back, kid." His voice is steel. His hand moves towards his holster. No guns, but he has a Taser. My legs go all trembly. I used to think that's just an expression, but they're literally trembling, the weight of my body suddenly too much to bear.

Other kids start to arrive. Thank god. With only me here,

I won't be able to do much. But with more people around, we'd be able to stop them. We'd—

The guy next to me takes out his phone and aims it at the struggling girl.

Video evidence. Yes. The more the better. This is so clearly wrong. But as I scramble for my phone, the guy stops recording and starts tapping on his phone, smiling. Then he says to his friend, "Sent to DD!"

Everyone around me looks at their phone. Smirks appear. A couple of kids are openly giggling at whatever they see. Some are still recording the struggling, but I don't think they're doing it to help her. They're watching her futile fight with a hungry light in their eyes, shark grins on their faces.

What the hell's wrong with them?

I take a step forward. A hand clamps down on my shoulder.

"Lia!" Beth says. "Don't."

"We need to help her!"

The girl's voice has broken, her screams now hoarse, unintelligible moans. The desperation in her voice makes my chest tighten. I need to—

"Stay out of it. Seriously." Beth is tiny, but her grip is unforgiving.

I'm about to pull away when someone steps out of the same building the girl and the cops came out of. An adult. Relief floods my veins. He'll do something.

But he doesn't. He strolls down the stone steps slowly, leisurely, holding something to his face. A bloodstained handkerchief. Something about him makes me instinctively shrink away.

Someone in the distance shouts. A boy, gangly, with a mop of dark hair. "Sophie! Soph—what's going on?"

The phones are whipped around and aimed at him.

At the sight of him, the girl renews her struggle. "Logan! Help me! You gotta tell them! It wasn't me! It was him!"

"Stay back," the campus police thunders, shoving the boy away with a meaty hand. The other two officers strengthen their grip on the girl. Her feet scrape uselessly across the gravel as they carry her away. I move toward them, but Beth stops me again.

"Seriously, Lia. Don't. You don't wanna be involved in the mess that is Sophie Tanaka."

"But—"

Something makes me look at the man with the handkerchief, his blond hair dazzling in the sunlight. He's closer now. Close enough for me to see his expression. He's not smiling or anything, but I know, I would bet money on it, he's enjoying this. He stares at the girl until she's almost out of sight, and he doesn't blink. A predator watching its kill's last breaths.

"Poor Mr. Werner," Beth says. "Looks like Sophie punched him in the face. Man, see what I said about not getting involved with that brand of batshit?"

I just stand there stupidly, gaping at her. "What's gonna happen to that girl?"

"They'll put her somewhere safe until her parents pick her up."

"Where?"

"You know, I've never thought of that." She taps a nearby girl on the shoulder. "Elle, do you know where they're taking Sophie? Do we have like, a little school jail or something?"

Elle shrugs. "Probably to the medical center so she can get sedated."

The guy next to Elle snorts. "It's gonna take a hell of a lot of drugs to get her down. She's probably high as shit right now. Did you see her eyes?" Then his gaze rests on me. "Oh, hey. New kid."

Heads turn. Eyes crawl over me. My skin bursts into gooseflesh. I want to run, to dive behind the first bush I come across.

"Enough of that," Beth trills. "You guys are going to scare her away." She steers me away from the crowd. "Sorry about that. I promise you that's not an everyday occurrence here."

I try to shake off the weight of my schoolmates' gazes on our backs. God, what is this place? Dread has suffused every single one of my veins. "Is that girl going to be okay?"

Beth waves off my concern. "She'll be fine. Sophie used to be in our year, but she started doing drugs—not the cool designer ones, but the really gross, common ones—and she just went in a downward spiral. Came to class one day barely dressed, started ranting about all sorts of crazy stuff. They kicked her out after that."

The sense of dread is quickly replaced by a sense of *what the hell?* "Cool designer drugs?" Has Chanel started foraying into pharmacology?

"You know, like Spice, or Gravel, or Molly."

What the hell is Spice or Gravel? I've heard of Molly, but the others are new to me.

Beth laughs at my expression. "I'm kidding, Lia! Obviously we don't do such things here. I have no idea where Sophie got her drugs from, but yeah, it was scary. I hope she gets help. I don't know how she got back in here. Security's pretty tight. Speaking of security..." She rummages in her handbag and hands me a card with my name and picture on it. "Here is your student ID. You need it to get into all the buildings and to pay for your meals and stuff."

"Thanks." I almost take my wallet out but decide against it at the last minute. Show Beth my ragged, little cotton coin purse I'm using as a wallet? Nooo, thank you. I stuff the card into my back pocket.

"Anyway! Back to the tour." Beth's already walking ahead. "That's Highland Hall," she says, pointing to the building that Sophie had been dragged out of. "It's where all most of the freshman and sophomore classes are taught."

Looking at the pristine, majestic building, it's hard to imagine that just moments ago, we witnessed someone my age being dragged bodily out of it.

Beth leads me past Highland Hall and points out over a dozen more buildings as we walk. By the time she takes me to a building called Mather and tells me it's the girls' dorms, I feel dazed. There's no chance in hell I'm going to be able to remember where everything is. And why can't they call the buildings what they are instead of naming them after dead people?

"That building over there's Mansfield. It's the boys' dorm. We're not allowed in each other's dorms after six p.m. Though there are ways around it, of course." She winks at me, then unlocks the front door of Mather with her card and sweeps inside.

"Holy crap." The lobby of the girls' dorm is so grand, it takes my breath away. Not exaggerating; I actually do feel winded, surrounded by the gorgeous interior. Lots of mahogany and ornate furniture that looks way too breakable to be part of a high school. Larger-than-life oil paintings of women in historical garb line the wood-paneled walls. Rosa Parks, Rosalind Franklin, Marie Curie. That's one hell of a bar to set.

I hurry after Beth down a side hallway, where the bedrooms are. A whiteboard hangs outside each room, each one filled with all sorts of doodles and notes. A few of the doors are open, and I catch glimpses of girls listening to music, playing on their computers, or chatting with each other. A couple wave and smile at me, which is somewhat surprising. In my old school, new kids are examined with sullen suspicion before being shuffled into one of the accepted categories—shanker or shanked. I'm kidding. Or am I?

A couple of the rooms we pass are empty, with their doors open. Shiny laptops and speakers lay unattended on the desks.

"Uh, how come people here don't lock their doors?"

Beth looks confused.

Am I really going to have to explain the concept of theft? What kind of amazing bubble have I entered? "Aren't people afraid that stuff might go missing?"

"Oh!" Beth laughs. "Draycott's super safe. We've never had any problems with anything like that." She hesitates. "What's your neighborhood like?"

Metal detectors. Lockers wrenched open and looted. Cars stolen right from the school parking lot. "Um, not like this." Abort, abort. I most definitely do not want to be talking about South Melville to anyone here. "What about you? Where are you from?"

"I'm from San Marino."

"Wow." I've been there once, when some fluke had us competing with San Marino Prep. The houses there are gigantic, bordered by rosebushes, Benzes and Lambos in the driveways.

"Yeah, it's nice. I miss it sometimes. Anyway, here is your room. I'll let you do the honors."

My heart thuds. My own room at last. The apartment I live in with Ibu is a one-bedroom. Enough said.

I push open the door and pause for a moment so I don't lose it and start squealing.

My new room. It's beautiful. Okay, it's probably pretty standard, as far as rooms go: single bed, study desk, wardrobe. But it also has a huge window overlooking the quad. Dappled sunlight streams through the window, dust motes glittering as they swirl lazily above the study desk (MY study desk!), and quite honestly, it looks magical AF. I take off my shoes—I'm not a caveman—and run to the window. I was going to fling it open all dramatically, but it's old and not the flinging type. I end up grunting as I struggle to slide it up, where it wedges about a foot up. Well, never mind. The rest of the room more than makes up for it.

"Do you like it?" Beth is actually biting her lip, as if worried I might be disappointed by the room. I want to hug her.

"I love it! This is—it's totally cool." I try, and fail, to wipe the idiotic grin off my face.

Beth smiles. "I'm glad to hear that. So this is where your tour ends. Any questions?"

I shake my head.

"I'm just two doors down if you need me."

"Cool."

After she leaves, I start unpacking and find something lukewarm at the bottom of my duffel bag. Ack. Ibu had insisted on packing me some of her homemade pisang goreng. I told her no, it would be the death of me to have everyone see me unwrapping this greasy package of fried bananas, but since when does she listen? And I hate to admit it, but I'm sort of glad she'd ignored me.

I'm in the midst of inhaling the homey scent when a shrill giggle from the corridor makes me jump. A couple of girls gallop past my room, shouting and laughing in that obnoxious louder-than-necessary way.

"—see her boobs? They got crazy big over the break!"

"Uh, yeah, all thanks to Dr. Carroll. Krista said they cost her like ten grand."

"Are you serious? That's such a steal. Oh my god, I'm totally going to ask my mom for a pair when we go back for summer—"

I release my breath only after they're out of earshot. Then, hating myself, I stride to the trash can and throw the package away. *Sorry, Ibu.*

I go back to unpacking, pulling out a faded blue-and-gold shirt. My old track uniform. It's a security blanket for my soul, albeit a ratty, smelly one. After locating an ideal spot above a chest of drawers, I take a pin from my bag and stick it in. But as soon as I let go of the shirt, it slides off the wall and ends up behind the drawers.

Dammit. I grip both ends of the drawers and pull. As it moves, I catch a flash of red written on the wall behind it.

WERNER IS GUILTY.

The words are scrawled in red, ground into the wall with so much force, I can almost taste the hatred behind them. Oh-kaaay. This is weird. It is, right? Graffiti's everywhere in South Melville. But here? It seems weird. Also, who's Werner and what's he or she guilty of? The name sounds familiar.

Beth's voice comes back to mind. "Did she punch Mr. Werner?" she'd said, as we watched the girl being taken away.

So. Mr. Werner's that creepy teacher who looks like a possessed Ken doll. Which means...this room belonged to Sophie. The girl with the desperate eyes, shrieking like a lamb at the slaughterhouse. She's flunked out, and here I am, taking her place.

CHAPTER 2

It's none of my business. It's not my fault she got kicked out. Even as my heart thunders a sickening beat and I feel like ripping my skin off, I keep myself busy unpacking. But in the silence of my room, I can hear Sophie's animal shrieks, and guilt churns in my gut, as though I were the one who expelled her. Finally, I put my earphones in and dive into arranging all my stuff around the room until it feels less like Sophie's old room and a little more like mine.

By the time I'm done, I'm starving. I comb my hair and look for my student ID, so I can go grab some dinner, but it's nowhere to be found.

I can't possibly tell Beth I've lost the card right after she told me not to. She'll think I'm a giant flake. Welp. I'll just starve until I can get a replacement card. Food is overrated anyway.

Later that evening, I stand outside of the main building and peer through the windows like one of those sad newspaper boys in old movies. The school has the fanciest dining hall ever, complete with a seven-foot fireplace. A board outside announces that tonight's dinner is roasted, free-range chicken with thyme jus accompanied by winter vegetables. I have no idea what "thyme jus" is, but I know I want to put it in my face. I wander to the side of the entrance, kicking at the grass despondently.

I haven't eaten much the past two days, because the very thought of leaving everything behind and coming here made my insides clench up and go, *Nope.* And now I'm stuck out here, with my stomach telling me I'm a complete idiot. Tears prick my eyes.

Do not cry. Don't you dare cry.

But I can't help it. Everything's coming down in a sudden crush, and it's just. So much. I'm a thousand miles away from Ibu. Okay, more like eighty-seven miles, but it's as good as a thousand. I want my mommy, dammit.

I sink to the ground and hug my knees to my chest. "God, I'd kill for some of that pisang goreng," I moan. Why did I throw it away? My stomach grumbles again. "Shut up," I say to it.

"Um…sorry. Was I thinking too loud?"

I look up, and whoa. It's the most beautiful guy I've ever laid eyes on.

Everything about him is positively edible, and I swear I'm not just saying that because I'm so freaking hungry. His hair is a carefully crafted mess, his gaze steady in a non-creepy way, and he has that classic, masculine superhero jaw. There's even a hint of a cleft in it. I've never met anyone in real life with an actual butt chin. It's indescribably, ridiculously cute. Would it be completely awful if I say I fall in love then? Just a little bit of falling. More of a trip, really. People have fallen in love for far stupider reasons, right? Well, I definitely fell in lust, anyway.

Quick, must say something mind-blowing. Something so hilarious and brilliant that he'll immediately fall in love with me. I open my mouth. "Bwuh?"

Damn it, self!

He smiles. "I said, 'Was I thinking too loudly?'"

"No." I stand up, busying myself with brushing invisible lint off my jeans so I don't have to look at his ridiculously perfect face. "I was just talking to myself. It's a thing I do sometimes. It helps me think. And stuff." He's smirking. He's smirking *at me*. I end the sentence in a mumble.

"Sorry, I wasn't laughing at you. I talk to myself too. Not because it helps me think. More because, you know, I'm pretty charming, so I can't resist myself."

I can't help laughing.

He holds out his hand. "Danny. Danny Wijaya."

"Wijaya? No way. Are you Indonesian?"

His eyes widen. "Wow, you're like the first person to get it right. I'm Chinese-Indonesian."

"Me too!" I cry. "Uh, I mean, I'm native Indonesian. Not Chinese. Well, I'm half-Indonesian. My mom is Indonesian. My dad's Chinese-Indonesian." Could I possibly say *Indonesian* more? But seriously, what are the odds that I'd meet another Indo here?

"Waduh, ngga sangka bisa ketemu orang Indo disini," Danny says.

"Right? I was just thinking the same thing! What are the chances?"

We both laugh. Then there's a moment of silence as we both grin widely at each other.

"Sorry, my Bahasa is terrible," I say. "I can understand it, but when I try to speak it, the accent's all wrong, and... yeah."

"Sounds like how I am when it comes to Mandarin. You never told me your name, by the way."

"Oh. Right. Lia. Setiawan."

"Did I hear you say something about pisang goreng?"

My instinct is to deny it, but he's Indo. He's even pronouncing it right, rolling the *r* in *goreng* with the tip of his tongue tickling the back of his teeth so it comes out sharp and thin, not at all like an American *r*. It reminds me so much of Ibu that my heart squeezes painfully, just for a second. "Yeah, my mom makes the best pisang goreng. She even drizzles homemade caramel sauce and grates some cheese over it—"

"Okay, I need this pisgor right now. You have some, right?"

It makes me grin to hear him do what Indos do all the time—combine two or more words into one short one. "Um, actually, I kind of freaked out a little and threw it away. Sorry," I mumble.

"Coming here does weird things to people. The first week I was here, I was so homesick, I cried myself to sleep every night."

"Aww."

Danny puffs out his chest. "I mean, I cried in a very manly way. Real masculine tears."

"Oh, I'm sure."

"I even tried to grow a beard to show my grief."

"A beard of sadness?"

"Exactly. But I hadn't really started growing facial hair yet, so the beard didn't happen."

"To be fair, you'd probably still struggle now."

"Ouch." He mimes a dagger stabbing into his chest. "But yes, you're right. It's a curse on us Asians."

"Speak for yourself, I grow beards just fine."

By this time, we're both grinning so hard, my face is actually hurting.

"How come you're not having dinner?"

"Oh." This is awkward. "Uh." Quick, think of a good reason that doesn't involve me losing my ID on my first day. "I already ate," I say, just as my stomach gives a growl so loud, it sounds like it's right next to our heads. Damn you, stomach. Read the room!

Danny raises his eyebrows.

"I lost my student ID."

"Oh, pfft. Come on, I'll swipe you through."

I'm so hungry by now that I'm contemplating eating my own foot. "Thanks. I'll buy you your next meal," I say, as we walk into the bustling warmth of the dining hall.

"Nah, don't worry about it, it's no big deal," he says, and the last three words drop like sizzling coals all the way into my hollow stomach. I'm in a place full of kids whose parents are paying upward of sixty grand a year in school fees alone. Of course, paying for a meal is small change to him. It makes me feel tiny. And stupid. And really, really poor.

I'm about to tell him to forget it when he takes out his phone.

"Sorry, gotta take this call," he says. I didn't even hear it ring. "Hey, Uncle. What's up? Gah, did I do that? Thanks for checking. I'll be there." He hangs up and turns to me. "I gotta go. I left my laptop in my uncle's car."

Probably the randomest reason anyone has ever used for flaking out, which means it must be true.

Before I can tell him it's fine and that I don't need him to pay for my meal, he leans toward me—holy shit, we're standing so close, I can see the freckles on his cheeks, aaaah—and swipes his card across the machine. The little gate swings open and Danny ushers me through. "I'll see you around, Lia."

"Wait—" I don't want your stupid handout! (Just make out with me!)

But he's gone, jogging out of the dining hall with the kind of athletic grace that pulls the eye to his butt. I mean, really now. You can't not look.

"Checking out Danny's butt?"

I start, my cheeks bursting into flames. Beth's right behind me. Jesus, the girl prowls as noiselessly as a leopard.

She laughs, shaking her head. "Don't look so guilty. We've all done it. Danny Wijaya's butt is a gift to Draycott. C'mon, you're super late. We're all on our entrees already." With that, she leads me to her table, where a Black girl and a white girl are eating. They wave at me with friendly smiles. The Black girl is Samantha—"But you can call me Sam"—the white girl is called Grace, and they're both very pretty and intensely likable.

"Saw you checking out Danny Wijaya back there," Sam says, winking.

My cheeks burst into flames. "I wasn't—"

"Hey, there's no shame in that. That boy is too hot for his own good," Grace says.

"Uh-oh," Sam says, "should I be worried?"

"Shut up, you know you'll always be my bae," Grace says, rolling her eyes. She turns back to face me. "Tell us about yourself, Lia. What's your origin story?"

Cute butts and friendly people. Maybe I can get used to boarding school.

First thing on the agenda the next morning is to get a new student ID. Luckily, all it takes is a harried explanation and one super judgmental eyebrow arch from the admin lady, and less than a minute later, I'm walking out of the admin building—sorry, Castor—with a shiny, new card.

Outside, I run into Beth and quickly stuff the card inside my bag.

"I'm on my way to sketch the roses in the Eastern Gardens. Wanna come with?" she says.

"Sure." I've never known anyone in real life who actually sketches flowers in the gardens, and I want to hug Beth because gosh, could anyone be more wholesome?

The sun is out in typical Californian glory, spilling over the grounds like liquid gold, making every color jump. The rolling grounds are crossed with small, undulating paths lined with pink peonies and deep-purple hydrangeas. It's the kind of place that makes you want to be a better person, just so you don't spoil the scenery.

Beth chooses a spot and sits on the grass. I sit next to her and watch as she takes out a drawing pad and several pencils. "How're you liking Draycott?"

"This place is unreal."

"Unreal in a good way or in a Jordan Peele girl-get-outta-here way?"

I laugh. "Definitely not the Jordan Peele way. It's just—look at you!" I gesture at Beth, who's sitting there in a pristine, knee-length dress, her feet tucked underneath her, drawing pad on her lap. "You look like an Insta model. Except you're not even posing for a picture, you're naturally Insta-ready."

"Ha! Well, I'm definitely far from perfect," she says, starting her sketch, her hand moving in sure, strong strokes across the page.

Something about the way she says it reminds me of what Sophie wrote on the wall of my dorm room. I'm about to tell her about the graffiti when her phone *boops*.

"Ooh, new Dirt!" She puts down her pencil and slips her phone out of her pocket.

"New dirt?"

"Did I not tell you about Draycott Dirt? Okay, you need to download it ASAP."

Less than a minute later, Draycott Dirt has been downloaded onto my phone and Beth is walking me through it. Which is good, because the app is overwhelming.

"It's basically like a PostSecret app," Beth says. "You create a username, then you post new 'Dirt' and people can upvote or downvote and make comments or whatever. The only rule is that it's all got to stay anonymous."

My head swims as we scroll through what seems like hundreds of thousands of posts revealing all sorts of nasty little secrets. So-and-so's a junkie, so-and-so's self-harming, so-and-so is smashing so-and-so's boyfriend. I can almost hear the kids behind each post, whispering, their voices layering on top of one another until it becomes a cacophony that threatens to drown me. And yet, somehow, I'm unable to tear my eyes away from the app. I want to know every piece of dirt there is to know.

"You can sort through the posts using the different categories or by date. Here are the latest posts—oh." Her mouth sets into a grim line as she reads.

Posted by: @MagicHands

Anyone seen the Sophie replacement yet?

Bangable—yes, no? #askingforafriend

Reply from: @SoDafferent

Eh. Bangable with beer goggles. A downgrade from Sophie for sure, even if she's not batshit insane. #meh

Reply from: @Scribofile

Y'alls are forgetting the most important thing,

which is that she's not here to replace Soph. She's here on a track scholarship, which means she's here to replace @TrackQueen, LOL.

Reply from: @TrackQueen

I would love to see the bitch try. #whatever

There's a moment of thick silence. Beth clears her throat and pats my shoulder gently. "People tend to be idiots on DD."

I manage a small smile. "Do you know who's who on there?" As in, who the hell is @TrackQueen and why am I here to replace her?

"I have my suspicions, but don't try to figure out who's who on DD, because there are plenty of trolls and it'll just drive you crazy."

I want to tell her that not knowing who's talking shit about me is going to drive me crazy, but Beth's already turned her attention back to her painting, and not wanting to irritate the first friend I've made here, I press my mouth shut and swallow the knot of unease. Staying out here in the garden makes me feel even more exposed, and not for the first time since I arrived at Draycott, I get the feeling of being watched and scrutinized. A coil of dread stirs deep in my gut. What if they find me lacking? Would I be the next Sophie?

CHAPTER 3

Somehow, I manage to stop thinking about all that's off about this place long enough to finally fall asleep that night, but I jolt awake what seems like moments later.

It's not even light out. My mouth is sandpaper dry, my heart doing its own mid-distance sprint. I'm about to have my very first track practice. At my fancy new school. The whole reason I'm here. Holy shit.

I roll out of bed and take out my new clothes. Draycott provides its athletes with all the bells and whistles—I even have socks in matching school colors. I put the whole thing on and look in the mirror. Okay, I look ridiculous. All this maroon and gold.

"Hey, I'm Lia," I say, striking a pose.

Nope. I take off the outfit and put on my old gear instead, but as a compromise, I leave my new socks on.

The school grounds look so different now, in the half dark. There's no one around, and the grass is all dewy and cold. It feels like I've walked into a fairy-tale forest.

I'm the first one at practice. Now what? I walk around the track for a bit, getting a feel for it. Look at this rubber. No holes or tears. And in the middle, the grass is pristine, uniform in length. The grass is way greener on this side, no doubt about that.

The clang of the stadium doors startles me. A tall, white girl with purple hair walks through the doors, yawning and stretching her neck.

"Hi," I call out.

She stops mid-yawn and stares at me.

"Um. I'm Lia." I hold out my hand for her to shake, but she just looks at it without moving. I tuck my hand into my pocket, my cheeks burning. "Anyway." I turn away, pretending to be busy with...something. Anything.

"You a transfer student or something?"

"Yeah!" Take it down a notch. "Yeah." God, I'm not doing well. But she's my teammate. And I want—no, I need—to fit in with my new team. I need it so much, it's almost a physical ache.

"Freshman?" she says, and her voice is almost accusatory. Maybe I don't have to get along with this particular teammate.

"Sophomore. You?"

"Huh. Didn't know they let non-freshmen in," she says, and then she turns and starts jogging around the track.

That went well.

I keep my eyes down and focus on stretching my hamstrings, trying to ignore the awful, squirmy feeling in my stomach. The stadium doors clang open again, and this time, it's the coach.

Without breaking stride, she calls out, "Hey, girls! You're here early. Is that a new hair color, Stacey?" She grins wide when she gets to me. "New kid. I've been looking forward to meeting you properly. I'm Coach Iverson," she says, catching my hand in a strong, reassuring grip. "You've got some impressive records, young lady. Glad to have you here."

It's impossible not to return the huge smile. "Glad to be here, Coach."

"Good timing too! Heard about the budget cuts at your old school."

I feel the smile slipping at the reminder that there's no longer a track team at South Melville High. If I don't cut it here, I have no chance at a college scholarship.

"Did you get an invite to the team's Google Calendar? It's got all of our meets on it and reminders to see the school nurse every two weeks."

"Every two weeks? What for?"

"Drug test," Stacey pipes up from behind me. She reties

her ponytail with a smirk. "Ever since Sophie got busted for drugs, the school's cracking down. You don't have anything to hide, do you?"

What's her problem? The squirmy feeling in my stomach hardens into iron. "Do *you*?"

"Hey, no. None of that," Coach Iverson says, clicking her fingers between us like we're two naughty dogs. The doors swing open again, and a few more girls walk into the stadium. Coach Iverson waves them over and has us stand in a circle. "Girls, meet your new teammate, Lia Setiawan. She's a mid-distance runner, freshly recruited from South Melville."

At the mention of South Melville, lips curl into a sneer. One girl snorts out loud.

"Is that how you're gonna treat our new star runner?" Coach Iverson says.

Oh god. I'm sure she said that to be funny, but she doesn't know the stuff that's been said on DD. All that crap about me replacing TrackQueen. Which one of these people is TrackQueen? Everyone here is wearing her very best resting bitch face. Anyone here could be TrackQueen. My nerves are so tightly wound by now, I just want to crawl into a hole and hide.

Coach Iverson tells everyone to introduce themselves for my benefit. I forget all their names almost immediately, except the mean one with the purple hair. Stacey Hoffman.

I try to ignore the dirty looks as Coach divides us into

our training groups. As we go through our warm-ups, I start feeling better. Who cares if my new teammates hate me? I'm not here because of them. I'm here to run. We go into position. This is it. Time to shine.

The whistle blows, and everything—all the bullshit like DD, Danny, and my new teammates' attitude—is shaken off. There's no room for anything else but me and the track. I'm a shooting star, blazing past everyone, and the only sound in my ears is the pounding of my blood and my feet on the rubber. I hit the finish line way before anyone else does, and Coach whoops and rushes forward then hugs me, raving about breaking records and colleges and I don't know what else.

I know I'm being petty as hell, but when I catch Stacey looking at me, I give her a wink. She freezes, then turns away. Ha.

A couple of the other girls actually congratulate me, which is really nice.

When practice ends, I trudge to the locker room, exhausted but happy, half-listening to the chatter among my teammates. Someone slams into my shoulder as she walks past.

"Ow." I'm trying to see who it was when someone else shoulders past aggressively. "What the hell?" And then it feels like the entire team brushes past, shoulder after shoulder thumping into me until I'm suddenly alone, the girls' laughter fading away.

I've dealt with worse. This isn't anything new. Still. My breath is coming out all rapid, and it has nothing to do with running. Tears burn the backs of my eyes and I take a shuddery breath. Don't cry. Don't you dare cry.

"That's why you shouldn't show off during practice," someone says.

Ugh. Surly Stacey. Still, her sudden appearance jars the tears away, and I ignore her and head for my locker.

"Did you hear what I said?" she says.

I open my locker in time to see my phone screen light up. A DD post. My stomach takes a dive and spatters at my feet.

"I know you can hear me, so I'm just gonna say it: Stop showing off. It's not going to win you any friends."

I give her my best side-eye, ignoring the painful thump of my heart. "I don't care about winning over people if they're so insecure, they can't take competition."

"It's not that. It's Mandy Kim."

Mandy. An image of one of my new teammates flashes through my mind. Tall. Cheekbones a Kardashian would kill for. Or at least hire someone to kill for. "What about her?"

"There's only room for four mid-distance runners on varsity."

"So?"

"There are already four mid-distance runners on varsity."

Welp. "Not my problem."

Stacey laughs. Not a pleasant sound. "Oh, yes, it is.

Mandy's the slowest mid-distance runner. If you get on varsity, she's out. If you knock her out, there's going to be so. Much. Shit." She narrows her eyes at me. "Don't knock Mandy out."

Now it's my turn to laugh. "Are your heads so far up Mandy's ass that you can't see having me on your team is a good thing?"

"Mandy has dirt on everyone. Everyone. If you get on her shit list, you're done. You can kiss your scholarship goodbye."

"And if I don't make it to varsity, I'm also done. So I appreciate the advice, but I think this conversation is over."

My entire body is trembling by now.

Luckily, Stacey chooses to leave me alone after that. I sink onto the bench and pat my cheeks. Could've sworn they're on fire. My phone beeps. I struggle to swallow. Only one day and I've learned to dread that stupid DD alert. I unlock the screen and tap on the hated icon.

And.

It is so much worse than I expected.

There's an actual picture of me, talking to Danny outside the cafeteria. Whoever it is has put a blur filter over it so they don't break any rules, but it's very clearly me.

Posted by: @SweetNothings

Red alert! Heard the new kid was a total C U Next Tuesday on the track this morning! Grosssss. Why are we letting these people in, you guys?

Reply from: @Flapjackbro
Blame it on the school's "diversity" push or whatever. #PCpolice

Reply from: @Dollface
Why do we need a diversity push? The student body's like, literally half Asian. It's why we need #MAGA.

Reply from: @TrackQueen
Half EAST Asian, morons. Newbie is Southeast Asian. East Asian =/= Southeast Asian. SE Asia is the armpit of Asia, basically. That's where my fam gets our servants from.

Reply from: @Dollface
Isn't the whole of Asia the world's armpit? LOL.

Reply from: @TrackQueen
STFU, white trash.

Reply from: @SweetNothings
Omg so she's basically a maid like in that #Parasite movie?

Reply from: @TrackQueen

LMAO yesss, basically. Omg, that's the perfect name for her. Our little Parasite!

Reply from: @SiliconBrains

Uhh, are you all really as stupid as you seem? You've completely missed the point of that movie, which is about the rich preying on the poor.

Reply from: @DollFace

Uh, no it's not. It's about the servants being parasites, duh. It's exactly what the new kid's doing, because she's totally sucking up all our resources, too cheap to pay her own way here. #Parasite!

Reply from: @TrackQueen

Riiight? Anyway, babies, don't you worry, #Parasite will be out by midterms, I guarantee it.

The screen blurs, and that's when I realize I've got actual tears in my eyes. I wipe my eyes quickly, stuffing the phone back in my pocket before gathering all my things and running back to the dorm. I can't face another second in the locker room, knowing my teammates are going to come out of the shower at any moment.

Of course, back at the dorm, everyone's getting ready for the first class of the day, so there's a long line for the showers. Damn. At least here there's a chance people haven't checked DD—

"That's her," someone in the shower line whispers. Eyes turn toward me.

Okay, so everyone's checked DD. Great. It's fine. Totally fine. I can stand here, all sweaty, clutching my basket of toiletries, and pretend I can't hear what they're saying about me, a.k.a. Parasite. (Seriously, can't they have at least come up with something more creative?) I'm fine. Sure, I end up sobbing quietly in the shower, but only a little bit.

I can't face the thought of going to the dining hall all alone, so I stop by the common room to grab a couple of granola bars. There are three girls in there, scrolling through their phones. I recognize one of them as Anya, my next-door neighbor. I give her a hesitant smile, which she ignores, before saying in a loud whisper to her friends, "What is *that* she's wearing?"

"Bet she shops at Target," her friend replies, to which they all laugh.

"Actually, it's Walmart, so all of you can suck it." I get a flash of bitter satisfaction at their horrified faces. Then I grab the entire basket of breakfast snacks—muffins, granola bars, little individual boxes of cereal—and march out of there. I dump the basket in my room and rage-eat two entire muffins before my body goes, *Pls stop, kthx*.

Aaand now I'm stuck with a whole basket of food I can't possibly go through on my own. Also, I'm pretty sure this counts as stealing? This is so not the fresh start I'd had in mind. I wonder if Beth's seen the stuff they're saying about me on DD. Who am I kidding? Of course she has. What will she think? Will she no longer like me? I take the basket back to the common room, which is luckily devoid of Anya and her friends, and plonk it on the table.

All the way to my first class, I catch snatches of whispers and unfriendly stares. Inside my pocket, my phone is constantly buzzing with new replies to the DD post about me. I keep my head down and briskly walk into the building. It's worse inside the hallway, where the stares are more obvious and I can actually hear what they're saying about me (nothing nice). Room 2-C, where the heck are you?

My breath comes out in a whoosh when I finally locate the classroom. I just want to sit in the farthest, darkest corner of the room and put up my hood. Except I don't have a hood, because we're not allowed to wear hoodies in class. Argh.

Heads pop up meerkat-style when I walk inside the room. I ignore the looks and make my way to the back.

"Ew, do you smell that?" someone says.

Mandy. Oh man. She's in the same English Lit class as me? Why, universe?

Next to her, a boy with overly gelled hair grins and nods. "I sure do. What is it?" he says, theatrically.

Another boy leans over from behind them and says, "Smells like...some sort of parasite."

My insides knot so tightly, tighter than they already were, and that's saying something. With very little effort, I think I could actually puke right in their stupid faces. Do parasites even smell?

Somehow, I manage to make my way past the giggling asshats and fold my leaden body into a chair in the back row. I'm fine. This is fine. The teacher will be here soon, and—

As though thinking about the teacher summoned him, a tall, bespectacled man strides into the classroom. Oh no.

It's Mr. Werner.

He of the psychopathic smile who watched benignly while Sophie shrieked and struggled.

Okay. Chill.

I mean, for all we know, Sophie just lost it and took it out on him. Also, she'd punched him in the face, and he was probably grimacing instead of smiling. Yeah. Also, even if he was smiling, it has eff all to do with me. So. Head down, mind your own damn business, and everything will be fine.

"Welcome to English Literature 20B. I'm Mr. James Werner. You'll have seen on the syllabus that this is a tightly packed course, reserved only for the most advanced students—" He stops. "Oh. I see a face I don't recognize."

It's me.

He's staring right at me with his dead-fish stare.

"What's your name?"

"Lia. Setiawan." So many eyes on me, none of them particularly friendly.

"Students are normally required to do an interview before they can enroll for this class. Please stay behind for a bit after we're done."

An interview? Nobody told me that. When I was signing up for classes, the guidance counselor was all, "Great choices, Lia. You're good to go!"

I didn't think it would be possible for me to feel even worse than I already did, but yep. Feeling so much worse right now. There is no way I'm going to be able to pass an interview on English Lit, but I need an English Lit class to fulfill my core requirements, and this is the only one that fits in with my hectic track schedule.

"At least we won't have to deal with the smell for long," Mandy says, just loud enough for me to hear. The kids around her snicker. Mr. Werner does nothing. Figures.

I struggle to pay attention to the lesson, taking notes like my life depends on it. Maybe it's not so bad. The reading list is super packed, but I can make it work. When the class ends, I pack my stuff with sweaty hands. I wait for the others to file out of the room before making my way to Mr. Werner's desk.

"Bring up a chair, Lia."

My hands are so slick, the chair keeps slipping out of my grasp, but somehow, I manage to do as he says.

"So how are you finding it here?"

It seems like a really toxic environment, thanks to this app called DD, which should really get shut down. "Um. It seems really nice? The facilities are amazing." That, at least, is true.

"Good, very good." That possessed-doll stare again.

I squirm a little. It's impossible not to, under that soulless gaze. What could possibly be behind it? It's too easy to imagine some sort of wormlike alien creature lurking behind Mr. Werner's face, trying its best to seem human.

"You seem nervous."

Is that a question? Should I respond? "A little."

"Tell me about the literature classes you took at your old school. South…Melrose?"

"Melville."

"Right." His eyes narrow for a second. Distaste? Silent laughter? I honestly can't read any of his expressions.

"Last year we studied mainly American lit. We did, uh, *To Kill a Mockingbird*. And a few short stories."

"What did you think about *To Kill a Mockingbird*?"

That it's yet another white savior story in which the narrative is focused mainly on a privileged, white family and how racism affects its members.

But nobody wants to hear that. "I enjoyed it," I lie through gritted teeth. "It's really a story about courage in different forms." For the next few minutes, I yammer on about how inspiring TKAMB was and how it made me want to go to law school. Completely untrue, but teachers love that stuff, right?

"I see," he says, when I finish.

I beam at him.

"All right, I think I've heard enough. Please don't take this personally, but I'm advising you to drop this class."

Wait, what?

"Well, you have some good thoughts about *To Kill a Mockingbird*, but I'm looking for more depth. I treasure out-of-the-box thinkers. What you've shared with me so far, while competent, isn't very different from what you might find on, say, CliffsNotes. My class moves very fast. Even students who have top marks and who were here as freshmen find it a challenge to keep up with the pace."

Oh my god. I should've been honest with him, told him how I really feel about TKAMB. "Hang on. Truth is, I think the book's a dumpster fire of white saviorism," I say.

His eyebrows rise.

"I'm sorry. I didn't think you'd like my honest take on it. All of my teachers have loved TKAMB."

Mr. Werner smiles. "I appreciate your honesty. But again, I'm looking for something deeper. Your scholarship is dependent on you passing all your classes. I would hate to see you lose it. Why don't you switch to Mrs. Brown's class? It's much less challenging than mine."

"I could write you an essay on it—"

"There's no need. I'll write a note to Mrs. Brown. She'll be happy to have you, I'm sure."

What the hell. Could this guy be any more condescending? He says he wants an out-of-the-box thinker, and clearly, I've managed to challenge his preconceptions, but no, I'm still not good enough for him. He's not even giving me a fair chance.

What he doesn't know is that I live off moments like this. Every time someone tells me I can't do something, all it does is fuel me. I'd take their nay-saying and pound it into a hot, angry kernel, and whenever I'm tempted to give up, I'd hold that kernel in my mind's eye and let the rage push me forward. Pure fuel.

"With all due respect, Mr. Werner," (everyone knows "with all due respect" really means "you're ridiculous") "I'm not going to move to Mrs. Brown's class. I've read your syllabus, and I know I can manage it. I'll be okay here, I swear."

Mr. Werner frowns. "I really don't think you are well-suited for my class."

"Mrs. Brown's class clashes with my timetable. I don't have a choice." I'm all fired up now and every atom inside me is banging the war drums. I'm going to ace his class if it kills me.

Mr. Werner regards me again for what seems like a heck of a long time. Finally, he sighs and says, "All right. I can see your mind's made up, so." He raises his hands. "I'll see you Wednesday."

I rush out of his class. There isn't really time before the next one, but I slip into the bathroom and lean over the sink, taking deep breaths. What the hell just happened? It takes a while before my breath returns to normal.

The rest of my classes are also filled with snarky classmates. When lunchtime comes, I eat a couple of granola bars in the bathroom. Not the most pleasant of meals, but it beats risking going to the cafeteria to find Beth, Sam, and Grace ignoring me after all those posts on DD. I really need to find a way to deal with the whole DD mess. Later. Gotta get through the day first.

By the time school ends, I. Am. Beat.

I drag myself out of Highland Hall and across the quad. I can't wait to flop into my bed and veg out over Netflix. Or maybe a short nap. Maybe a short crying session?

But when I get to Mather, I see Danny standing outside my room. My heart quickens.

"I came to say hi."

I actually get tears in my eyes. That is how starved I've been for some friendly human interaction.

"This is a really nice surprise." My voice comes out slightly choked with emotion.

Danny scratches the back of his neck. Now that I'm closer to him, I notice that he's standing all weird, like he's trying to hide something. I crane my neck to see what's behind him, and he moves so he's right in front of me, blocking my view. "Wanna grab a hot chocolate?"

"What's going on?"

He gives me the world's fakest smile. "Come on, let's have a hot drink."

I have no patience left. I put my hands on his arm and push him aside. And that's when I see it. The whiteboard outside of my room. Yesterday I'd spent some time doodling my name in a pretty font, but someone's erased it and written: *PARASITE.* Underneath that is a caricature of my face, complete with cartoonish balloon lips and the words *we know where you sleep.*

It feels like a punch in the stomach. I swipe my palm across the board, but the letters don't come off. I rub harder and harder still, my vision blurred by tears.

There's a gentle pat on my shoulder. "I think they used permanent marker," Danny says. "I—um—I've asked Beth for a new board. I was going to switch it, but I didn't get a chance to."

I nod wordlessly. I can't look at him, or I'll burst into tears.

"Come on." Danny places his hand gently on my back and guides me to the common room, which is thankfully empty. "Sit down. I'll make us a drink."

I sink into an overstuffed couch and hug a throw pillow, and suddenly, I'm exhausted. I just want to go home. The thought, so tiny and pathetic, makes my eyes wet. Again. I take a deep breath and blink furiously. Quick, before Danny finishes making the drinks. We're nowhere near familiar enough with each other for me to bawl into a throw pillow while he pats my head. Get a grip, please, self.

Inhale. Shuddery with throat tears.

Exhale.

Inhale. Better.

Exhale.

Okay, tears successfully cockblocked. Crisis over.

Just in time, because Danny's walking toward me, holding two steaming mugs. He puts them down on the coffee table, and then grabs a plate and loads it with cookies. I take a sip.

"Whoa."

"I know, right?" Danny says, settling into the seat next to me.

"What is it?" I take another sip and close my eyes. I can't not. It's the kind of drink that makes all your muscles melt.

"Hot chocolate with a sneaky bag of green tea. One of my mom's signature drinks."

"Your mom's a genius."

"She's…complicated. Makes good hot chocolate, though."

For a while, we sit in silence, drinking and letting the hot chocolate melt us further into the sofas.

"Rough first day, huh?" Danny says.

"Is it always like that here?"

"Like what?"

I shrug. "The Dirt app, my whiteboard. The whole mean girl thing."

"Ah. Okay, well, DD is always like that, yeah. But it moves on pretty quick. By tomorrow, there'll be a post about some other kid and the heat will be off you. And the mean girl vibe...most girls and guys here are pretty chill. I think it's really all down to one girl."

"Mandy?"

"Mandy."

I groan. "Someone told me I should stay off varsity just so I won't piss Mandy off."

"Not a bad idea."

"I'll lose my scholarship!"

"Oh." Danny takes a cookie and chews it slowly. "Well, in that case, you gotta do what you gotta do."

I snort. As much as I like Danny, I can't help but feel frustrated at how easy he assumes everything is. Of course, he's never had any need for any scholarships or financial aid, so he can't grasp just how huge this is for me. And it's not his fault he's privileged, it's just...ugh.

"You got this, Lia."

"I really don't."

Danny holds up his hand to my face. "No buts. Ini masalah kecil. Elu pasti bisa."

You can do this. It's what Ibu always says to me.

"But—"

"No buts." Danny gives me the Look. It's the look that every Asian kid knows, this kind of "don't even try it, kid," look. He does it so well, I instinctively sit up straighter.

Ridiculous as Danny's little pep talk is, I actually feel better, like he's given me permission to go ahead and do whatever the hell I want. Okay, not whatever I want, because what I really want is to sharpen my toothbrush into a shank and stab Mandy with it, but you know. "You make a good Asian auntie."

"Ha! Yeah. It's 'cause my mom is like, the biggest Asian auntie around."

A face pops into the doorway. "Did someone mention Asian aunties?" Beth says, grinning.

I can't help smiling back. It's been a shit day, but it's quickly improving.

Beth squeezes next to me on the sofa and grabs my drink. "Damn, this is so good! So are we talking about Asian aunties, 'cause my mom is officially the biggest Asian auntie around."

"Nuh-uh," Danny says, shaking his head. "My mom has that title. Singaporean aunties have nothing over Chinese-Indo aunties."

Beth laughs. "Not true! My mom is like, 'Hanh? You want to be painter? Painter your head, ah! You think painter can earn what money, ah? You wear Prada—which she pronounces Pra-ta, by the way—and Burberry—which she pronounces Blur-beh-ly—and you want to be painter? You better take business module or else, ah!' See? Can your mom beat that?"

By now, all three of us are laughing so hard, I nearly choke on my hot chocolate.

"What about you, Lia, is your mom like that too?" Danny says.

I shake my head. "Sorry, guys, but my mom's totally laid-back."

"Whoa, a chill Asian mom. I thought those are a myth," Beth says. "My mom's the reason I'm working my ass off with my part-time job."

"What part-time job are you working?" I say. Having one seems pretty hard-core, given how competitive classes are here.

"Ugh, just a super annoying thing. Not gonna bore you with that. I'm really only doing it to prove to my mom I can take care of myself, even if I were to go to art school."

"Here's to proving our folks wrong," Danny says, raising his cup.

"Here's to proving everyone wrong," I say, raising mine.

CHAPTER 4

Danny's right about DD; that very same night, Aaron Presley and his buddies take his Bugatti Chevron or Chevy or whatever to party in downtown SF and then proceed to drunk-crash his car into the rose garden when they get back. Everyone's fine, except for poor Kaylyn Crawford—one of her new silicone boobs exploded, and DD can't have enough of that nasty piece of info. All those posts about me are quickly drowned out by GIFs of balloons popping.

I feel awful for Kaylyn, I really do, but I can't lie. I'm sort of slightly relieved that she's taken the heat off me, even if just for a while. I spend the next few days keeping a very low profile. The lowest. Asian parents everywhere would've been proud of the amount of time I spend hitting the books the next couple of weeks. When I'm not on the track, I'm burying my nose in books. I'm just living to see the look on Mr. Werner's face when I totally crush his biweekly test.

When he finally hands out the test paper at the end of the second week, I almost LOL. The test consists of five short-essay questions, and the questions can't possibly be any easier. The answers shoot through my mind so fast that my hand gets a bit of a cramp writing the answers quick like a bunny, or you know, quick like me doing a hundred-meter dash. There is no way. No way I'm not acing this one.

I don't even bother wiping the smug smile off my face when I hand in my paper.

The next class, I basically strut into Mr. Werner's. Just another straight-A star athlete coming through. Mandy, who's been eating my dust on a regular basis, gives me one of her very bitchiest bitch faces, but I just swan past her.

Mr. Werner gives me this sort of bemused smile, like he can't possibly imagine what I'm so happy about. *My A+*, I want to snap at him. *I'm happy about proving you wrong.*

Instead, I fold my hands and sit in my seat as prim and proper as can be, and I keep still as he goes around and hands us back our papers. I pick mine up with a small smile.

And freeze.

D minus.

No. Not possible. I know I've aced it. I know it in my bones, the same kind of feeling I get right before I blast through the finish line. What the hell is this thing—this grade that's so unfamiliar to me, it practically looks like a hieroglyph?

Sophie flashes through my mind. She's flunked his class. Maybe I'm headed down the same path. A wave of black despair surges through me. It takes a huge effort not to scrunch up the paper. My answers have been slashed through hideously. Bleeding red into the margins. An army of red swarming the page.

WEAK ARGUMENT.
WHERE'S THE EVIDENCE TO SUPPORT YOUR STATEMENT?
THAT'S QUITE A LEAP IN ASSUMPTION.

I look up in time to catch Mr. Werner watching me. Something about his expression makes me start. Then I realize why. It's the exact same one he was wearing as he watched Sophie get dragged away. An expression that says, *Poor little cockroach. Now do please fuck off before I crush you.* My hand squeezes into a ball, crushing the test paper, and he turns away.

A folded-up note plops onto my table. First note I've received at this school. I unfold it.

Did you ever think you were gonna pass this class?
Bye, bitch. ☺

Mandy's watching me over her shoulder. When I catch her eye, she smiles and blows me a kiss. I give her the finger, but that only makes her smile wider.

I don't have the energy to face other humans at lunch, so I trek through the obnoxiously beautiful grounds and go back to Mather. Maybe I'll take a power nap. Maybe I'll just veg out and watch TikToks until my brain drips out of my ears.

The dorm's eerily silent. Of course it would be. Everyone's at lunch. My phone *boop*s and I take it out without thinking about it. Then I realize the sound means it's yet another DD update, and that it's about me. I really should unfollow #Parasite, but it's an itch I haven't been able to stop myself from scratching.

Posted by: @MagicHandzz
Someone PLEASE take a pic of @TrackQueen's face when she sees this?? #Parasite #trackdrama

Below that is a screenshot of a piece of paper with a list of names.

MATCH LINEUP. FIRST DIV, MID-DISTANCE:

1. Lia Setiawan
2. Stacey Hoffman
3. Arjuna Singh
4. Elle Brown

Joy dances through my mind, flashing with a multitude of bright colors. I'm in. I've done what I came here to do. I'm one step closer to that college scholarship.

But just as quickly as it arrives, the bubbles of joy are swallowed by a sudden stab of dread. Mandy's name is nowhere on the list. I've done the thing. The thing Stacey told me not to do on pain of death. I've kicked Mandy off varsity.

And suddenly, I find it hard to swallow. My mouth might as well be a desert. How much trouble am I gonna be in with her now?

The next morning, I try to shake off the feeling of dread as I make my way to the track for my first meet of the season. As usual, I'm the first to arrive. I'm a chronic early bird.

"Lia!"

I look up to see Danny jogging over to me.

"What're you doing here?" Not that I'm complaining.

He smiles, suddenly looking shy. Honestly, is there

anything hotter in the world than a cute, shy guy? "I just… you know…wanted to wish you good luck, so…good luck on your match."

Yes, there is. There is something hotter. It's a cute, shy guy who comes early to your match to wish you luck.

"Thank you." We smile widely at each other. Maybe it's the mess of nerves that I've become lately, but there's something magical about the moment. I lean closer to him. My chest gives a painful squeeze. Maybe we can have our first kiss right now, on the empty track—

A shout jerks us apart. "Hey, what're you doing here? Athletes only!" Coach Iverson strides toward us, pointing straight at Danny, her expression deathly serious. Danny looks like he's ready to make a dash for it when Coach breaks into a grin. "I'm just messing with you. But seriously, though, get off my track. Go on, get outta here."

"Yes, ma'am. See you, Lia," he says, giving me a look that's a cross between a smile and a grimace. His cheeks look about as red as mine feel.

"Thanks for coming down here," I call to his retreating back, then I turn back to Coach, cockblocker of the year. "Hey, Coach." I don't wait for her to reply before crouching into the first of my stretches. I don't want her to see the flames on my face. Oh my god, that was almost my first kiss.

"Slept well? Ready for the race?"

No, and definitely not. "Uh-huh."

Coach Iverson pats my shoulder, shifting her weight from one foot to the other. She's nervous. Which makes me even more nervous. But I can deal with nervousness over athletics. Been dealing with that my whole life.

"Don't worry, Coach. I've got this." I sound a lot more confident than I feel.

It's just as well that my teammates start arriving, because I'm out of small talk, and Coach's nerves are contagious. First one who gets here is Elle Brown. I smile at her, but she rolls her eyes and turns away with a hair flick. I don't even get a chance to smile at the girl behind her—Arjuna Singh—before *she* gives me the cold shoulder (minus the hair flick). Wow. I know it's dumb to expect anything aside from this, since they've been ignoring me ever since my first day, but I guess part of me had hoped that they'd get over it on match day. Well, whatever. I swallow the lump in my throat and go back to my warm-ups. When we're done warming up, I go sit at the bench, but Elle scoots over to block the remaining space on the bench.

"Seat's taken."

Watching her and the other girls there, smug smiles on their perfect, manicured faces, I'm suddenly enraged. A small crowd has gathered on the bleachers, but I can't hear them anymore, not over the roar of my blood. I want to grab my teammates by their hair and bash their heads in. To them, being here's just a fun after-school activity, something to add to their college applications. To me, it's this or bust. If I don't compete, I don't get a scholarship, and without a scholarship, I can't afford college. Not unless I'm willing to take out a student loan that will debilitate my future.

I quickly walk off before I say something they'll no doubt make me regret. Inhale. Exhale. I jog in place, shaking out my arms.

Our event is called, and I walk into position. Someone in the crowd yells out my name. I see Beth sitting next to Danny. They wave at me and shout something. Danny's going to see me run. I can't decide if that's amazing or terrifying. I wave back before refocusing on the track. On my left is a girl from St. Theresa's, our biggest rival, and on my right is Elle.

"Suck a dick, Lia," Elle mutters, as we crouch into position.

"Not if I see you first." I really need to work on my comebacks. Elle looks confused for a moment, then shoots me another dirty look.

I ignore her. All sound is muted, like I've dipped my head underwater. There's just me and my lane. Exhale.

Ready.

Set.

The pistol pops. I shoot forward. Wind whips into my face. Every muscle in my body contracts and pushes. My feet pound the track like gunshots. Just me and my lane, and I'm tearing through it at the speed of light. Everything falls behind me—all the bullshit, Mr. Werner's class, Elle and TrackQueen and all the other mean girls, all the crap posted on DD about me—I outrun them all, and for the first time since I arrived at Draycott, I feel nothing but undeniable, unshakable peace. I was made to do this. God, I wish this feeling could last forever.

Then, suddenly, I feel the tautness of the ribbon against my stomach, a split second before it rips. Reality comes rushing back with the roar of an asteroid breaking through the atmosphere. Someone grabs me in a giant hug.

"You did it! You broke your own record!" Coach Iverson shouts, practically lifting me off my feet.

"Seriously?" I pant. A laugh wobbles its way up my chest. It's like a light's been turned on, chasing away the darkness. Hope. Everything's still shit, but it's gonna turn out okay. I laugh again. I turn to the crowd and wave. There aren't many people—it's not football or lacrosse—but the ones who are there cheer for me. Okay, some of them are actually booing, but I'm brimming with so much joy, nothing can possibly touch me right now. Beth and Danny are clapping madly, and that's good enough for me.

"That was amazing! Never seen anything like it." Coach's babbling as we walk toward the benches.

Kat, Coach's assistant, approaches us. Instead of congratulating me, she leans toward Coach Iverson and says, "We need to talk."

"Be back in a sec," Coach Iverson says to me, and walks off with Kat.

I look at my time. 2:06. Joy bubbles through my veins. Coach was right, I really did break my own record. If I keep this up, I'll get a full ride to college, no doubt. I dig my phone out of my duffel bag. I've gotta call Ibu. The notification screen is full of new posts from DD.

Okay, I was wrong about nothing being able to touch me, because some of the bubbles inside me deflate at the sight of the new post notifications. I really should delete this damn app.

Instead, I click on it.

Posted by: @TrackQueen

A little bird told me someone's about to get kicked out of varsity... #NoMoreParasite

Reply from: @Scribofile

Oh??

Below that is a GIF of a man resting his chin on his hands and saying, "Do tell." The replies that follow are along the same lines. Everyone can't wait to see what @TrackQueen has in store for me.

My heart does a nervous stutter, and I fight to get it to calm the hell down. It's just trash talk. I've blasted through my first race. There is no way—

"Lia!"

Coach Iverson is storming toward me, her expression thunderous. My throat dries up painfully. No way. I've done nothing wrong. I'm okay. Everything is okay.

"Yeah, Coach?" I try to keep my voice calm.

"You got a D in English Lit?"

What does that have to do with anything? "Yeah."

Coach closes her eyes and mutters a curse. "Did the guidance counselor not explain our rules to you when you were admitted? You need to pass all your classes, otherwise you're not allowed on the track."

My mind goes blank, like someone's unplugged it.

"I'm sorry, Lia. It's school policy. This will be your last match until you bring your grades up."

"What?" The word rips out of me like a gunshot. No, this can't be happening. It can't, it just can't. I feel as though I'm drowning.

Heads turn to face me. Whispers, snatches of laughter. Everything seems to be spinning. I catch a glance of Stacey, doing her stretches and watching me out of the corner of her eye. Blood roars in my ears.

"I'm sorry, that's our rules. But hey, I have faith you. You'll get your grades up in no time. Take the time you're not on the track to study." She claps me on the back before turning around and shouting at the other girls, "What're you all doing just standing there looking pretty? Get ready for the next event!"

Stacey smirks at me and jogs onto the track, her ponytail swinging like a pendulum. The other girls get into position, and just like that, I'm forgotten. A speck of dust, so easily lost in the wind. Despair clutches at my gut. I think I might throw up. Kicked off varsity? I can't—it doesn't compute.

My phone beeps again.

Posted by: @TrackQueen

Buh-bye, Parasite! #thankyounext

Below that is a picture of me, shoulders slumped, standing on the track. It's taken from afar and it's been blurred out, but it's still clearly me. Someone here is taking pictures of me. The back of my neck prickles. I look around at the cheering spectators, the girls on the track. No one seems to be paying me any attention. Even Danny and Beth are busy watching the next event. Which is just as well. I don't really want to interact with anyone right now.

I gather my stuff and walk off the track, glancing behind my shoulder as I go. My feet, flying across the track just moments ago, have turned to lead. I'm off varsity. Tears prick my eyes and my cheeks burst into flames again. I quicken my step.

I manage to hold it in long enough to get in the shower and turn on a blast of hot water, then I sob my heart out. Mid-sob, it strikes me that I'm doing a lot of crying in the shower lately. The thought makes me cry even more, which is massively pathetic, I know, but I can't hold back anymore.

The cry shower clears my mind a little, and by the time I get back to my room, I'm clearheaded enough to realize that I need to tackle the root of the problem. Mr. Werner's class.

I take out my phone and do a search for his timetable. As it turns out, he has office hours for the next forty minutes today. Okay, time to grovel.

The walk to Collings Hall, where the teachers' offices are located, is terminally long. I want to say I'm imagining the stares, but these kids aren't bothering to be subtle. I keep my head down. One foot in front of the other. And then I'm in front of his office, staring at the little brass plaque on the door which says *James Werner*. It takes about four aborted tries before I manage to will myself to actually knock on the door.

In the second it takes Mr. Werner to reply, I almost convince myself to run the hell away. Somehow, I make it through the door.

"Lia." He looks genuinely surprised, straightening up and hurriedly clearing a space on his desk. "Do we have an appointment?"

"No. Sorry, do I need one?" I have no idea how office hours work.

"Yes. I'm expecting another student any time now—"

"Please, Mr. Werner, I just need two minutes. Please." A

month ago, I would've made gagging noises at how pathetically desperate I sound. Now, I'm ready to go on my knees and beg.

Mr. Werner's mouth presses into a thin line as he watches me. Studying me. "Alright," he says after a while. "Two minutes. What can I help you with?"

"Thank you." I scramble through my bag and grab my test paper. I rush through his comments. "Um, okay, so here, you said I need to be more in-depth. Can you tell me how in-depth I should go with my answers?"

"Much more in-depth than that," he says and gives me an apologetic smile. "Okay, that wasn't very helpful." He takes a long breath, leans back in his chair. "Look, the thing is, I expect my students to go beyond the surface. Like I said during our interview, your answers aren't necessarily wrong, but they're also not groundbreaking. I want innovation. I want answers no other student outside of my class would be able to come up with."

What in the hell? God, could this prick be any more pretentious?

I must've looked like I was ready to strangle something, because he says, "You're probably sitting there thinking I'm being too harsh, but I assure you most of your classmates performed just fine on the test. It's not an impossible standard."

No, just one I failed to reach. Okay. Think outside the box. "Can I write an essay for extra credit, or—"

His blond eyebrows crash into each other. “That wouldn’t be fair to your classmates. No, I’m afraid I can’t give you special treatment like that, Lia.”

And now I feel like an absolute brat, coming here and asking for favors. Shame burns through my face. My scalp feels like it’s two sizes too small. “I’m sorry. I’m just kind of freaking out ’cause I’ve been suspended from competing, and—”

“And you’re here on a track and field scholarship. I know,” Mr. Werner said. “But I did warn you about my class.”

“I’ve missed the deadline to switch,” I mutter with a sinking feeling. “I won’t be able to replace it with another class. I need to take at least twelve units to keep my scholarship.” I scramble for another solution. Anything. “Do you have any advice for the next test?”

“Study hard,” Mr. Werner says, like it’s the most obvious answer in the world. I guess, in a way, it is.

“I meant more of like—”

There’s a knock at the door, and Mr. Werner straightens up. “That’s my afternoon appointment. Don’t let me keep you, Lia.”

Head down, I open the door.

“How much—oh.” Mandy does a double take when she sees me. “Ew,” she says under her breath, wrinkling her nose and stepping aside so I don’t end up touching her as I walk out.

Mandy sweeps inside and the door swings closed with a click. I'm left alone in the corridor, clutching my bag and smelling the remnants of her scent—a mix of high-end hairspray and perfume I've come to associate with the smell of Satan. I don't know what I was expecting. Something a lot more helpful than "study hard." But "study hard" was all I got. The disappointment crashes down so fast, I almost crumple right then and there, and start crying.

I walk out of Collings in a daze and startle when my phone beeps.

Okay, universe. I think I've dealt with enough crap today not to have to read through more hateful crap about me on DD. I mean, really now. You know what, I'm gonna delete that awful app. I really am.

I unlock my phone, but instead of a Draycott Dirt notification, it's a new email.

Sender: SiliconBrains@gotmail.com

Passing Mr. Werner's tests is impossible. I can help, but it has to be our secret.

CHAPTER 5

I'm not dumb. The D minus in English Lit notwithstanding, I'm really not. So, even though everything inside me is scrambling to reply to SiliconBrainsand go, "Omg YES PLS TELL ME EVERYTHING," I don't. Because, folks, I can smell a trap a mile away. And this smells bad, like something Mandy's cooked up with her gnarled witch hands. (Mandy's hands are actually really nice and smooth because she bathes in the blood of babies under every full moon, but go with me on this.)

Once I get back to my room, I do a search online for Mr. Werner. Very impressive résumé. Undergrad at Brown, followed by a master's from Stanford. Must be nice to be able to afford all that. I click on his LinkedIn profile then sigh when I find it's set to private mode. I do a search on Facebook, but there are about twelve thousand other James Werners. I'm about to close the tab when I see that one of the search results has *James Werner* tagged with *Wijaya*. I click on the link.

It takes me to the profile page of a woman named Yoana Wijaya. I don't know her, but the name Wijaya—oh.

Danny Wijaya. Well. That's one hell of a coincidence.

I close the tab and flop onto my bed. I'm chasing ghosts here. Despair wells up once more, threatening to overwhelm me. I close my eyes to keep from bawling again. Then something makes me open DD and do a search of Mr. Werner. There're a whole bunch of posts, mostly bitching about how much homework he gives, but one post catches my eye.

Subject: English Lit

Teacher: Mr. James Werner

Vote now! Do you find this teacher's class:

A. So easy it's basically a joke
B. Relatively easy
C. Relatively challenging
D. Impossible to pass

Poll results:

A. 27% C. 53%

B. 0% D. 20%

Reply from: @Boyatthebeach

Can I just point out that when I took the class last semester, I noticed that only the richest kids got As? #JustSayin

Reply from: @Jinxxy

Omg right? There was this girl in my class when I took it who's dumber than a brick but her family's loaded, and she somehow got an A and I got a B-.

Reply from: @TrackQueen

Jinx, maybe your too stupid to pass? Next time, instead of blaming the teacher, maybe you should try actually studying.

Reply from: @Jinxxy

Uhh, that's rich coming from someone who doesn't know the difference between "your" and "you're."

Reply from: @TrackQueen

[This message has been deleted by Admin. Reason: Please do not out fellow members.]

Some strange, dark emotion unfurls inside me. The replies are weird, right? I'm not just being paranoid? Or am I?

There's a knock on my door. I bound up and open it to find Beth.

She gives me a big hug before I can say anything. "Oh my god, you were amazing! You killed the competition! Just slayed them all!"

It actually takes me a while to realize what she's talking about.

"You okay?" she says. "Danny and I looked everywhere for you after the meet. He had to go work on some extra-credit project. What's wrong?"

And I burst into tears.

I end up telling Beth everything—Mr. Werner, the failed test, how I got kicked off the team, and of course, all the posts about me on DD.

"I'm sorry about DD," she says. "But everyone's got Dirt on them on the app. God knows I've got my own share of DD gossip."

"Really?" I sniffle. It's hard to imagine Beth being gossiped about. She's so nice, she's like a sitcom character.

Beth sits up. "I have just the thing to cheer you up."

"A passing grade in English Lit?"

"Okay, I have the second-best thing to cheer you up. Tonight, get dressed and meet me outside my room at nine."

"Why? What's up?"

"Just meet me there at nine. Bring a jacket."

Five minutes to nine, and I'm standing outside Beth's door, armed with a fake cold. I feel bad about flaking out, but after spending the rest of the afternoon alternating between worrying about track and worrying about English Lit, all I want to do is curl up in bed and sleep this terrible, no-good day away.

"You're early!" Beth says, by way of greeting. She's super dressed up—a bright-yellow, figure-hugging dress with flowers up one shoulder, hair all glossy and curled, heels that go all the way up to the sky. She pauses as she takes in my grubby *Futurama* shirt and greasy hair. "Well, good thing we're early." And then she yanks me into her room.

"I don't—" I stop and stand there, gaping at the sight of her room. Wow, I had no idea a dorm room could look like this. How do I describe Beth's room? It's like a Buzzfeed intern was given unlimited funds to decorate it. The walls are painted a light peach, there are white, faux fur throws everywhere—even her chair is lined with white, faux fur—and clumps of healing crystals here and there. It would be really pretty, if not for the incredible mess—there are mounds of clothes strewn everywhere.

"Put this on," she says, grabbing something from one of the mounds and throwing it at me.

I catch it. It's a silver dress made of the softest material I've ever touched. The label says Chanel. "I—wait, I can't—this is Chanel." It probably costs more than an entire month's rent.

"Yeah, you're right, Chanel is so basic. Okay, um...how about this one?"

"No, that's not what I meant—" I catch the second dress before it hits the floor. The label says Dior. "All this stuff is way too expensive."

"That's what you're worried about?" She sighs, and I know she's about to say something condescending that will completely ruin our friendship. "Lia, honey." My heart skitters. Here it comes. Time stutters. Her plumped lips move in slow motion. "Look at your abs. You were made for Dior."

God, I love Beth. Even as I laugh, she's rummaging in her closet. She resurfaces with a pair of sparkly heels.

"Shirt off! Come on, let's get going."

There's no use arguing with her. I hurriedly undress and slip the dress over my head, and oh. Whoa. Is that really me? The dress doesn't show cleavage or anything, but somehow, I look unbelievably hot. I move this way and that, marveling at the way the material moves with me. The dress goes surprisingly well with my kris necklace.

"Oh, to have your body," Beth sighs. "Okay, Cinderella. Let's go."

Outside, the air is bracingly cold. It doesn't take long before my teeth start chattering.

"Where are we going?"

"Dude, don't be so loud, or we'll get caught."

What? I'd assumed—I don't know why, maybe because

Beth exudes Good Asian Kid out of every pore—that the school allows parties once in a while. But now that I realize we're breaking school rules, I don't know. I'm excited, but mostly I really, really want to run back to my room and hide under the covers.

We creep all the way to the far end of the Eastern Gardens, where a ten-foot-tall hedge borders the grounds.

"I can't climb that in this dress," I say. The thought of ruining one of Beth's thousand-dollar dresses is enough to make me sweat despite the frigid weather. I fan my armpits desperately. How do rich people keep from getting sweat stains on their expensive clothes?

"We're not climbing anything, sa gua." She creeps along the hedge, one hand trailing across the leaves. "Here it is." She gets to her hands and knees and burrows into the hedge. Within two seconds, she's gone.

We've gone full Narnia. I stand there, hesitating, and jump when Beth says, "Hell-ooo, come on, Lia. We're all just waiting for you."

We? All?

I scoot my dress up a few inches and kneel on the grass, wincing at how cold and wet it is. At a glance, the hedge seems solid, but when I look closer, there's a hole behind a layer of leaves. I push my hand through it, revealing a hole just big enough for me to squeeze through.

"Alright, Lia!" It's Sam, looking stunning in a blue,

body-con dress. She helps me up and gives me a quick hug. “Glad you could make it.”

Grace stands behind her, equally gorgeous in a backless, red dress. She smiles and waves at me. What’s going on?

“We’re really sorry you’ve been getting so much crap on DD,” Sam says. “Um. We’re kind of too chickenshit to say anything publicly, but we thought we’d take you out clubbing to make up for it.”

“Oh. I mean. That’s just.” I turn away so they can’t see how full my eyes are. “Thank you.”

Sam waves me off and takes something small and black out of her purse. She hits a button. Next to her, Grace does the same.

Lights flood the grove. My mouth drops open. Two cars are parked a few paces away. Not just any cars. They look like something Batman would drive to Pride.

“You got the Aston in pink?” Beth says. “That is the cutest.”

“Wait till you see the inside. I got it all blinged out. Lia, you’re with me. Beth, you slum it in Grace’s Porsche.”

I’ve never been in a sports car before and getting in is a lot trickier than it seems, especially because the car sits so low. I feel gigantic and awkward, all knees and elbows, but once I’m in, it’s surprisingly spacious.

“Belts on!” Samantha says, sliding in gracefully. The engine turns on with a rumble. It sounds hungry. “Ready?”

My reply turns into a squeak as the car leaps forward. I

clutch the side handle, getting that sick roller-coaster feeling of my guts being pressed into my spine. I want to yell SLOW DOWN, AAAAHHHH, but then maybe Samantha won't like me anymore and OH GOD, A TREE—

With a practiced flick of the wrist, the car swings left. I glance at Samantha. She's perfectly relaxed. I force myself to swallow the bile that's risen up my esophagus.

We zoom down the empty streets, and before long, we pass by a YOU'RE LEAVING DRAYCOTT sign. Sam won't tell me where we're headed, and my mouth drops open when the Golden Gate Bridge suddenly looms before us. The lights of the city twinkle in the distance, and in no time at all, I find myself in the heart of San Francisco.

Sam swerves smoothly to the front of a beautiful, redbrick building. The car doors hiss open, music flooding in from the building, and she slides out, tossing her car keys to the doorman. There's a line of people waiting to get inside, but Sam merely nods to the bouncer, and he opens the red velvet divider and lets us in.

Holy wow.

I've been to clubs before. I'm not totally uncool. But this place. I mean. It's like stepping inside a diamond. There must be more than a thousand people here, all of them beautiful. The music is so loud that even when I cover my ears, I can feel its vibrations through my chest. We go up a winding staircase to a balcony that overlooks the dance floor.

The second floor is beautiful, dazzling lights everywhere, and sleek, leather furniture on which many of my schoolmates are lounging and drinking from champagne flutes. They've all transformed from high school kids to gorgeous celebs. They don't look at all like teenagers.

"Come on," Sam says, leading me to one of the leather booths. I hesitate.

"You okay?" Sam says.

Do I want to face these people right now?

"Don't be nervous, these are all kids who don't buy into Mandy's mean girl bullshit," Samantha says.

I try to believe her. As we approach, the kids in the booth look up and smile. They seem genuinely glad to see us—or rather, they seem glad to see Sam and not un-glad to see me. I spot Stacey among them, looking as sullen as usual. Okay, she's someone who's totally bought into Mandy's mean girl shtick, but whatever. Someone hugs me from behind. Beth, who's finally arrived with Grace.

"You met everyone?" Beth shouts over the music.

I nod. I share classes with most of the people here. We slide into the booth and someone puts a champagne flute in my hand. We clink glasses and I take a careful sip, but someone else—Sam—pushes the bottom of my glass up so I end up finishing the whole thing in one go.

"Holy crap," I sputter. I put my glass down, and instantly, a new flute is plopped into my hand.

Someone touches me softly on the shoulder, and I look up to see Danny smiling at me. "Glad you made it."

It's impossible not to return that smile.

"You look really nice," he says, sitting down next to me.

It feels like my entire body is blushing. I feel both glamorous and ridiculous in Beth's outfit. Does that make sense? I can't tell anymore. The champagne is bubbling through everything, and the night feels electric, like anything can happen.

"You look nice too," I say. Very original, Lia. But he does. He really, really does. He's wearing a sleek, gray shirt with the top button undone, and his hair is all mussed up, and his jaw is—okay, I mean, it's unchanged, still very much the same jaw as before, but I'm really noticing just how strong of a jawline it is. And we're sitting so close to each other that if I leaned over a few teeny inches, our jaws would touch. Uh, or our lips. Because that would be less weird. I lean forward a little, the champagne giving me courage.

Danny leans toward me.

So close, I can almost feel his heartbeat.

Henry McDonnell, a guy I recognize from American history, clears his throat loudly. "Okay, ready for tonight's stash?" Goddammit, Henry. Read the room!

Danny and I separate, my chest deflating.

Henry takes out a small, velvet pouch with the gravitas one reserves for an ancient artifact. He tips the bag and a bunch of little packets spill out. More cheers. Despite my irritation, I'm curious. I pick one up.

It's a pretty, little packet made of thick paper, velvety to the touch. There is a letterpress logo on it in the shape of wings.

"What is it?" I say.

"Sky," someone says, like that should mean something to me.

I open the packet and inside is a single blue pill with the same wing logo. Oh shit. I drop it on the table and wipe my hands on my dress. Drugs. Like, drug-drugs.

Everyone else has quickly swiped a little package each. Phones are taken out.

"What's the damage?" Beth says.

"Two hundred each," Henry says.

"Dollars?" I blurt out. For one of these tiny pills? Good lord.

"No worries, I've got you covered," Beth says.

"No, wait, I don't—"

"Too late, I've just Venmoed Henry the payment for two of these babies," Beth says, showing me her phone screen. And she really has. Sent four hundred bucks, just like that.

"I can't accept that. I mean, I've got homework to do. And like, I'm pretty sure I'm already drunk from the champagne." I'm babbling. Someone help me.

"I'm sitting this one out too, guys," Danny says.

"What? But you sat out the last one too!" Henry says.

"Yeah, I've got a ton of homework due. I can't afford to be hungover."

"What homework?" Grace says. "We're in pretty much all the same classes, and I don't have homework."

"Yeah, come on, bruh," Henry says, waving one of the square packets in Danny's face. "Don't ruin the vibe."

Danny grimaces. "No, I really don't—"

"Take the pill," Henry starts to chant. "Take the pill." To my horror, the others are picking up the chant. "Take the pill. Take the—"

Without warning, Danny grabs Henry's wrist and yanks hard enough to make Henry fall to his knees with a squeak. Danny's voice comes out in a deadly hiss. "I said I don't want any."

Everyone is silent, a few mouths agape.

"Jesus, alright, man!" Henry squeals.

Danny hangs on for just a beat longer before releasing him. Henry stumbles back, landing on the sofa with a loud thump.

Welp. He definitely ruined the vibe. Everyone looks so uneasy, I want to fold myself into a little tiny square and jump into someone's pocket. Danny turns away from the group and I catch a glimpse of his face—panicky with a clear "WTF did I just do" expression. Despite myself, I feel awful for him. He did overreact, but Henry was being really pushy and putting him on the spot.

"That just means there's more for us," I blurt out.

Everyone looks at me—oh god, oh god—but a beat of silence later, Henry laughs and says, "Good point!" and pops two pills into his mouth. The tension melts away, and everyone else takes their pill, smiling and chatting. "Hey, new kid," Henry says, "take your poison."

"Oh yeah, I already swallowed mine. Mmm, so, so high right now." I wave my empty packet at him.

Next to Henry, Stacey rolls her eyes. She's not buying my bullshit. The pill is burning a hole in my fist. I have no idea where to put it. I want to flush it down the toilet, but it seems wrong flushing something that cost $200 down the toilet. Why did I even lie about taking it? I shouldn't have. But I want these kids to like me. Or at least to not dislike me.

"Let's go dance!" Beth says, and everyone cheers and heads toward the dance floor.

Danny touches my arm. "Thank you for saving me back there."

I want to tell him it's okay. I want to ask him why he got so angry all of a sudden. I want to ask him if he'd get out of this place with me, maybe take a little walk, but then Beth and Samantha give my arms a yank, and off we go onto the dance floor.

The next few hours pass by in a blur. Flutes of champagne continuously appear in my hands, until I'm so tipsy, I can't keep up with anything. It's all just a whirl of smiling faces and moving bodies, and then at some point, the lights come on and the music stops, and everyone groans. The magical night is over. We trudge outside, where a line of limos await us because everyone's too drunk and/or high to drive back to school, and the whole drive back to Draycott, I wear a stupid grin because I've realized that not everybody hates me. Beth was right; this was just what I needed.

Unfortunately, the magic of that night doesn't last. In the morning, the fact that I'm off varsity crushes me as soon as I awake. For a few moments, I'm threatened by the darkness of despair, but somehow, I manage to fight it off. I don't have time for self-pity. If I want to get back on varsity, I need to pass Mr. Werner's class.

The next few days, I devote myself to nothing but studying. In class, I nearly get a cramp writing down literally everything Mr. Werner says, even stuff like, "Nice weather today, huh?" There is no way in hell I'm going to give the man another chance to flunk me.

The night before the next English Lit test, I'm so engrossed in my notes for *Lord of the Flies* that I completely forget about dinner until my stomach suddenly decides this whole not-eating thing is bullshit and makes my life a living hell. "Okay, okay," I mutter, as it gives a growl loud enough for the entire library to hear. I pack my stuff up and hurry to the dining hall. Only fifteen minutes left before dinner ends. My phone's full of messages from Beth and Sam.

As I walk across the quad, I hear Mandy's voice. Over the past few weeks, her voice has ingrained itself into my mind the same way a chimp would familiarize itself with the growl of a lion. Instinctively, my shoulders tighten, and I grip my books close to my chest. I can't see her—ah, behind the hedge. I'm about to veer off course just to avoid her when she says, "Oh god, she's not going to pass."

Ugh. You're only saying that because you don't know how hard I've been studying, witch.

"I've made sure of it."

What? Instinct overtakes me, and I turn and run away. As soon as I round the corner, all my strength leaves me and I sink to the ground, trying to catch my breath. She's "made sure of it." Made sure that I'd flunk Mr. Werner's next test. But I don't understand, I can't—

I start shaking.

I believe her. I have no doubt that Mandy's done something to sabotage me completely, and I feel so utterly defeated. All those hours I spent studying. What little hope I have of getting back on varsity, my dreams of a college scholarship. Crushed with one wave of Mandy's manicured hand.

I take my phone out and open SiliconBrains's email. With shaking hands, I type out a reply.

"*Help me.*"

I hit Send.

"You okay?"

I yelp and look up so fast, the back of my head smacks into the wall.

"Ouch. That sounded bad. You okay?" It's Danny, crouching and tilting his head to look at me.

My head is throbbing, but the pain is actually grounding me a little, stopping me from spinning out completely. I don't want to lose it in front of Danny, so I turn away, wincing so he thinks I need a moment because of the head smack. Take a deep breath, Lia. Good. And another one. When I feel a bit less like I'm about to shatter, I turn back and force a small smile. "I'm okay."

"Okay..." He doesn't look convinced.

I start gathering my books so I don't have to meet his eye.

"Oh, you taking my uncle's class?"

For a second, I have no idea what he's talking about. Then I recall my Facebook search. "Mr. Werner is your uncle?"

"Only by marriage. But we're pretty tight."

I blink a few times, trying to digest this weird connection. "How come you're not taking his class?"

Danny smiles sheepishly. "I wanted to, but he told me no. Said it would be way too hard for me."

I don't know what to make of that, and the last thing I want to do is discuss Mr. Werner right now, when my mind is such a mess, so I quickly change the subject. "How come you're not at dinner?"

"Um. I'm on a diet?"

I stare at him.

Danny sighs. "Okay, truth is, I can't really afford it. Please don't tell anyone. Not even Beth."

Now I'm really staring. "Aren't you like a crazy rich Asian?"

"My parents are. But things aren't going so well with them, so."

Huh. I think back to how angrily he'd rejected the Sky pill. Oooh. He didn't want to take it because he couldn't afford it. "I'm sorry to hear that."

"Eh, I'm not hungry anyway. Food's overrated," he says, just as his stomach gives a horrible growl. "Plenty of granola bars and muffins in the common room."

This is too sad. "Come on, I'll take you out for dinner."

And just like that, without meaning to, I've asked a boy out on a date.

CHAPTER 6

We're not allowed to leave school grounds without a permit on weeknights, so we head for the Narnia hole. The wind's picking up, and once again, I am woefully underdressed for the chill of Norcal nights. In my defense, I wasn't expecting to go around asking dudes out on impromptu dates.

"So."

"Yep."

Okay, so my first-date conversation really needs work, but so does his.

"South Melville."

"Yep."

"What's that like?"

I side-eye him. "Are you thinking of like, gang

violence and I dunno, Trump-esque visions of inner-city communities?"

Danny grimaces. "Uh. Sorry, I just. I really have no idea what anything outside of the OC is like."

"You're Indonesian, dude."

"Oh, well. Yeah, but Indo's different. You know how it is, you just get driven from high-end mall to high-end mall."

"Actually, I don't know how it is. My parents took me once, when I was a baby, and then shortly after that my dad died, and my mom just never went back."

"Shit. I'm sorry."

"It's okay. I mean, to be honest, my dad's family is super racist toward native Indonesians, so they were really against my dad marrying my mom, and then when he died, they blamed her for it, and it's just a bunch of bullshit I'm glad I don't have to deal with, you know?"

Wow, talk about killing the vibe. Why did I have to bring my pathetic origin story up?

"On behalf of the Chinese-Indo community, I am so, so sorry."

"It's not your fault." I snort, though to be honest, it feels kind of good to hear it from him.

Our hands bump. We pretend not to notice. A thick, charged silence hovers over us as we crawl through the Narnia hole.

"Last time I did this, Sam and Grace had their cars parked here. It was crazy."

"Yeah, this is pretty much everybody's rendezvous point. I don't have my car with me right now, so I'm afraid we have to walk."

He looks so genuinely sorry that I can't help but laugh. "It's okay. I'm not going to melt or anything."

He gives me a grateful smile. There's a little dimple on his left cheek that's only just visible when he smiles. This boy, I swear.

"I didn't think the school has student parking. Sam was telling me she parks her car at a private garage off campus."

"Yeah, mine's parked at my uncle's place for now. He's cool like that."

"Are we thinking of the same uncle, 'cause I'm having a bit of a hard time seeing Mr. Werner as 'cool.'"

He laughs again. "Okay, admittedly, Uncle James has his quirks, but once you get to know him, he's really cool. Last Christmas, we built an actual drone from scratch and flew it all over the place until one of our neighbors got sick of it and shot it down."

Wow, Mr. Werner. Who would've known he has it in him to be a public menace? The mention of him reminds me of Mandy and SiliconBrains and everything that is wrong in my life. I can't bring myself to banter with Danny. I don't know if he notices the shift in my mood, but he doesn't say anything.

Before I know it, we've walked all the way to downtown Draycott. Built during the Gold Rush, the town's maintained its Wild West charm. Most of the buildings on Main Street have these wooden balconies. I've watched *Westworld*; I know what those balconies are for. As we walk down Main, I can totally imagine hookers—ahem, sorry, ladies of the night—leaning over and flapping their boobs and catcalling customers. Now, the shop houses are mostly places that use the word *artisanal* a lot. There's an artisanal bakery, an artisanal candle shop, an artisanal deli. Scattered in between the artisanal shops are candlelit restaurants featuring fusion food and hipster cafes where you can get iced coffee in Mason jars for ten dollars.

It's all really pretty and also really, really expensive. Which is right about when I realize I have completely failed to think this whole "treating someone else to a meal" thing through.

As we walk, I sneak glances at the menus outside of the restaurants. The cheapest dish I can see is a side salad that costs fourteen dollars. Commence panic breathing.

"Um. Sorry, Danny. I don't know if I can—"

"Uh-oh. Am I getting dumped before our date even starts?" He looks genuinely concerned.

He referred to this as a date! A date that is about to end prematurely because we're both broke AF.

"I'm sorry, I didn't realize how expensive everything is here. I mean, that last restaurant we passed is selling roasted kale salad for twenty bucks!"

"Don't worry about it, we're not going to eat at any of these places. Where we're going is a lot more affordable."

I narrow my eyes at him. "Your definition of affordable may be very different from mine."

He grins. "So cynical. Trust me."

And he leads me into a dark alleyway. Which is when I realize I don't actually know this boy very well, and then I think maybe it's time to reach for that pepper spray in my bag. But before I can do that, we come out of the other end of the alleyway, and it's like we've stepped into a whole different world.

We're in some sort of food market. There's stall after stall selling all sorts of street food and drinks, and even though it must be close to ten by now, the place is full of people walking, eating, and generally just having a blast. Multicolored lights crisscross above our heads like stars on wires, and after weeks of being in Draycott, it's like I've finally found something authentic.

"This is amazing."

"Right? Come on, I'll show you the best part of this entire place."

He takes my hand super casually and leads me past various stands. I'm torn between "Holy shit, we're holding hands!" and "Wow, those tacos look good." Finally, he stops at a stand selling—

"Nasi goreng!" I cry. Seriously? I haven't had nasi goreng

since, well, since coming to Draycott, and I haven't even realized how much I've missed it until now.

"Not just any fried rice," Danny says. "This is nasi goreng terasi cabai hijau. It's bellisimo." He kisses the tips of his fingers dramatically. "Halo, Om," he says to the stall vendor. "Apa kabar?"

"Danny, sudah lama sekali tidak kesini," the old man behind the stall says. His smile is missing a few teeth, but it doesn't take away its warmth.

"Yeah, it's been way too long, Om. This is Lia."

"Orang Indo?" the man says, leaning forward and squinting at me.

"Yes. But I don't really speak it well," I add apologetically.

"Ah, no problem, no problem. You like fried rice?"

"Very much."

"Good, good. I make you best fried rice." With that promise, he gets to work, throwing all sorts of stuff into his wok. Shallots, green chili paste, complete with the terasi—fermented shrimp paste. The smell of terasi, in all its delicious cheesiness, is basically the smell of home. When he hands us our plates, I try to pay, but he just waves me off with a frown. "Cepat makan," he says.

It's something Ibu always says to me. *Eat quickly*. Now my eyes are wet, and it has nothing to do with the stinging smoke of frying shallots. The old man smiles and nods. He gets it.

"Terima kasih, Om," I say.

He waves me off and I follow Danny to a nearby bench.

"Ready to have your mind blown?" Danny says.

I roll my eyes. And then I take a bite of my green chili fried rice, and WOW. I inhale the entire plate within minutes.

"Wow, you're hungry," Danny says.

I stare pointedly at his empty plate.

"I've been eating nothing but granola bars and muffins the past week," he says, laughing.

This stuff is like crack. Om Ah Fei gives us seconds, and by the time we're done, we're both stuffed and happy. I leave his stall with a huge grin and a full heart.

I buy cups of freshly pressed cane juice, and we stroll around downtown Draycott. The trees lining Main are draped in lights, and there's sugar in my mouth, and carbs in my belly, and a cute boy at my side. This night is pure magic.

"Did you like the fried rice?"

"It was so good. I wish my mom could try it. She'd love it."

"You guys are really close, huh?"

I'm so relaxed, I don't even consider how uncool it is to admit that I'm close to her. "She's my best friend."

"That's so wholesome. Like, in the best way. I wish I were that close to my parents."

"I thought Chinese-Indo families are super tight." Or at least it's always seemed like that to me. My 87,621,679 cousins back in Jakarta are all besties with one another. Their Instas are full of pics of them hanging out together. Without me, the mixed-race outcast. Not that I feel sorry for myself or anything.

"Well, my family's really close, but we also have way too much drama. We're like a real-life Korean drama. You don't even know. Like, one of my cousins got engaged to this white guy last year, and my uncle and aunt went nuts, and the whole family intervened and broke them up."

"Wow."

"Yeah, they're pretty intense. Anyway, I've never gotten along with my parents. I'm too much of a bad boy." He wiggles his eyebrows at me.

"Oh yeah, with that clean-shaven K-pop face and that sweater vest, you are clearly a gangster."

"Hey, I'm bad. I even ran away from home."

"You ran away? Really?"

He shrugs. "Kind of. I went to my uncle's place."

"Again, clearly, you are a gangster."

"Okay, running away definitely qualifies for gang behavior in our culture."

"True." I like how he says "our" culture.

"So I pretty much stayed with Uncle James all through summer. It turned out to be a good summer, actually. He was pretty happy to have me around. I think he's been struggling since his divorce."

The mention of Mr. Werner sours the sugarcane juice in my mouth. I shove aside the thought of him and try to focus on Danny, who's suddenly looking shy.

"Um, I haven't told anyone about me being broke. I only have enough credit left on my student card for ten more meals, so—"

"I won't tell a soul," I say quickly.

"Thanks." He sighs. "I just don't know if anyone at school would get it. I mean, not that I'm special in any way, just—"

"You're right, they won't get money troubles, and it sucks to have to hide shit from your friends because you don't want them to look at you different." Wait. If he's only got enough money in his student account for ten more meals... "That first night we met, when you swiped me in—"

He grimaces. "I was hoping you wouldn't remember."

"What, that I wouldn't remember you paying for my meal? So you've been scrimping and saving all this time, but you paid for my meal? Why? We'd only just met then."

"I don't know." He looks down at his shoes. "You seemed really hungry, and you were sort of crying a little. Anyway, I'd had a big lunch that day, so."

"You pretended you had to go get your laptop because you couldn't afford to buy dinner for yourself after swiping me through?"

He doesn't say anything. The air is charged. Electric. Full

of magic and light, myriad possibilities at my fingertips. I take one step toward him, then another, until a single, lonely inch separates us. I want to remember all of him, in this moment, the way his hair flops messily across his forehead, the dark mahogany of his eyes, reflecting the fairy lights above us. Then I rise on tiptoes and our lips meet, and every cell in my body glows as bright as the stars.

CHAPTER 7

In the morning, I float out of bed before my alarm goes off, and not like in a gloomy, ghostly way but like in an angels-singing, forty-year-old-virgin-who-just-got-laid way. Not that I got laid last night.

I reach for my phone and see that I have an email from SiliconBrains.

The floaty sensation disappears, and I crash back to reality.

There's something attached to the email. I click Open. It's today's test paper, complete with answers. Oh shit. I close it quickly and jump out of my bed, feeling disgusted at myself.

I'm not a cheater. Ibu raised me better than that.

My reply is swift and angry. Wth? I'm not gonna cheat

on a test! I hit send and pace with righteous anger. Who the hell does SiliconBrains think I am?

There's a boop. I pounce on my phone.

FFS. You don't get it, do you? Mr. Werner sells grades to the wealthiest students. It fucks up the bell curve, but people haven't really noticed. They just assume it's because his class is really challenging. He makes his tests ridiculously hard so he can nitpick on the answers and control your grades that way to make it look like he's got a normal bell curve. So unless you've got the money to pay for a passing grade or know the answers to these obscure questions, this is your only chance of passing.

God, I feel sick. My thumbs fly across the phone screen.

Prove it.

I have nothing to prove to you. Take my help or leave it, I rly don't give a shit.

Argh. They have a point, but still.

I can't deal with human interaction, so I choose to have breakfast in my room after track practice. And then, hating myself more than I can possibly imagine, I open up SiliconBrains's message again, and this time, I actually read the test paper. And SiliconBrains is right. These questions are so difficult, so obscure, they would've driven me mad.

But I won't cheat. I won't. I'll come up with my own answers.

My phone beeps with a message from Danny: So last night was sort of awesome.

Yeah, very definitely sort of awesome. I look for an equally adorable emoji to add, but nothing beats nerdy smile, not with its two buck teeth and glasses. I settle for closed-eye smile emoji. Not as standoffish as slightly smiling emoji, not as thirsty as grinning emoji.

See you at lunch?

Sounds good

Our conversation makes me smile, but as soon as it's done, anxiety resumes squeezing my stomach

By the time I'm seated in Mr. Werner's classroom, I'm so jumpy, I feel like a meth head in need of her next fix. Mr. Werner meets my eye and I look away like his gaze burnt me. When he hands out the test paper, I pounce on it, and—

Everything stops.

Because it's the exact same paper that SiliconBrains sent me. My stomach sinks. I mean. Just. This proves it. Mr. Werner is really selling test papers.

Hang on, it doesn't actually prove that. All it proves is that SiliconBrains managed to get his hands on a test paper, either by buying it or, more likely, by stealing it. Argh, why does everything have to be so complicated?

My stomach boils as I fill out my name. Is this what it feels like to have guilt eating away at you? It actually does feel like my stomach is eating away at itself, gnawing the same way a dog worries at a bone when it knows it's done something bad. I grip my pencil so hard, it snaps. The top half bounces off my desk and clatters to the floor. In the hushed room, it sounds super loud.

"Sorry," I whisper to no one in particular. Oh god, I can't do this. I can't cheat on a test. Ibu would freak the eff out. *I'm* freaking the eff out.

But as I pick my pencil up, I catch sight of Mandy. She's leaning back in her chair, twirling her pencil, wearing the world's most bored expression. Which, you know, that's weird, right? Or maybe that's just her thinking face? Yeah, she's probably deep in thought—

And then Mr. Werner catches her eye and gives the tiniest shake of his head. Mandy sighs and moves her hand over her test paper, scribbling. But from where I sit, I can see that she's not actually writing anything on her paper. It's all swirls and doodles of vines and flowers.

Oh.

My.

God.

SiliconBrains was right. Mr. Werner is selling test papers, and now I know for sure who one of his customers is.

At first, I'm just so shocked that my head is devoid of any thought. Then, like a faucet turning on, rage pours into every fiber of my being.

I got kicked off varsity because of this. Because of *them.*

I'm seething, fire spitting out of my eyeballs. God, I could just—

Breathe, Lia. In, out. In, out. I don't have to fail. Not anymore. Not with SiliconBrains's help. But then I'll owe SiliconBrains. I'll worry about that later.

I look at my test paper, and I see it in a new light. I see how the questions are worded in the most confusing way possible. Designed so he can mark people's tests up or down. I write down my answers so hard, I tear a hole in the paper. Many of the questions focus on the most obscure parts of the text, which Mr. Werner never touched on during class.

By the time I finish the paper, my hand's cramped from gripping my pencil too tight. I look over my answers. Crap, I totally forgot to choose the wrong answer for a couple of questions. I can't turn in a perfect paper. It'll look so suspicious. I'm hopeless at this whole subterfuge thing. I erase two of my answers and write something different. There.

Satisfied, I look up.

Mr. Werner's looking straight at me.

I lower my head. Shit, shit, shit. He knows. HE KNOWS. I sneak another peek. He's typing something on his tablet. And exhale. He doesn't know.

When the bell rings, we hand our papers to Mr. Werner on our way out.

"There goes another faaail," Mandy says under her breath.

One day, I will punch her right in the face, and it will be worth it. Instead, I say, "Were you surprised by question three? It has your name on it."

I'm rewarded by a widening of her eyes as she quickly checks the paper. Gotcha.

"What're you talking about? My name's not on it."

"Oh? My bad. Maybe you should read the actual test paper next time." I give her a sweet smile and stroll out of the classroom.

CHAPTER 8

There's no way in hell I can focus on anything after the test, so instead of heading to the dining hall for lunch, I change my outfit and head for the track. It takes nearly four laps before I feel less like I'm about to explode into a million fire ants. I cheated on a test. No matter how many times I tell myself that it was justified, that I had no other choice, I still feel so slimy, I want to rip my own skin off. I mean, that's probably a normal reaction to cheating, right? That is how a human with a soul should feel.

I put in a burst of speed, until every part of my body is screaming, and sprint through the final lap. I collapse on the rubber track, wheezing. I'm utterly exhausted, but I also feel lighter, like I've finally outrun the weight of my guilt.

A pair of shoes crunches into position next to me. I look up to see Danny smiling at me.

"Hey," I say, scrambling up. I stand up way too fast and the blood rushes to my head, and I end up doubling over, trying to catch my breath. Real smooth.

"You okay?"

"Yeah—(gasp)—just—(gasp)—ran—(gasp)—a bit—(gasp)—too fast."

"Ah. I didn't mean that. I mean…um, well, I sort of missed you at breakfast. And at lunch. Um. You know, if you feel uncomfortable about last night, I totally respect your space. Except I'm here now, but like, if you wanted me to leave, I totally would—"

"No, no! Last night was amazing. Really!" I bend over again. Come on, breath, be caught already. I straighten up again, slower this time, and meet his eye. Suddenly, I'm feeling shy myself. "I had a really good time last night."

He smiles. That wayward dimple shows up again. "Me too."

"I was going to text you, but I got a bit distracted." By Mr. Werner's test. God. The test. The memory of it comes rolling back like a giant, nightmarish wave, and now it's so much worse. Because I'm looking right at Danny, the guy who worships Mr. Werner. And then a little voice whispers, *Is he in on it?* And it's like poison seeping into the atmosphere, killing everything good, and suddenly, I need to know if

Danny knows about Mr. Werner's side business. A burning need. "What do you know about your uncle's class?"

Danny frowns. I search for any traces of anything off—guilt, fear, anger—but there's none, only pure confusion. "What do you mean?"

Okay, now I'm starting to feel ridiculous. "Has anyone ever complained about it?"

A shrug. "I mean, sure, but people complain about every teacher. No one's ever said anything overly terrible about Uncle James to me, anyway. Probably 'cause they're scared I'd tell him. Not that I would."

"Have you ever heard anything...off?"

He looks at me closely. "Is everything okay?"

No, it's not, your uncle's running a cheating ring and I'm caught in the middle of it. The words are almost out before I stop them. I can't do this to Danny. I have no real proof. Plus, what am I planning to do about it, anyway? Blow the whole thing open? Get Mr. Werner fired, Mandy kicked out? And then what? Be known as the school rat? DD would explode. What would they say about me? Worse, what might they *do* to me?

"Nothing, I'm just struggling a little in his class, but I'll be fine." I give him my best convincing smile.

"Wow, that looks hella forced. You need to work on your fake smile."

That turns it into a real smile. "Yeah, let me put that on my to-do list. Work on fake smile."

"It's an important life skill to have." He leans closer to me.

I feel like I'm at the precipice of something. In a good way, the way you do at Christmas morning, right before you pull the ribbon off the first present. Our eyes close at the same time, and then our lips meet in a slow, sweet crush.

It's like watching fireworks in slow motion. I'm dazzled by the spectacle of it, but all of my senses are also supremely heightened. I can feel every caress of his lips against mine, the slightest flutter of his eyelashes on mine, his hand gentle on my chin.

Our phones beep at the same time. We pause, look at each other, and laugh. And then I recognize the beep as the DD notification. My laughter dies, just like that. There's a new post, and they've tagged it with something both Danny and I follow. That's not a good sign. Without a word, both of us take out phones out.

There's a picture of us from last night, kissing. As always, it's been pixelated so you can't see any facial features, but to me at least, it's painfully obvious who it is.

Posted by: @TrackQueen

Seen last night: A certain Prince Charming kissing a certain frog. #asianprince #parasite

Reply from: @Jazzy

Eww! Better wash that mouth with bleach afterwards, #asianprince!

Reply from: @TrackQueen

Methinks someone is about to get in trouble for cavorting with the pheasants...

Reply from: SiliconBrains

It's "peasants," moron, not "pheasants."

Okay, that's not as bad as I thought it was going to be.

"Damn, I get *parasite* as my hashtag, and you get *Asian friggin' prince* as yours?" I totally expect Danny to laugh it off, but when I look up, his face is drawn. "Everything okay?"

"Huh? Oh yeah." He stuffs his phone into pocket and gives me a smile that's closer to a grimace.

"Seriously, what's up?"

His smile looks less fake this time, though it does look tired. "You don't know much about the Asian community, do you?"

I shake my head.

"It's nothing," he says. "I'm probably just worrying over nothing. But—"

His phone rings then. And his expression is awful. A scared little kid who knows the world is about to crash down on him. He looks down at the screen. It says *Papa*. "Shit," he whispers. We both continue staring at the screen as the phone rings. I'm dying to know what's going on, but it feels wrong to say anything. The phone stops ringing. We both exhale.

The screen lights up with another phone call. This time, the name that pops up is *Mama*. Danny takes a deep breath and hits Accept.

"Ma." He shoots me an apologetic look and turns away.

I know it's dumb, but I feel...shunned. Though he's still right there, I sense a sudden rift between us.

"I don't—what did Auntie say to him?" Danny sighs again. "Can we talk about this later? I'm about to go to class."

He's not about to go to class. He just can't talk because I'm here. I look down at my shoes, wanting to disappear. And then it gets even worse. He switches to Mandarin. "Nǐ shì zhǒngzú zhǔyì zhě. Wǒ zhīdào bàba huì nàyàng, dàn wǒ yǐwéi nǐ huì gèng hǎo."

I swear my insides are actually twisting to get away from here. Any moment now, they'll burst out of my belly and writhe away, squeaking, "THIS IS SO AWKWARD." Because I may be half-native Indo, but I'm also half-Chinese, and one of the things Ibu has always been adamant about is me going to Chinese class every Saturday so my Chinese family doesn't have yet another thing they can look down on me for. So, in a very awkward twist of events, I know that Danny has just called his mom a racist, and it doesn't take a genius to guess who she's being racist about.

Exhaustion takes over. I just want to slump onto the track and sleep the rest of the semester away. I can't believe Ibu spent half her life trying to please my dad's racist family, and now I'm in the exact same situation. Why did I think anything would be different?

"Wǒ bùxiǎng zài gēn nǐ tǎolùn zhè jiàn shìle," Danny hisses. Then he pauses and looks at the phone disbelievingly before shoving it back in his pocket.

"Sooo," I say. "Your parents found out about us, then?"

"Lia, I'm so sorry. Hang on, how did you guess—"

"I speak Mandarin."

Danny's entire face falls. He looks so utterly miserable, I can't help but give him a hug.

"It's okay," I say, which is stupid because it didn't sound okay, and it's not okay, and it feels like nothing in my life is okay.

"No, listen." He tucks his hand under my chin and gazes at me. "It's really not okay, and I'm so sorry you had to hear that. It's one of the many reasons I don't get along with my folks. But you know what? They don't control me. They cut me off months ago. They've done their worst. I don't care what they think. I think you're pretty freakin' amazing, so fuck them."

"Thank you, I think I'm pretty freakin' amazing too."

He laughs. "You're supposed to tell me that *I'm* pretty freakin' amazing too."

"You're alright." And then I go on tiptoes and kiss him, because really, what else is there to do in this moment?

A shrill ring slices through our kiss. It takes me a second to realize my phone's ringing. I break apart from Danny and fumble for it, my heart racing. Nobody ever calls me. Everyone just texts. Something's wrong. Please don't let be Ibu. Who the hell—

"Hello?"

It's not Ibu on the other end. It's Mr. Werner, and he wants me to go to his office right now.

CHAPTER 9

By the time I make it to Mr. Werner's office, I'm this close to puking. He knows. I'm busted. I'm going to be kicked out of school. That's basically worse than dying.

I watch as my hand rises and knocks on his door.

"Come in," he says. Doesn't even ask who it is. He knows it's me, the dirty cheater who deserves to be expelled.

No. I'm not the dirty cheater. *He* is. *Remember that.* I turn the doorknob and walk inside. I have to remind myself not to hunch my shoulders.

"Sit." It's delivered as a command, and my body reacts instinctively, practically falling into the chair opposite of Mr. Werner. I can't even look at him. I look at my hands and find that they're wringing tightly. *Loosen up, hands.* They refuse.

"Do you know why you're here?" he says.

I manage to give a small shake of the head.

"You're here because I've just finished grading the last test."

Is that a question? Should I say something? I should stop looking down at my stupid hands, at least. I try to meet his eye. Fail. Settle for his neck instead. "Uh-huh?"

"You did very well, Lia."

I internally scream at my face until it stretches into a smile. "Yay."

"Yay indeed. To be honest, I wasn't expecting such a dramatic improvement."

"I studied really hard for it," I say, as earnestly as I can. I mean, to be fair, I really did study hard for it.

"I'm sure. Tell me, what are your thoughts on question number five?"

I can practically smell my brain cells frying as my mind short-circuits itself trying to think of an acceptable answer. "That's the question on uh—"

"Why was the severed sow's head nicknamed the Lord of the Flies?"

"Oh right. Yeah." I struggle to recall my answer. Or rather, SiliconBrains's answer. "Because. Um."

"You said because it literally has flies swarming around it."

"Ah, yes. Uh-huh."

Mr. Werner narrows his eyes. "Lia. That wasn't your answer. You said because it symbolizes Satan, who is sometimes called the Lord of the Flies."

"Did I?" Oh god, I'm going to throw up. "I've had a really long day, I can't remember all of my answers."

"Because you cheated." He says it so simply, like he's telling me I've got ketchup on my blazer. I feel like my entire face just caught fire.

"I didn't—"

"You did," he says, and he's still so calm, like yep, you totally did, whatever. "We have a zero-tolerance policy on cheating. I'm afraid I have to report you to Mrs. Henderson—"

"If you do that, I'll tell Mrs. Henderson you're selling grades to your students!" And it's out, just like that. Holy shit, I can't believe I said it. My entire body is pulsing, like my heart's taken over everything, and I'm just one giant BOOM, BOOM, BOOM. Somehow, I'm glaring at Mr. Werner, and I can't look away, can't tear my eyes from his pale gaze, and whoa, I'm on my feet, when did I stand up—

Mr. Werner blinks. Then he throws his head back and laughs, this totally eerie laugh that makes me want to claw my face off because it's so discordant, so wrong, he's most definitely a possessed doll come to life.

"That's just the most—oh god, this is hilarious. Excuse me, but it's just so ridiculous—" He goes back to laughing madly.

"I have proof!"

"Oh? Do tell." He's still grinning like a shark.

"I—" I don't. Why did I say I have proof? All I have is the test paper from SiliconBrains, someone I don't know.

Someone who probably stole it from Mr. Werner in the first place. “I have proof,” I say again, “and trust me, you don’t want to tell Mrs. Henderson.”

His face twitches. “Don’t tell me what I want or don’t want. Know what I want? I want to keep my job.”

“Am I in the way of that?”

An eternity passes before he answers. “My in-laws.”

“Come again?” What the heck do I have to do with his in-laws?

That twitch again. “Daniel’s parents.”

Right. That bizarre familial connection.

“They called,” he says. “They don’t want you to keep seeing Daniel.”

Wow. This is not real. This is—no. “Did I just step into a K-drama? What’s going on?”

“You’re not stupid. You know why.”

The phone call from Danny’s mom. Danny telling her she’s racist. My own mother’s struggle to be accepted by Papa’s family. There’s a feeling in my stomach, this horrible clench like when you bite into a piece of fruit and realize it’s rotten. I’m thinking of Ibu now. Realizing just how much of this hate she’s had to go through. Papa’s whole family seeing her as nothing more than a brown woman.

“I’ll stop seeing Danny,” I say, desperately. “We’ll just be friends. Please, don’t report me.”

“I don’t think they’ll believe that.”

"So I'm going to be expelled because I started dating the wrong guy?" My entire future is about to be destroyed because I'm the wrong color.

"If it makes you feel better, that's not quite true. You're going to be expelled because you cheated on my test." He picks up his phone and starts dialing.

And then. Something magical happens.

The door to his office swings open, and Mandy strides in, saying, "Here's the rest of the money—"

The only thing wider than my eyes is my mouth. And Mandy's mouth. It's just for a second, then she quickly recovers and says, "For the school trip. What're you doing here?"

"What school trip?" I say.

Mandy glares at me. "The school trip from last semester."

"Where did you guys go?"

"The museum," Mandy says.

"Which museum?" I'm relentless. I'm a shark that smells blood.

"MoMA. In SF."

"Why would an English Lit class go to the MoMA?"

"Enough." Mr. Werner's voice silences us both. "Come back later," he says to Mandy.

She shoots me her very best bitch face and then stalks out with a hair flick. I turn back to look at Mr. Werner. I have no idea if I have enough to report him—in fact, I probably don't—but this is enough to shake the board, surely?

"So you were telling me about how you're not selling grades to your students?" My voice comes out a lot calmer than I'm feeling.

Mr. Werner looks almost bored. "It'll be your word against mine."

Shit, he's right. It'll be me, a struggling kid from a neighborhood known for its delinquents against him, a well-respected teacher. I struggle to remain confident. "Yeah, but if I reported you, they'll have to do an investigation, just in case."

"And they'll find nothing. I'm nothing if not meticulous. This is a service I'm offering only to a select few of my students. It doesn't affect the other students' grades overmuch, certainly nothing that would look off to anyone else."

"What if I paid? Like the other kids do?"

"You won't be able to afford it. There's a reason why only the wealthiest students can take up my offer. An A costs twenty thousand dollars."

My hand goes to my kris pendant, squeezing it, my thumb going over the familiar grooves on the sheath. "I don't need an A. I just need to pass."

"A C goes for ten thousand. Per test."

I glare at him, searching every part of my mind for something. Anything.

"Sophie!"

"Yes, what about her?"

Talk about grasping at straws. But you know what? Even

straws are better than nothing. "She knows what you're doing." A flash of Sophie, kicking madly. "We've been talking." If her gouging cryptic messages on my wall counts as talking. "She says she's got proof. I wasn't sure before, but if there's two of us reporting you, they'll investigate—"

"And, like I just said, they'll find nothing."

"Maybe not on you, but what about the kids?" I'm on to something now. I can feel it, same way dogs can sense the hunt. "Your customers. Not all of them are going to be as anal as you. Look how careless Mandy was. It's not gonna take much to find something on her or any of your other customers. We're *kids*!" I spit the word at him.

Mr. Werner doesn't say anything for a while, but his jaw clenches and grinds as he watches me. He doesn't look bored anymore, so I know—I know—I've got him. He can't take me down as easily as he thought. "I don't have a choice, Lia."

"You do! You could—" What? What can he do? "Just give me some time. Just—I'll look into transferring out of here." Crazy. Completely nuts. But I can't think of anything else right now. "I'll tell them it's a family emergency or whatever. I'll make it work. Please, Mr. Werner." My voice comes out trembly with tears. "I can't—I need this. For college."

He closes his eyes. "I'll think about it."

He won't. But maybe I've bought myself a bit of time.

CHAPTER 10

Not that I have any idea what to do with that time. Once I get back to my room, I fire up my computer and do a search on schools, but I know it's futile. Even if Mr. Werner were to write me a glowing recommendation—which is hard to believe—what respectable school is going to let me join in the middle of the school year, especially when I've started at Draycott not long ago? Too many jumps in such a short time. They'll know something's off.

No, what I need to do is find irrefutable evidence of Mr. Werner's cheating ring. I open my email and type out a message to SiliconBrains.

I need your help. I swallow the lump in my throat and hit Send. God, please send me help.

Luckily, SiliconBrains replies almost immediately. Whoever they are, they've got their phone surgically attached to them. Which doesn't narrow down the possibilities.

If you want another test paper, you're going to have to do something for me.

I don't actually need another test paper. I need to know how you found out about Mr. Werner's cheating ring. Send.

Why?

Why? Because racism. That's fucking why. Non-Asians wouldn't understand the hierarchy that exists between different Asian cultures. To them, we're all just one big giant category. And if SiliconBrains IS Asian, then chances are, they've probably got the same bias that everyone else does, so. It's hard to explain, but basically, I need proof of the cheating ring, otherwise I'm outta here.

Silence.

Okay, now I'm desperate. Please. I'll lose everything if I can't prove it. I hit send. Almost instantaneously, I get a reply.

> Delivery to the recipient failed permanently:
> SiliconBrains@gotmail.com. Reason: This user
> does not have a gotmail account.

No, no, no. I must have typed in his address wrong. Except I didn't type in his address, I just tapped on the Reply button. I try it again, replying to an older message of his. Just in case it's a glitch in Gotmail. I get the same error message. I try typing in the address manually, but my hands are shaking too hard, and I end up dropping my phone.

"No," I whisper hoarsely, choking back my tears. SiliconBrains has deleted his account. He's gone, and I still have nothing on Mr. Werner.

I find Danny at the quad, throwing a Frisbee around with Aiden R. and Aiden B., and for a moment, I just stand there, watching. They're all wearing woolen sweater vests, and they're all broad-shouldered and tall, and the entire scene looks like a catalog page from J. Crew. Danny, with his openmouthed laugh and that hair flopping across his forehead, looks so wholesome. I'm the wicked witch, come to destroy this all-American scene. Maybe I should just go.

But then Aiden B. spots me and gestures to Danny. He looks over and his eyes light up. My heart does this weird skip-hop. I smile weakly as he jogs over to me.

"Hey, you," he says. I always think I know how he looks, and then I see him close-up and realize I've totally underplayed how amazing he looks in real life. He's literally breathtaking. I mean, I'm actually finding it hard to breathe, though that probably also has to do with what I'm about to ask him to do.

"Hey. Can we go somewhere and talk?" The two Aidens are within hearing distance, and Aiden B. goes, "bow chicka bow wow." I flip him off, but my heart's not in it.

"Sure." Danny takes my hand, and we walk off the quad. This time of day, with the sun dipping low and painting the sky with pink streaks, everyone's out enjoying themselves. Every bench is taken, and every tree has a picnicking group under it.

"Narnia hole?" I say.

"Narnia hole."

I feel über-conspicuous as I crouch down and crawl through the hole. Any time now, some teacher is going to see us and yell, "WTH are you kids doing?" And then I'm gonna end up getting the Narnia hole closed up and—

We make it through the hole. No one yells at us, no alarms are raised. I'm half-relieved, half disappointed. Because now I actually have to do the Thing. Okay, just say it. Swallow the Band-Aid. Rip off the frog.

"Your uncle is running a cheating ring!"

I clap a hand over my mouth. Okay, that could have been said with a lot more tact and lot less volume.

Danny blinks, a confused smile on his face. "My uncle's what now?"

"Running a cheating ring."

"A cheating ring? Like, men who cheat on their wives?"

I groan. "No." It takes some time getting him up to speed,

and by the end of my rambling, Danny's no longer smiling. Very definitely not smiling. Then he snorts.

"Okay, you got me. That was a good one. Kind of bizarre, but very creative."

An ugly knot forms in my stomach. "I'm not kidding. Mr. Werner really is selling grades to students."

He lets go of me then, leaving a cold emptiness on my arm where his hand was. "Do you have any proof?"

"I've got the emails from SiliconBrains, and Sophie's writing on the wall in my room—" I wish my voice didn't come out so shrill. But desperation has me in its claws, and I can't back down. Not right now.

"You know how crazy this sounds?"

I can't lose him too. I think of something else. "Your parents."

Danny smiles, but it's not a nice smile. It reminds me of Mr. Werner's smile, no heart in it whatsoever, and the knot in my stomach turns to ice. "You gonna tell me they're involved in this cheating ring too?"

"No. But—" An idea strikes me, and I grab it. "Remember the phone call you got from your mom? Telling you to break up with me?"

And, against all odds, Danny's face goes slack as realization dawns. The knot in my gut loosens, just a little, and I dive in.

"Mr. Werner is selling grades, which makes it hard for

me to pass his class, but even if I manage to pass some other way, he's still going to fail me, because he needs to have me kicked out of school. Because your parents called him and told him to get rid of me." I pause then add, "Okay, I know how that sounds, but if you think about it within the context of a Chinese-Indo family, it's actually not that unrealistic."

Danny's rubbing his forehead like he's got a giant headache. "No," he says, after a while. "It doesn't sound totally nuts. Not for my parents."

"Yeah! I mean, not about your parents specifically, but just thinking of my dad's family and the shit they pull. Anyway, so maybe Mr. Werner was, you know, pushed into doing it..." Except he wasn't, but if getting Danny on my side means I have to paint Mr. Werner out to be some tortured saint, then so be it.

"I need to talk to him."

"No!" I cry. "What's he gonna say? 'Yes, Danny, I'm being threatened by your parents to get your girlfriend kicked out of school'?"

Danny sighs, all his earlier anger melting from his features. "I don't know. This all sounds so. I don't know. Uncle James is the best person ever. And my aunt Joanna—man, you don't even want to know. She's my mom's younger sister. And she's pretty insistent on their kids living with her in Indo, so she's vying real hard for custody. I just can't see Uncle James doing anything that could potentially lose him custody, you know?"

My frustration threatens to boil over. I mean, seriously. *The best person ever?* If things weren't so fucked, I would've cackled at that. How could Danny be so ignorant to the truth? Somehow, I manage to keep my voice calm. "Maybe that's what your parents are using to make him do this."

He sighs again. A long, defeated one. "God. You know what the worst part is? The worst part about all of this is that part of me isn't surprised. Because part of me felt that something was off. Nothing like what you're saying," he says quickly, when I straighten up like a meerkat. "More like, I don't know—he's been drinking a lot more, and he's a lot quieter. And a couple weeks back, he left this brown leather ledger on the back seat of his car, so I picked it up to hand it to him, and he like screamed at me and grabbed the ledger really quickly. An actual scream. He was so panicked and angry. I thought maybe it was legal documents for his custody case, but who knows?" He meets my eye. "I'll look into it."

I can't believe it. "Really?"

"You don't have to look so excited about me trying to find out if my uncle's guilty."

"Sorry," I say hurriedly. "It's just—my entire future's kind of riding on this, so."

"I know. Don't get your hopes up, though, okay? I have no idea where that ledger is—I haven't seen it since."

Don't get my hopes up. Kind of hard when just moments ago, they were way beyond rock bottom.

What I should be doing over the next few days: focusing on school and track, and keeping my head down.

What I do instead: spend all of my free time poking around campus for clues and shooting Danny hopeful looks whenever I come across him. It always makes his cheerful expression somewhat less cheerful, and he'd give a small shake of the head, and I'd get this horrible pit opening up in the base of my stomach.

After a couple of days of this, I finally gather enough courage to bring up an idea I've had. A horrible, awful idea. We're walking in the Eastern Gardens when I say, "You mentioned before that you sometimes have dinner at Mr. Werner's house?"

"Yeah?" Danny says.

"Um. Maybe you could. Um. Poke around his house and see if you can find something?" I once watched a really weird sci-fi movie starring Natalie Portman. There's a scene where these guys who're trapped in an alien, radioactive zone start to mutate, and they decide to carve one of their friends open, as you do. There's a close-up of the poor dude's intestines all twisting and creeping and sliding around like snakes, and that's exactly how my insides feel right now. They're twisting around painfully because of how incredibly shitty I'm being. I can't believe I'm actually asking Danny to snoop around his uncle's house. This is how low I've sunk. Or maybe I've always been this low, I just never had an occasion to prove how low I really am. “I’m sorry, never mind—”

“I’ll do it.”

“What? No, I was just—it’s a ridiculous idea.”

“No, it’s not. He has a home office where he keeps all his folders and whatever. I’ll have a quick look. I probably won’t find anything, but it won’t hurt to check.”

“What if he finds you snooping around in his office?” My voice is shrill now. I can’t bear the thought of Danny getting caught by Mr. Werner. That weird laugh of Mr. Werner’s. No matter how hard Danny tries to paint his uncle as a wholesome family guy, there’s something more lurking under the surface.

“Then I’ll tell him I was looking for something else. Like…my passport or something. He’s got a bunch of my documents for safekeeping ’cause my parents don’t trust me to keep hold of my own stuff.” He sounds so sure, so confident. Maybe he’ll find something.

“Thank you.” I squeeze his hand, not daring to let myself hope for too much and yet unable to stop myself from doing it anyway.

On Saturday, I do everything I can to take my mind off what Danny’s about to do. I run myself ragged on the track. I hang out with the girls and try my best to take part in normal human conversation. Then, halfway through dinner, as Sam tells us about some Netflix show she and Grace are watching, realization strikes me.

Danny's at Mr. Werner's house. Which means Mr. Werner is sure to be off campus. Which means his office will be left unguarded.

CHAPTER 11

I can't really just leave the dining table halfway through the meal without at least giving a good excuse. Or can I? Would it look really suspicious? The thought of stealing into a teacher's office turns my hands to ice. I'm about to fake food poisoning when Beth's phone goes off. She checks it and straightens up, her shoulders going rigid.

"I gotta bounce."

Sam and Grace groan. "Seriously?" Sam says.

"Sorry, work calls," Beth says.

This is my chance. I stand up as well. "I'm going too."

As we leave the dining hall, I worry that Beth's going to ask me why I'm skipping out on the meal too, but it seems she's got other things on her mind. I've never seen her this quiet. But when I ask her what's bothering her, she says, "Just some logistical issue on my site."

We both hurry back to the dorms, and Beth shouts a quick "Bye!" before slamming the door to her room. A second later, I hear the click of the lock on her door. I go back to my own room and pace around, trying to sort out my chaotic plan.

I'm going to do it. I won't get another chance like this. I mean, yes, technically, I am aware that Mr. Werner probably leaves his office every night, but tonight I am 100 percent sure he's not going to be there, so this is it. Do or die.

I change into black pants and a black top, decide it looks way too suspicious, and change into a navy-blue top. I grab a handful of bobby pins and stick them in my hair. Let's hope Mr. Werner has flimsy locks in his office that I can pry open with the help of a bobby pin.

As I make my way to Collings Building, I have to keep reminding myself to walk normally instead of like someone's who's about to break into a teacher's office. My body has completely forgotten how to move like a human. Every step feels wrong, the way my arms swing feels weird, and it feels like there's a neon flashing sign on my head that says GUILTY. Somehow, I manage to make it across the quad without running into anyone. The front door to Collings is locked. Of course it's locked. Why wouldn't it be? I go around to the side, where there's an entrance for the janitors, and yes! The side door opens smoothly.

Once inside, the enormity of what I'm doing catches up in a sudden swoop. Maybe it's the emptiness of the place. In the daytime, the hallways are always bustling with students getting to class. Now, it's half dark, with only a few of the lights on, but more than that, it's the silence that gets to me. Every step I take is thunderous, the sound bouncing off the walls. I swallow, and I swear the gulp is audible from the other end of the hallway.

I tiptoe as quietly as I can—which isn't very—toward the stairs. Teachers' offices are on the fourth floor. Just as I round the corner on the third floor, I hear footsteps. I slink back down the stairs and hide behind a corner. The footsteps come closer, then stop some distance away. Keys jingle. A door is opened. The footsteps recede. I chance a peek in time to see the janitor pushing his cleaning cart into a classroom. I keep going.

Fourth floor. It seems more menacing than the other floors, somehow. Maybe because in Chinese culture, the number four is the unluckiest number. Guess which office is Mr. Werner's? 404. Everything about the man is a bad omen.

I creep forward, realize that slinking toward his office while keeping my entire back to the wall looks suspicious as hell, and decide to just walk normally. If the janitor or anyone else finds me here, I can tell them I'm turning in a paper, slipping it under a teacher's door. Except I don't have any papers with me. I rip a couple announcements off the nearest bulletin board.

Here it is, 404. Mr. James Werner. I try the doorknob, expecting it to be locked, but to my surprise, it turns easily. That's strange. Someone who's involved in the kind of shady shit that Mr. Werner is should be more paranoid, right? Maybe he just forgot to lock it today? Okay, never mind, I'm not one to question such good luck.

I slide inside and, keeping my eyes on the door, gently push it shut. My breath releases with a *whoosh* and I lean my forehead against the door, shutting my eyes

God, it feels wrong to be in here. My stomach does that alien-gut-twist thing again. It's the smell. Mr. Werner's cologne hangs heavy in the dead air, reminding me that this is his space and I'm not supposed to be here.

Okay, never mind that. Focus. I need to get moving. But before I even turn around to look at the office, I hear footsteps from the hallway. My heart jerks painfully. Calm down, it's probably the janitor. He'll walk past this door, I'm sure of it. But whoever it is doesn't walk past Mr. Werner's door. They stop right outside. There's a pause, during which my mind screeches at a million miles an hour. Then the doorknob starts to turn.

There's no time for me to hide before the door swings open. Light floods the office, blinding me for a second, and when my eyes adjust, I find myself face-to-face with Stacey.

"What the hell?" I blurt out.

"Shut up," Stacey hisses as she shuts the door. "Do you want the whole school to know we're here?"

"What the hell are you doing here?" I whisper.

"None of your business. What are you doing here?" she snaps.

I gape at her for a second too long. She shoulders past me with a sigh and says, "Just stay out of my way, okay?" She takes a few steps into the deep gloom of the office and stops with a gasp.

"What is it?" I hurry over, and that's when I see it. Shoes. Attached to someone's legs. Lying on the floor, the rest of their body hidden behind Mr. Werner's desk. My chest seizes. I feel as though I'm having a heart attack. But somehow, I keep walking, as though whoever is behind Mr. Werner's desk is calling out to me.

"What are you doing? Stop, Lia!" Stacey hisses at me, her voice cracking with fear, but I can't. My feet are moving on their own accord.

Another step, and another. I understand now, why people say "my heart was in my throat." It genuinely feels as though my heart is lodged in my neck, like I'm being slowly strangled from the inside. And when I finally reach the other side of the desk and I see the small, limp shape, the face shining sickly pale from moonlight streaming through the window, I think I might faint.

It's Sophie Tanaka, the girl I'd seen my first day here, the one who had punched Mr. Werner in the face, the girl I'd replaced. And from the way her eyes lie open, staring unblinking at the ceiling, one thing becomes excruciatingly clear.

Sophie is dead.

CHAPTER 12

I have to give it to Stacey. While I stand there, frozen in shock, she takes out her cellphone and dials 911. She sounds scared but somehow manages to tell the 911 operator that we've found a dead body at our school. She even retains enough lucidity to tell them exactly which building we're at and what room we're in.

"Come on," she says after hanging out. "We should wait outside."

"But." I can't tear my eyes off Sophie.

Stacey takes my arm gently and starts to tug me away. "No," I say, my voice coming out surprisingly loud. I pull my arm away. "We can't just leave her. She'll be alone then." Tears spring to my eyes, hot and stinging. Sophie looks so helpless and tiny, like a child. I don't want to leave her here, in the office of the man she blamed for everything. It feels wrong, somehow.

"Seriously," Stacey says. "They said to wait outside. It might be dangerous here."

That shakes me out of my daze. Dangerous? I stare at Sophie with renewed horror. I'd assumed she'd taken her own life, but what if I was wrong? What if it was murder?

Suddenly, I can't get the hell out of the office fast enough. Stacey takes my hand again, and together, we rush out of the office and hurry down the stairs, not stopping until we're outside. The cold air feels sharp on my skin, and I take deep, shaky gulps of it. God, did that really just happen? Did we really just come across a dead body? Stacey walks a few paces away, hugging herself and shaking her head, muttering something like, "It's okay, it's okay, it's okay." She does not sound okay. A small voice inside my head whispers that I should go comfort her, but I do not have it in me to comfort anyone right now. My mind's a mess. My breath is coming in a high-pitched wheeze, and I can't seem to stop my hands from shaking.

"What the hell happened in there?"

It takes a second to realize that I've spoken out loud. Stacey's head jerks up, her face looking haunted. "I don't know," she mutters.

"Was she—did someone—"

"I don't fucking know, okay? Stop asking such fucking stupid questions!" With that, Stacey buries her face in her hands and utters a strangled cry.

I focus on trying to breathe. Just inhale. Exhale. Inhale. I keep seeing Sophie's thin legs sprawled on the floor. Bile rushes up my throat. Maybe she was just passed out. No, not with her eyes open like that. Oh god. She's dead. She's DEAD. And that's when it hits me. She's not just dead, she's dead in Mr. Werner's office. Mr. Werner, the man who has a really shady business going on. The man whose house I've sent Danny to snoop into.

It's as though every cell in my body has exploded. I feel hot, like I'm suddenly running a high fever. I need to get a hold of Danny. I yank my phone out of my pocket and my palms are so slick with sweat that I immediately drop it. I grab it, my fingers all thumbs, unlock it, and call Danny. There are two rings before it abruptly goes to voicemail. My stomach drops. I hit Dial again, and this time, it goes to voicemail right away. Oh shit. What does that mean? Did he get caught by Mr. Werner?

But just as I'm about to freak out, Danny sends a text: Can't talk now, will call in a bit.

I'm in the midst of typing out a reply when lights flash in the darkness. A few feet away, Stacey gasps, "Thank god, finally!" The ambulance has arrived.

A crowd has gathered, hungry eyes watching as Sophie's body is carted out on a stretcher by paramedics. My gaze keeps straying from the cop who's taking my statement to the stretcher. The paramedics have covered Sophie with a blanket, but I can't stop imagining her underneath that white cloth, her face so blank, devoid of any expression. As they load the stretcher into the ambulance, a boy breaks through the crowd, his eyes wild. I vaguely recognize him as the boy who tried to help Sophie that first day.

"Logan! Stay back!" someone shouts.

He ignores them, making a beeline for the stretcher. Before he can get to it, a police officer steps in his path. "Calm down, son," the cop says.

"Fuck you!" Logan shouts. "Let me see her!"

The cop lays a heavy hand on Logan's shoulder and gently but firmly leads him away. The other kids are all aiming their phones at him, recording him as he shouts and struggles and begs the cop to let him see Sophie. My insides twist with sympathy and fear and what feels like every emotion there is.

"And what were you doing in there at this time of night?" the officer says to me.

I blink and snap back to the cop in front of me. "Uh." Belatedly, it hits me that I haven't thought of a good explanation as to why I was in Mr. Werner's office so late at night.

"It was a dare," Stacey says. I turn and find her right

next to me. I haven't even been aware that she'd been here all along.

The officer frowns at Stacey, who shrugs. "I'd dared Lia to break into the teachers' building."

The cop narrows her eyes, obviously doubting Stacey.

"It's true," I blurt out loud. "We dare each other to do stupid stuff all the time. Sorry," I mumble.

The cop shakes her head with a sigh. "I was a teen once. I know what it's like. So you were dared to break into the building. What made you go into this particular office?"

Think fast! My mind screams. "Um, the door was left open." I go over what I just said, picking it apart for flaws, finding none. "Yeah, it was like halfway open, so I went to close it, and that was when I saw um. The body." Those two words feel like stones coming out of my mouth. So alien, so wrong.

The officer nods, writing this down in her notepad. "That's unfortunate," she says sympathetically. She turns to Stacey. "And you were with her the whole time?"

"Yeah," Stacey says quickly. "I was the one who called nine-one-one."

The cop nods. "Alright, sounds good. If we have any questions, we know where to find you."

Is it just me, or does that sound really ominous?

Just then, Mrs. Henderson arrives, her hair all messy, her eyes raw from interrupted sleep. Her arrival causes a few murmurs to rise from the crowd, as she pushes her way toward us. "Officer, I'm the school principal. What's going on?"

The cop who's been questioning me leads Mrs. Henderson away, speaking in a low voice. I catch Mrs. Henderson's soft gasp and the words, "Has anyone called her parents?" before they go out of earshot.

Stacey clears her throat. "Hey, so—"

"Lia!" someone calls out, and relief surges through me because it's Danny, oh, thank god, he's okay. I hurry over to him, forgetting everything else. The whole time, my head is just going, *He's okay, he's okay!*

"Danny, thank god!" Everything else I'm about to say dies halfway out my mouth because right behind Danny is Mr. Werner. But Mr. Werner isn't looking at me or even in my direction. He's staring at the ambulance, his mouth parted and his eyes wide with horror.

"James," Mrs. Henderson hurries over, and the cop talking to her follows.

"Sir, are you James Werner? Your office is in that building, room 404?" the officer says.

Mr. Werner nods. "What happened?"

The officer leads him and Mrs. Henderson away from the crowd, out of earshot. I turn to Danny, grasping his arms tightly. "Oh god, Danny. I'm so relieved you're okay."

"What happened?" Danny says.

At that, the everythingness of it all crashes down on me

and I sag into his arms, my face crumpling into ugly, uncontrollable sobs. Danny gently leads me away from everyone while I cover my face and try without luck to control my crying. I barely register where we're going until the doors swing shut and I realize we've gone inside a building.

We're inside the boys' dorm. I'm too upset to register anything else aside from the distinct smell of sweaty gym socks and Axe body spray. I try to control my sobs as we walk down the hallway and into Danny's room, and once we're inside, we sit down on his bed and he holds me tight, keeping his arms around me as I fall apart.

It's a long while before I run out of tears. I rest my head on his shoulder as he strokes my hair gently. I haven't felt this spent in a long while. My insides have been carved raw and empty. Danny asks if I'm okay to talk about what happened, and I release a wobbly breath and nod. I start with getting the idea to sneak into Mr. Werner's office to look for the ledger and tell him all about running into Stacey. I'm stalling, I know it. I don't want to talk about Sophie, about seeing her shoes first, followed by those skinny, long legs of hers. I don't want to relive that moment, the worst moment of my life, of realizing that there's a dead girl in the same room, someone I can't help, no matter how much I want to. But finally, I do.

"Wait, you found—what? Sophie? As in, Sophie Tanaka?" Danny's voice is sharp. Under my head, his shoulders stiffen, and he stands up so abruptly that I'm taken aback.

"Yeah. The girl who—uh, well, you know."

"How the hell did that happen?" he cries.

I gape at him. "I don't know. I think Stacey said it looks like Sophie overdosed on something."

"No, I mean how the hell did she manage to sneak back in here? She's not at Draycott anymore. And last I heard, she was a total druggie, but somehow she managed to sneak back onto campus? Did you know that she assaulted my uncle not long ago?"

Okay, this is not the reaction I was expecting. Danny actually looks…angry. Maybe under normal circumstances, I would be more patient, but I'm done with this cursed day. I have no fucks left to give. "Who cares how she snuck back in here? The school grounds cover hectares of land, I'm sure there's a ton of ways to get inside. And you're missing the point, which is that a girl's dead, Danny! What the fuck?"

The raw panic in my voice catches Danny, and he stops pacing. He sighs and grimaces. "You're right. I'm sorry. I just freaked out because yeah, you're right, holy shit. A girl's dead. A girl I knew. We were in quite a few of the same classes last term. Jesus." He sinks back down onto the bed next to me and rubs his forehead, looking suddenly very, very tired. "And she was in my uncle's office?" When I nod, he groans and slumps down on the bed, staring at the ceiling. "Poor Uncle James."

Poor Uncle James? I want to scream at him. Poor Sophie!

Am I the unreasonable one here? Sophie's the victim, not Mr. Werner. He screwed her over so badly with his stupid cheating business that she took her own life in his office, and we're sitting here feeling bad for Mr. Werner? I can just imagine Mr. Werner right now, talking to the police. He'd be saying all the right things, murmuring about how awful he feels, how disturbed Sophie had been. He'd probably even bring up the fact that she punched him a few weeks ago. At the end of the day, Mr. Werner would get out of this unscathed, and Sophie would still be dead.

The thought bolsters me, infusing me with renewed anger. Enough to say, "So, um, I hate to ask right now, but did you manage to find anything at Mr. Werner's house?"

Danny releases the longest sigh in the history of sighs, which immediately makes me feel like such a terrible person for asking him that at this moment. But still, tonight's events serve as more evidence that Mr. Werner doesn't deserve to be a teacher.

Danny closes his eyes for a long moment before opening them and sitting back up. But even when he's sitting upright, he keeps his gaze at his lap, avoiding my eyes. "Sorry. It's been a shitty night. I mean, not as bad as yours, obviously. But." He sighs again. "My cousins are in Indo and weekends are always hard on Uncle James, especially in that big house all alone. And then I asked him to look for my old baseball cards, and while he was looking for them in the garage, I went through his home office. It was just—I felt like such a shit, and I didn't find anything. I'm sorry."

The disappointment is crushing. Sickening. I haven't realized just how much hope I've pinned on him finding something until this point.

"It's okay." It's not okay. It's so not, but there's no use in pushing him. He's tried his best, and he looks so deflated, I can't bear to say anything else.

Danny takes my hand, interlaces our fingers. "We'll find another way," he says.

It's all I can do to bring myself to nod. Another way. I close my eyes and try not to think of Sophie, lying alone in Mr. Werner's office, staring forever at his ceiling.

CHAPTER 13

The next morning, I take a longer time than usual brushing my hair into a neat ponytail and making sure my uniform's flawless. Shirt: crisp. Blazer: ironed. Skirt: three fingers above the knee. Socks: four fingers above the ankle. I force myself to focus on each task with a fierce intensity so I don't have to think about last night, but Sophie haunts every minute I'm awake. Every time I close my eyes, her blank, unseeing face flashes through my mind until I can't take it any longer. I need to talk to someone. A grown-up. Someone who will solve everything.

I can't stomach the thought of going to breakfast. I haven't even dared to look at my phone. I know DD has probably blown up with stories about last night, and I don't want to know all the nasty gossip that must have been posted about Sophie. I don't want to see my classmates' faces at the dining hall, eating while gossiping with barely concealed glee about Sophie. Once I'm dressed, I head straight to the principal's office.

The receptionist is a kindly old lady who takes one look at my pale face and somber expression and says, "Let her finish her coffee first. It'll be best for everyone." I give her a weak smile and sit there, wringing my hands, until the receptionist nods and tells me it's probably safe for me to go in. My legs are all wobbly when I get up.

Mrs. Henderson sits behind a stupidly huge mahogany desk. It's the kind of desk a dude might buy to compensate for smaller things. Or maybe the kind of desk one buys to intimidate the shit out of problematic students. It's working. I feel tiny and dispensable.

She looks up when I enter, and I swear she actually sighs. "Ah, Lia Setiawan."

Why does she know my name? Does she know the name of every student here? Considering there are over a thousand students in this school, probably not, which brings us back to the first question: Why does she know mine?

"Sit down, Lia."

I do as she says, reminding myself not to pick at my fingernails or fidget or anything. Mrs. Henderson looks harried, the lines on her face deeper than usual, locks of hair flying loose from her usually flawless bun. I realize belatedly that she must have spent all night putting out fires everywhere and that maybe this isn't the best time for me to…do whatever the hell it is I'm trying to do.

"What can I do for you?" Mrs. Henderson says with a small, tight smile. A smile that obviously takes a lot of effort to put on.

"Um, I—um, I came here to talk about, um—" *Stop saying* um. "Ummm…" I clear my throat. My fists are clenched. "I wanted to talk about last night."

Mrs. Henderson's lips tighten, like a purse whose strings are being tugged closed. "I'm sorry, but I cannot discuss any details regarding last night."

"No, I know, I'm not here to talk about Sophie—well, I sort of am—but only in relation to Mr. Werner."

Now a frown appears on her face, and she clasps her hands and leans forward. "Mr. James Werner, your English Lit teacher? What about him?"

God, here it goes. My hands clench tightly. "Um, it's going to sound really crazy."

She utters a sharp, bitter laugh. "Given the night we've all just had, I think it's safe to say nothing else will faze me now."

"Okay," I manage. I take a deep breath, then I tell her everything. Mr. Werner's class, track and Mandy, dating Danny. She frowns when I tell her about failing English Lit, looking concerned. With shaky, sweaty hands, I lay out all the pieces of evidence I have—printouts of my emails with SiliconBrains, the copy of the test SiliconBrains gave me, pictures of Sophie's messages on my walls, and my English Lit test papers.

Mrs. Henderson flips through the papers, and the whole time, the groove between her eyebrows deepens, but she says nothing as I babble on until I get all the way to last night. "And I think he was doing the same thing to Sophie, which was why she—"

"Let me stop you right there," she says, holding up her hand. "We're not going to make wild guesses on Sophie Tanaka or any other students or ex-students here, okay?" She sounds so stern that my insides shrivel up and I quickly nod.

"Yeah, of course. Sorry, I didn't mean to be disrespectful."

She makes a "hmm" noise, like she's not convinced, then she frowns at me again. "Is that why you were at Mr. Werner's office last night? You told the officers that it was a dare. But it wasn't, was it?"

My mouth opens, but no words refuse to come out. Why would she ask me about that? Who cares why I was there, especially after everything I've just told her?

Seconds crawl by painfully before I finally manage to say, "Uh, sort of. I just. Um, ignoring the events of last night, because you're right," I add quickly, "I'm not here to gossip about Sophie at all, I guess I'm here because I needed to tell you about what's been going on with Mr. Werner. About him selling grades to students."

Mrs. Henderson's eyes close, and she pinches the bridge of her nose like she's trying to wish away my presence. After a while, she clicks her tongue and says, "Alright. Hang on a second, Lia."

She picks up her desk phone and taps a number. "Morning, April. I need you to look into an email account for me. The address is SiliconBrains@gotmail.com. Yes, this person—oh right." She puts a hand over the receiver and says, "Lia, April has to go into your email account in order to trace the messages from SiliconBrains. Is that all right with you?"

"Uh." I mentally scroll through the latest messages in my email. Anything bad or embarrassing? Not that I can remember.

"Lia?" Mrs. Henderson is watching me expectantly.

"Yeah, okay."

"All right, April, I'll have her send you her email details. Thank you. Yes, right away, please."

She hangs up and instructs me to email the IT person with my account name and password. I do it, but wow, does it ever feel wrong. Still, once I hit Send, I kind of feel slightly… hopeful. April will find out who SiliconBrains is, and then we can summon SiliconBrains here. This stupid shitty tunnel has a light, after all.

"These accusations are quite disturbing," Mrs. Henderson

says, taking off her glasses and placing them carefully on the table. "Do you know how many applicants we get every year?" She doesn't wait for an answer. "Over ten thousand. And that's not counting the scholarship applicants." She gets up from her desk and walks around her chair to gaze out of her huge picture window. "We only accept two hundred students every year, so out of those ten thousand applicants, less than five percent will make it here. We review scholarship applicants with an even more stringent eye."

What does this have to do with me, exactly? I swallow, trying to still my stomach.

"Last year, one scholarship student graduated with a full scholarship to Juilliard for cello. The other one went to Caltech. The year before that, our scholarship student received a Rhodes award to study at Oxford University. In England," she adds, in case I'm one of those rare idiots who don't know where Oxford University is. She finally looks at me, and her gaze is one 100 percent disappointment. No traces of warmth or sympathy.

Dread seeps into my limbs, poisoning every part of me.

"And now we have you. Lia Setiawan. A rising star on the track. *Runner's World* referred to you as the female answer to Usain Bolt! Of course, once we saw that, we had to take a look at you. And wow, did you ever blow us away. We thought that with the right training, you could be Olympics material." Mrs. Henderson shakes her head. "We chose you over a student who invented a machine to test for liver toxicity that costs two dollars to make. But we chose you, Lia, because who can turn down the next Usain Bolt?" Her phone rings, and she holds up a finger in my direction, as though I were about to interrupt, and then picks up the phone.

"April? Yes. You got in? Uh-huh. Right. That's what I thought." She looks at me, and it's like a door just got slammed in my face. Whatever April's found, it's nothing good.

I want a do-over. I want to turn back time and talk myself out of coming to Mrs. Henderson's office. Why the hell did I think I had enough evidence to back up my claim?

Mrs. Henderson hangs up the phone. "Would you like to hear what April said?"

No. "Yes."

"Well, this SiliconBrains email address is being used under a proxy server."

"A what?"

"A VPN."

All I know about VPNs is that they're what people use in countries like Indonesia, where porn is censored, to—well—watch porn.

"It makes the email impossible to trace." Mrs. Henderson narrows her eyes at me. "Which means there's no way you can prove that SiliconBrains isn't…well, you."

"What?" I cry, jumping to my feet.

"Enough lying, Lia." She's not shouting, but somehow, her voice is so commanding that I'm struck dumb. As I stand there, gaping like a fish on land, Mrs. Henderson takes out a folder from a drawer and slides it across the table toward me. I catch it and stare.

LIA SETIAWAN—DISCIPLINARY ACTION NEEDED.

The words are written in all caps. They're being shouted at me from the page.

From afar, I hear Mrs. Henderson say, "I was expecting you to come to my office. I thought you might want to apologize and explain your atrocious behavior and performance." She reaches across the table and flips the folder open.

The first page is titled: *James A. Werner's report on Lia Setiawan, English Lit 210.*

"Mr. Werner has a very long list of complaints about you. Cheating in class—well, you confirmed that all right. Then we've got lying, harassing fellow students—"

"Harassing fellow students?"

She flips over to the second page. The title burns its way through my retinas.

Lia Setiawan—Harassment Report

Victim: Mandy Kim

"Mandy Kim?" I cry.

"Young lady, do not raise your voice at me," Mrs. Henderson snaps.

I try, I really do, to get myself under control, but the

world's gone crazy, and I can't believe the extent to which Mr. Werner has gone to screw me over so completely. Tears sting my eyes. My breath's coming in and out in short, wheezy gasps. I need to make this right. "I'm sorry, but Mandy's had it in for me ever since I got here—"

"It's not just her," Mrs. Henderson says. She flips to the next page, and the next.

Lia Setiawan—Bullying Report

Victim: Elle Brown

Victim: Arjuna Singh

Victim: Yoshi Kitagawa

When Mrs. Henderson speaks, her voice is pure ice. "We have a zero-tolerance policy on bullying, Lia. And a zero-tolerance policy on cheating."

"I didn't—" My voice catches in my throat. It feels like a fist is squeezing my throat. "Mr. Werner—"

"Mr. Werner has been a teacher here for more than ten years. He hasn't had a single complaint against him."

"Sophie!" I cry. The grip around my throat loosens. There's something, finally. No matter how tenuous. "Sophie made a complaint about him. My first day here, she came here and she said he made her fail!"

Mrs. Henderson's face goes cold. "How dare you use that poor girl against him? After what happened last night? Do you not have any compassion?"

"I do!" I'm speaking too loud now, practically shouting,

but I can't help myself. "I sleep in her room! She wrote on the walls about Mr. Werner! I have nothing but compassion toward her. Don't you see? She killed herself because of him!"

"Enough!" Her voice slices through mine like a crack of thunder. She points a finger at me, wielding it like a sword. "I won't have such slanderous gossip about my teachers or my students. Draycott Academy is a sterling institution that creates future world leaders. It's clear that you do not belong here."

"Wait, what?"

She shakes her head. "I blame myself for this. I should have known you wouldn't fit in."

Wouldn't fit in? Never mind swimming, my mind is drowning.

"Against my better judgment, I thought maybe we could take a risk. I'm sorry for the mess, Lia. I will be filing for your expulsion immediately. It'll be effective right after the next board meeting, which is in..." She checks her calendar pointedly. "Two days' time. I suggest you start packing your things."

And just like that, all my nightmares about being kicked out of school scream into reality.

I don't remember walking out of Mrs. Henderson's office. Everything goes by under a murky layer, like I'm seeing myself in a dream. Somehow, I make it back to my room, where I sort of just slump onto the floor and lie there, not crying or sleeping or anything. I lie suspended in that state, outside of time and space, and watch the world turn.

It's over. Everything is over. There's nothing I can do to save myself. I'm sinking into the deep and dark. My limbs are lead. I'm well and truly defeated.

And then, suddenly, the anger finds me. And I let it swallow me whole.

I'm going to go down, that much is clear. No school will have me, not now that I'm about to get expelled from Draycott. My future is over. There's no saving me. But I'm not going to go down alone. I won't be the next Sophie, self-destructing because of Mr. Werner. I'm taking him down with me.

CHAPTER 14

It's very nearly noon when I resurface from my trance and decide I'm about to rain hell on Mr. Werner's life. I don't know what I'm going to do, but I have to do something. Something to quell this fire raging inside me, the hatred that drives all my thoughts. Something to avenge Sophie's death. It's painfully clear to me that she overdosed because of him, because he drove her to it, and I can't possibly let him get away with it.

I look up his schedule, my teeth grinding at the sight of his name on the school roster. God, I hate him. Now I know what it's like to truly hate someone, to despise them with every fiber of your soul. I scroll through DD, unsure what I'm looking for, but lapping up everything ever posted about Mr. Werner and Sophie. Just as I had expected, there are dozens of posts, a couple of them with hundreds of comments, about Sophie. Only a handful of posts are sympathetic, the majority are more on the vein of gleeful shock-horror, people shamelessly trying to troll for more information to use as gossip fodder. I close the app, feeling sicker and angrier than before.

At lunchtime, my phone buzzes.

From: Danny Wijaya

Hey, I hope you're okay. I'm sorry about last night, and I'm sorry I wasn't more helpful about the ledger stuff. Are you coming to lunch? Would love to be able to talk about everything.

I smile sadly. I start typing: No. I'm getting kicked out. Mandy Kim and her friends filed some bullshit reports about me bullying them, and between that and your uncle, I'm done here. But then I hit Delete. I look at the blank screen. I just. I don't have it in me to get into everything with Danny right now.

From: Lia Setiawan

I'm not feeling great, I think I have food poisoning.

From: Danny Wijaya

Oh no! Can I get you anything? Do you have Norit?

From: Lia Setiawan

Of course I have Norit. What kind of Indo would I be if I didn't have it?

From: Danny Wijaya

Ok. I'll come by after class. ❤

Crap. He can't do that.

From: Lia Setiawan

No, don't bother, I'll probably be napping. And I don't want you to catch whatever I have. I'll see you tomorrow!

I spend the rest of the afternoon pacing about my room again, opening and closing my hands, talking myself into and out of and into my crazy plan. At 3:55 p.m., I wait outside of Collings. I lurk around the corner and pretend to look at my phone while scanning the faces of people trickling out of the building. I wish I could cover my head, but wearing something like a hat or a hoodie would only make me stand out here.

Finally, I catch a glimpse of brown tweed and blond hair. I stuff my phone in my pocket and follow Mr. Werner, careful to keep some distance between us. Even this far away, the sight of him ignites the hatred inside me. I want to rush up and strangle him. Somehow, I manage to wrestle those instincts to the ground and focus instead on my plan. No brown leather ledger, but he is carrying his briefcase. Maybe the ledger's in there.

We walk past the tennis courts, all of which have been booked out by students. Their steady whacks and occasional shouts make me feel even more bitter, more untethered. I should be like them, spending my afternoons running and playing with my schoolmates, instead of literally stalking my teacher.

Finally, we arrive at the teachers' parking lot, which is deserted. Mr. Werner takes out his car remote, and a hundred feet away, a champagne-colored Nissan beeps to life and unlocks.

Now! my mind screams. I hide behind a tree, take out my phone, almost dropping it thanks to sweaty hands, and send a message I drafted earlier in the day. Less than a second later, Mr. Werner's phone beeps. He takes it out of his pocket and looks at it. I memorized the message I just sent, and I wish I could see his hateful face as he reads it.

"Mr. Werner, this is Janice from the admin office. Mandy's mother, Mrs. Alicia Kim, is here to see you regarding an urgent matter."

Succinct, believable, and totally, undeniably unignorable. I couldn't hide my number, but I'm hoping the thought of Mandy's mom waiting in his office would be enough to shock Mr. Werner into rushing back. Sure enough, as I watch, Mr. Werner curses out loud and then turns and heads back toward campus.

No time to hesitate. I sprint from behind the tree to his car. My heart explodes into a gallop. Oh god, oh god, what am I doing—

I ease the back door open and crawl inside. Lean over the front seat—shit, where's the trunk release button—there. I pop the trunk open and hurry out of the car, my heart in my throat, my hands slick with sweat. It's got to be there. It's not in his house, and after last night, he must have removed it from his office, so it must be here, it MUST.

The trunk's empty. No ledger. Hope crumbles to ash inside me. I close my eyes. That leaves his briefcase, which he still has on him. God. Why can't something go smoothly for once? I want to sink to my knees and burst into tears. I slam his trunk shut, not bothering to be quiet about it. Let him catch me at his car; what do I have to lose?

Just as I'm about to close the back door, something comes over me. Something wild and dangerous, snaking its way through my guts and all the way down my arms and legs. I find myself sliding back inside the car and curling up as small as possible on the back floor. I pull the door closed behind me, and I'm cocooned in sudden, complete silence.

Oh my god. What am I doing? I can't be here. I can't, I should go, I need to get out of here.

But my body refuses to comprehend. Or maybe my brain refuses to send the necessary messages to get my body the heck out of Mr. Werner's car. I don't know. I can't tell anymore. What's the new plan, genius? The new plan is—

New plan.

Okay.

New plan: The ledger's clearly inside his briefcase, which he's still carrying. I'll hide in the car until we get to Mr. Werner's house, and then I'll steal out and go inside his house while he's in the shower or his study room or whatever, and then I'll grab the ledger out of his briefcase and then get a Lyft back to Draycott, where I will slam the ledger on Mrs. Henderson's stupid mahogany desk and tell her to read it, and then I'll watch as that smug expression melts off her stupid plastic face and gets replaced by the perfect combination of shocked horror and shame. Maybe I'll bring a little bell so I can pull a *Game of Thrones* moment and shout "shame" while she reads it.

New Plan is good. I'm going to carry out New Plan.

NO. Dumbass, New Plan is bad. VERY BAD. You are literally sitting on the floor of his car. He's going to find you!

Time does that weird taffy-stretch thing where it goes fast and yet slow as my brain battles my brain. I should go. No, I won't get another chance like this. I should stay. But it's dangerous. I should go. Yes, I should definitely go. What the hell was I thinking? I can't be here, lying on the floor of my teacher's car. This is insane. I should—

The front door opens. The swirl of voices in my head abruptly goes silent. Mr. Werner throws his briefcase onto the passenger seat before sliding in. The car fills with the scent of his cologne. The sound of my breath is deafening. He's definitely, for sure, 100 percent going to hear it. And what will happen then?

For the first time today, I feel a sense of true fear stabbing deep into my belly. I haven't given this crazy thing I'm doing much thought beyond *I'm out of options, must do something, anything!* But now, a small, insistent voice is whispering, *What if Mr. Werner turns out to be dangerous? What if he hurts you?*

He wouldn't. He's cruel, and greedy, and awful, but I can't see him physically hurting anyone. I think.

But what if he reports this to the police? What if he spins it so that I'm stalking him? Coupled with all those false accusations about me bullying, maybe this would land me in juvie. Holy shit. This is bad. This is so bad.

But then he turns the engine on, and the sound of the AC and the engine help mask other sounds in the car. I take the chance to steal a few deep breaths and try to bring my heart rate from Quantum Computer Whirr down to Mere Gallop.

Before long, we're out of Draycott and on the main road. Maybe this plan isn't too crazy after all. I'll make it all the way to his house without him even knowing I'm here. I breathe a small sigh of relief and relax my muscles a little. Then Mr.

Werner takes something out of his pocket. I tense up again. He's got his phone in his hand. What is he doing—

It hits me a second too late. He's dialing the number that sent him the message. As in, MY number.

I scramble for my phone just as it begins to ring.

"What the—" Mr. Werner turns in his seat, his mouth dropping open, his eyes going so wide they're almost cartoonish. The car swerves to one side, horns blare, and I yelp as the momentum throws me against the door. He regains control of the wheel, makes a sharp turn, and screeches to a halt. "What in the fuck?" he screams, jumping out of the car.

I clamber up onto the back seat and hit the lock just before he wrenches the door open. He curses, hits the Unlock button on his remote. I hit the lock again.

"Get out of my car!"

It takes a lot—it takes everything—to shake my head at him.

"What the hell do you think you're doing?" He's a blur of movement, prowling outside the car. The front door is open, but it's hard for him to try and reach me from the front. He throws up his hands. "You're insane! You know how much trouble you're in right now? Do you? Unbelievable. First Sophie, now this."

"Can't get much worse than being expelled. Which I will be after the next board meeting, apparently. Mrs. Henderson told me herself. And don't talk about Sophie like that."

That stops him dead. He sighs. "I'm sorry." Bastard actually sounds like he means it. "And I am sorry about Sophie. God, of course I'm sorry about her."

My voice comes out as a poisonous whisper. "I don't think you are. You pushed her into being depressed, into killing herself. And now you're the whole reason I'm about to get kicked out of school. And it's not even about staying at Draycott now." To my horror, tears are sliding down my cheeks. "No school will have me. I'm finished."

"Christ," he mutters. "Look, I'm sorry. I truly am. I wish there were another way." A woman comes out of a nearby shop, pushing a stroller, sees me crying in the car, and gives Mr. Werner a funny look. He blanches. "Come on, I'll take you back to school."

"No!" My shout's loud enough for the woman to turn her head.

Mr. Werner gives her a small smile and then leans through the front door and whispers, "Alright, we'll talk. But not here. Christ, people are probably going to think I'm kidnapping you. Lie low on the floor and don't let anyone see you." He straightens his hair and climbs back into the driver's seat. He takes a deep breath, starts the car, and rejoins the traffic.

From my vantage point, I can see a really huge vein throbbing on the side of his neck and the way he's strangling the steering wheel. I struggle to control my breathing. What just happened?

Mr. Werner sighs. "I'm not a monster, you know."

Something in his tone of voice catches my attention, and I still.

"My life was fine, up until two years ago. Then my wife decided she'd had enough of middle-class life and left me. Just took off for Jakarta. She missed the city, she said. I pointed out to her that Draycott is hardly a small town, but oh no, compared to Jakarta, it's tiny." His voice drips with resentment, but I get what his wife meant.

People always think that Indonesia's some third-world country where people live in shacks and bathe in the river. I guess in the rural parts of the country, it's like that, but Jakarta is a huge city with ten million people. Ibu describes it as a place filled with skyscraper after skyscraper, luxury hotels and shiny nightclubs and trendy hipster cafes all bunched together in a never-ending metropolis. Compared to Jakarta, Draycott is nothing but a sleepy little town.

"She took my kids. You don't know what that's like. Losing her—I mean, yeah, that hurt, but losing my kids… it's like—god." His voice pitches all weird, and I look away out of embarrassment. I don't want to see Mr. Werner cry. I wish he'd stop talking already. He's making everything so awkward.

"You know what's funny?" he says. "Help came from—of all people—Daniel's mother. My wife's sister. Can you imagine that family dynamic?"

"Indonesian families are complicated," I mutter.

Mr. Werner laughs. "You can say that again! I guess Daniel's mother has always had a thing against her sister. So she contacted me and said she'd help pay for my lawyer's fees if I look after Daniel.

"She wanted me to meddle in his life. Make sure he's taking the right courses to prime him for business school. Make sure he's spending his time with the right friends. I sent her reports on Daniel and she sent me money to pay my lawyer, my mortgage. I have to be honest with you, the idea that my wife's own sister is helping me fight my wife tickled me. But it's a challenge to steer someone in a direction they don't want to go into. Despite my best efforts, Daniel never showed an interest in business. Then, a year ago, he ran away."

I know this story. Danny told me about it on our first date. The night we first kissed, under the string lights. God, that feels like a lifetime ago.

"Daniel's mother was apoplectic. I managed to convince her that I could do more to influence him. But I knew I couldn't just depend on her for money. I had to find a different way. You know how little teachers earn? Private school teachers earn more than public school teachers, but not much, certainly not enough to cover lawyer's fees, and my ex-wife has an endless pool of money on her end, them being crazy rich Asians and all." He spits out the word *Asians*, which makes my whole body bristle, the way he says it.

"The answer came from one of my students. A student who was failing my class. He came to see me during office hours and offered to pay me ten thousand dollars to let him pass. That was when it struck me. The answer's been right in front of me this whole time."

It's true. I think of Beth and her totally blinged-out room, of Sam and her insane car, of Danny and his three guitars.

"I approached a couple of my wealthiest, laziest students and made them an offer. And they jumped at it. I would've stopped, you know, once the divorce proceedings are finalized."

He pauses and his gaze flicks toward mine in the rearview mirror. The corners of his mouth lift into a—a something. It's most definitely not a smile. "Then you came along.

"I don't care what you are. Daniel's parents do, though. His mother threatened to back her sister's case, provide her with a character testimony or whatever." He laughs, a bit hysterically, and gives the steering wheel another squeeze. "I can't take on another one of them. There is no way I can afford—and my kids—" His voice cracks. "I'm not a bad person. I'm truly sorry that you got caught up in all this, Lia."

I can't meet his eye. I can't see him like this, vulnerable, without his usual sheen of self-assurance. It makes it that much harder to hate him.

Maybe I should just back off. Accept my fate and leave Draycott, forget about all this.

But then I think about Ibu and how she'd react when I tell her I got kicked out of school. The worst part is, she wouldn't scold me. She wouldn't even say anything mean; she's not that kind of mom. She'd try to hide her disappointment, and she'd hug me and tell me everything would be okay, and all the while, she'd be blaming herself for somehow failing as a mother.

And I recall my meeting with Mrs. Henderson and how my folder had been filled with accusation after accusation, all of it arranged by Mr. Werner. How effectively he'd ruined my reputation. This whole vulnerable thing is nothing but an act.

I have to do it. For my sake, and for Ibu's. I have to go through with my plan. Even if it ends up destroying both Mr. Werner and me.

CHAPTER 15

I'm so busy wrangling my own thoughts that I barely notice where we're headed until Mr. Werner stops the car. I stare out the window. Nothing but redwood trees towering around us. A nearby sign says WELCOME TO ORANGE POINT.

Orange Point. I remember Danny telling me about it once. He'd said it's a scenic overlook near the school, though there's not much scenery there. Just a pathetic little ledge down a dirt road that overlooks the river. About a fifteen-minute drive farther up the hill is Strawberry Point, which is a lot nicer than Orange. And I'm out here all alone with Mr. Werner. I take out my phone and try to send a message to Beth to let her know where I am, but there's no reception out here.

Mr. Werner turns off the engine and gets out of the car.

I take a deep breath and try to calm my thoughts into something coherent before getting out as well.

He doesn't waste any time. "So what do you want, Lia? You have to leave Draycott, I'm very sorry. But I'm not a monster, really, I'm not. Look, here's some money..." He actually takes his wallet out and rifles through it, like he thinks forty bucks might just be enough to make me disappear.

Now or never. I brandish my phone like a trophy. Because in a way, it is. "I did my homework."

Mr. Werner sighs. "Can't wait to hear it," he mutters. He actually looks bored.

Again, the rage flares deep inside me, and I fight to control my voice. "Have you heard of an app called Draycott Dirt?"

"Sounds like the kind of thing you kids nowadays spend too much time on."

"Um. Yeah, okay, that's true." I mentally shake myself. "It's an app that lets you post secrets anonymously. All you have to do is make up a username, and then you can post whatever you want, no questions asked. Any secret you want to share. About anyone."

He's stopped looking so bored now. Understanding is dawning on his face, and I can't decide whether it's a good sight or a terrifying one.

"I hate the app. People use it to bully others. Mandy and her posse post all sorts of crap about me all the time. I can't stand it. But then I realized, hey, if there's so much on me, a new student, what will I be able to find on *you*?"

"Hang on—"

I tap on my saved posts and start reading out loud. "*Why are only the richest kids the ones getting As?* Oh, here's a really good one. *I paid for an A- but got an A instead. Thanks for being so generous, Mr. W!*" Despite my heart hammering its way out of my rib cage, I manage to raise my eyebrows at him. "Did you just decide to give that kid a freebie? That's not very lucrative."

"A couple of kids telling lies on social media? This is hardly evidence," he spits. He stuffs his hands into his pockets. I bet he's starting to sweat. Good.

"Yeah, except it's not just a couple of kids. There are over thirty of 'em." I hold the phone up so he can watch as I scroll through my saved posts. "And here's one from a user called LittleTokyo, posted a few months ago." A lump appears in my throat and my voice catches, but I make myself read it out loud. "LittleTokyo said: *Mr. W ruined my life. We'd agreed that I would get an A, but when I couldn't cough up the cash, he got so angry that he started failing me. I got rejected by every college I applied to because of it.*"

"That doesn't—"

"How much do you want to bet that LittleTokyo was Sophie Tanaka?" I say in a voice rough with emotion. Because when I found that post, buried under thousands of other newer ones, it had driven such sorrow in my heart. The post had been inundated with the usual unkind replies, other kids jeering at her for failing, for being unable "to cut it" and blaming it on her teacher instead. Only one other user had taken her side, probably that kid Logan, and the others had quickly made fun of him too. She'd bared her soul on DD and got eaten alive for it. Mr. Werner's mouth is a thin line, his eyes hot coals.

The thought of Sophie crying as she made that post months ago, followed by Sophie last night, defeated and broken, spurs me on. "Did Sophie confront you? Did you say something to her? Push her into committing suicide?"

"That doesn't prove anything," he says, but his voice lacks conviction.

"No, it doesn't, but when you take into account the thirty or so posts by other users about your cheating ring, Mrs. Henderson can't just ignore it. She'll have to look into it." Smiling is the last thing I want to do, but I make the corners of my mouth lift, just as a fuck you to Mr. Werner.

"Ha! Ha. Ha."

Okay that has got to be the weirdest, creepiest laughter I have ever heard. It's straight out of *Annabelle*.

Mr. Werner stops laughing and holds out his hand. "Give me the phone, Lia."

I take a step back. His laughter has triggered something inside me, some primal fear that makes me realize, belatedly, that I'm all alone in a secluded place with someone who just might be dangerous. I'd just assumed that Mr. Werner had made Sophie so depressed, she turned to drugs. But now I'm realizing—what if he'd actually killed her?

"Lia," he says, his voice a warning. "Give me the phone, Lia."

"Don't come any closer." Fear makes my voice wobble.

Mr. Werner looks confused. "What—are you scared of me? Give me the phone and we'll forget about all this. I told you why I needed to do it. I told you, I don't have a choice. Look, I even tried to warn you about taking my class. You were the one who insisted on taking it. How's that my fault? Now give me the phone!" He darts forward as he says the last sentence and suddenly catches my wrist in a painful grip.

I shriek, try to pull away, but he's got a death grip on me, and I can't—I kick, aiming my knee for his groin. I hit his hip instead, but the kick surprises him into loosening his hold. I wrench my arm away and do the only thing I'm good at. I run.

I bolt straight into the thick of the woods, weaving around the redwoods, narrowly dodging their branches. Oh god, oh god, what the fuck is happening right now? What just happened? My thoughts are scrambled, my breath coming in and out in a terrified, high-pitched wheeze.

"Lia!" Mr. Werner's shout comes from afar, a sound straight out of a nightmare. "Jesus, why are you kids so fucking melodramatic? My own fucking kids are like that too. 'I'm a spoiled little shit! I don't give a crap about everything you've sacrificed, Dad, I want to live with Mommy!'"

My mouth drops open. I can't believe the revulsion in his voice as he talks about his own children. Only minutes ago, he'd been moaning about not being able to spend time with them, but his voice right now is pure poison, devoid of any genuine affection. So all of that stuff he'd said in the car about missing them had been a lie designed to make me feel sorry for him, to let my guard down. God, how could I have been so stupid?

He laughs to himself. "Those little shits. Why the hell would I want to see them? All I want is to keep them from their bitch of a mother and teach her a lesson for the way she treated me. And now here you are, messing everything up, and for what? Come out, Lia. Let's be reasonable."

I glance behind me. Can't see him anywhere. Only trees around. My foot catches in a tangle of underbrush and I slam onto the ground. The breath is knocked out of me, and for a moment, I forget where I am, what's going on, and then it all comes back in a rush and I scramble to untangle my foot from the mess of leaves and vines. Too slow. I'm sobbing out loud, a wild, desperate sound. I'm all of five years old once more, caught in a nightmare, with a monster pursuing me. I should be quiet—otherwise, the monster might find me—but I can't control my breathing, my whimpering. I'm going to die here. Mr. Werner is going to catch me, and then he'll—I don't know how he'll do it, maybe he'll strangle me, maybe he'll just throw me over the cliff, but the point is, I'm about to die.

"Liaaa."

Pure panic bursts through my chest. I tear at the vines with my bare hands.

"Come out. I've told you my life story, shared with you the most vulnerable parts of my life. You see that, don't you? That I'm the victim here?"

I give one last hard yank and my foot finally comes free. Just as Mr. Werner comes through the trees and sees me. His mouth stretches into a grin, showing all his teeth.

"Got you." He leaps.

He crashes down on top of me, and I'm winded again. His body mass is sickening, terrifying, an alien grabbing me. His heat envelopes me, the weight of him shockingly real. So heavy, like a boulder crushing me. His hard flesh is on mine, and though I try to turn, he's too heavy for me to budge. He's too strong, too big for me to push off. I claw for something. Anything. A rock. I grip it so hard, its sharp edge bites into my palm. I swing it—sudden hot pain rips through my arm. He bit me! I shriek, dropping the rock. Mr. Werner lunges for it and swings at my head. I twist my head around, and the rock bashes into the ground, less than an inch from my skull. I feel the rush of wind against my skin, the savage *thunk* the rock makes. Mr. Werner isn't holding back. He means to crush my skull like an egg.

Terror pounds through my veins. I will die here. His rancid breath is hot on my face, and the weight of him on top of me is so solid, so real. Oh god, this is truly happening. I fling my fist at his face, but it barely does anything. We're both snarling, panting like dogs, limbs flailing everywhere, eyes barely seeing, uncomprehending what's going on.

Then, suddenly, survival instinct takes over and I kick up with all the strength in my legs.

This time, I don't miss his groin. His balls squelch sickeningly against my knee. He gives a weird half scream, half yelp, and grabs at my face. His fingers brush my head and my entire body lurches away from the touch. I shove myself to one side, but instead of getting up, I brace my hands against the forest floor, ignoring the way the sticks and stones on the ground bite into my palms, and I push, rolling into his legs with all my might. He pitches forward, arms pinwheeling.

There's a crack, so hard, so clear, I feel it reverberate through my entire body. He hit me with something, he must have. I paw at my head, expecting blood, expecting excruciating pain to overwhelm me at any second. Maybe he's hit me with the rock somehow, and this is a belated reaction—

No blood. What?

I look at Mr. Werner. He's on the ground. But getting up, slowly. His movements are all wrong somehow, lurching and alien, a broken doll jerking to life. Every alarm inside me is blaring at me to run, but I'm rooted to the spot. When he turns to face me, I scream in horror.

A branch is sticking out of his left eye. He touches it, his other eye widening, like he can't believe there's something sticking out of his actual head. His mouth moves. Words come out, but they're all wrong, jumbled and loose. I only catch the last one.

"*—bitch.*"

He reaches out for me with bloodied fingers. I stumble back, the tips of his fingers brushing against my cheek, then he's past me, tipping over like a falling tree.

Time stops. Or maybe it goes really fast. I don't know. I lose track of it as I stare at Mr. Werner. And then it's like my mind suddenly returns to my body and I start gasping again, oh god, what just happened, is he okay, no, he's obviously not okay, he's got a BRANCH THROUGH THE EYE.

"Mr. Werner?" I scramble over to him and grab his arm. As soon as I touch him and feel his warm flesh, it hits me. This is Mr. Werner. My English Lit teacher. Holy shit. Holy SHIT. "Mr. Werner! Get up. Get UP!" I cry, shaking him harder.

He coughs. He's alive. Relief rushes through me. Thank god.

I loop his left arm around my shoulders, take a deep breath, and try to pull up. He makes a sound that's somewhere between a gasp and a strangled scream, his limbs flopping around. He's heavy as hell. A guttural, animal grunt rips out of me as I lift him right up.

"Hang on, Mr. Werner. We'll get you to a hospital," I babble, staggering forward. One step. Two. I think he nods, or maybe that's just his head lolling forward. I try to remember everything I know about first aid. Keep them awake. I start babbling, the words tumbling out so fast, I barely register what I'm even saying. "Hey, Mr. Werner, you're a real asshole, you know that? Wake up, Mr. Werner. Please. Hey, um, what was the thing you said about *Lord of the Flies*? The one about the pig's head."

How far have I walked? Where's the parking lot? Everything around me looks the same. Just trees and more trees. Warmth dribbles down the side of my neck and onto the collar of my shirt. Blood. Mr. Werner's blood.

"Mr. Werner, the car—do you know where it is?" I can't look at him. I can't bear to see that thing sticking out of his head. I keep walking, but with every step, more of his weight settles on me, until it feels like I've got an entire world leaning against me. My legs are trembling, my arms are noodles, my back is screaming with pain. I take another step. And another. I trip over something. The forest floor rushes up to meet me, and I land with a thump that knocks the breath out of me. Mr. Werner's weight very nearly crushes me as he falls on top of me. I struggle to get back up, but all I manage to do is push Mr. Werner off my back. I can't stop sobbing.

"Mr. Werner, please, I need your help. I'm lost. I—"

There's no answer. He's lying very, very still. Unblinking. His one remaining eye, that is. Although the other one's probably not blinking either.

Suddenly, I'm crying. And screaming. At some point, I must've vomited as well, because my shirt is really wet and smells like hell, and I can't seem to stop screaming.

I've killed a man.

When I run out of air, I sit there for a while, staring blankly at nothing. What do I do? I should…turn myself in? Yeah. Probably that. It was self-defense. Self-defense is not murder. Thing is, that sounds an awful lot like something a murderer would say—

My phone rings. My heart explodes. For one ridiculous moment, I'm 100 percent sure it's the police, like they've got some sort of super-sense which alerts them to murders as soon as they're committed.

I take it out of my pocket. Ibu's face is on the call screen. Right. Ibu. That makes a lot more sense than the cops calling me. I take a couple of deep breaths and then hit Accept.

"Hello?" My voice comes out wobbly with tears. I close my eyes. I suck at sounding okay. In my defense, I haven't had much practice trying to sound okay after killing someone.

"Lia? Are you okay?"

I don't trust myself to speak, not with tears choking my throat, so I just go, "Mm-hmm."

"I miss you, baby girl," she says, and oh god, please don't make me cry right now, because I will never stop. Luckily, she rambles on and says, "Wah, I have so much to tell you. Auntie Janice actually replied to my messages on the family chat. She said you look so pretty, so grown-up—"

I close my eyes again and let myself sag, sinking into the comfort of my mother's voice as she fills me in on the family gossip. I can't believe it's only been a month since I left home. My old life seems like someone else's. God, what I wouldn't give to go home and forget everything about Draycott. I just want to go home, and put my head down on Ibu's lap, and cry forever while she strokes my hair and tells me everything is going to be okay.

Except it's not, is it? Here's Ibu, so happy one of my paternal aunts has deigned to reply to her messages after years spent snubbing her. What will it be like for Ibu when the news breaks, when everyone learns that her daughter has killed someone? She's been through so much already. And what if I get tried as an adult? I don't know how that works, why some teens are tried as adults. But the odds aren't good. Me, a half-brown girl, killing a white dude. Nope, definitely not great odds.

It's as though my heart stops beating. My brain shuts down. Blood stops flowing through my veins. It's like my entire being has hit the reset button. My mind is a complete blank, devoid of every thought. One thing remains. Ibu's voice, now happily telling me about her side of the family and how one of my myriad cousins has gotten engaged and how we're going to go back to Jakarta for the wedding next summer. I can finally wear her old kebaya, she says, the one she saved from when she was seventeen. It's emerald green with gold detail.

My mind clears. When I inhale, my breath's no longer shaky. I straighten up. "Ibu, I'm sorry, but I gotta go. I'll call you tomorrow, okay?"

"Okay, be good!"

Too late for that. I hang up and stuff my phone back into my pocket. I know now what I must do.

The body. I need to get rid of it.

The thought makes me ill, but I force myself to keep going down this path. I need to survive this.

Okay. How do I get rid of it? The river? If I could just push it uphill and throw it over the cliff, it'll go a long way before anyone finds him.

He's right where I left him. His good eye remains open, and I notice now that there's a drop of blood on it, spreading across the whites. Oh god, no. I gag and turn away. Okay, just gotta—just gotta do it.

Still averting my eyes, I put my hands under one of Mr. Werner's arms and pull.

My stomach lurches and I snatch my hands away. Touching him makes me want to rip my skin off. Okay, calm.

Down. Deep breaths. I go for his ankles. They're farther away from his head, which is less personal, somehow. They're still warm. They're still WARM. I gag again, but somehow, I manage to keep my hands on Mr. Werner's ankles. I sob out loud as I pull. He's a lot heavier than I expected. I plant my feet firmly and yank hard. He moves a couple of inches. The cuffs of his pants slide up, revealing skin. Strands of brown leg hair and a tattoo. Somehow, this sight is even more horrific, more sickening than anything. It drives home the fact that I've just killed a person. A person with a tattoo, a past, an entire life behind him. Tears course down my cheeks and I'm babbling apologies to thin air, begging the universe to forgive me.

I give another big yank, but my hands slip and I end up falling onto my back. My arms are dead. All the strength has gone out of them, and I feel tired, so goddamn tired. A sob burbles out. Come on, Lia. You can do this. I stagger back to my feet and try again, but it's no use. I'll never be able to drag his body uphill and push it over the cliff.

A twig snaps. I jump, looking around me, my breath caught midway through a sob. There's no one. And then, right at the edge of my hearing, I catch something. A growl. Goose bumps break out across the back of my neck. A wild animal, maybe? I stand there, frozen, sudden terror replacing the wave of guilt. It must be all this blood. It would attract all sorts of animals. What sort of animals are up here? Foxes? Bears? Mountain lions?

Survival instinct takes over for the second time today. I have to go. Now. I take one last look at Mr. Werner, and I run away.

By sheer luck, I go in the right direction, and not long after, I burst out of the woods into the parking lot. The sight of it is so sudden, so surprising that I stand there dumbly for a few moments, breathing hard and not doing anything. Then conscious thought crashes back through my head and I rush to Mr. Werner's car. I wrench the door open and use my blazer to wipe down all the insides and then the outside of the car.

Have I missed anything? My thoughts are a jumble. All I want to do is to run away and never look back. I force myself to stop and think for a second. I look at my phone. Six-thirty. Shit. I won't make it back in time for dinner. Panic claws at the edges of my mind and I shove it away.

I should—I—I'll send a text to Danny and tell him I'm swamped with homework or something.

But when I start to compose the message, my thumbs refuse to move. I can't. I can't send a text to Danny, knowing that I'm doing it to cover up my killing his uncle. A sob wrenches its way up my chest. I don't have it in me to send him a casual text.

Whimpering, I tap on Beth's name and send her a text instead. Feeling disgusted at myself, I shove my phone back in my bag without waiting for a reply and make my way downhill to the main road.

As I walk, clouds gather and blot out the setting sun. It starts to drizzle, then starts to rain in earnest, cold sheets of water that chill my entire body. Despite the freezing temperature, I welcome the rain. It feels fitting somehow, to be pelted by cold water. I wish for it to rain harder, for it to somehow wash away the memories of what just happened. My tears mingle with the rainwater and drip down my face, and still, I can't stop crying, can't stop hearing Mr. Werner's last gasps over the sound of the rain.

By the time I turn into Draycott's driveway, my teeth are continuously rattling. I walk around the edge of Draycott until I find the Narnia hole. I take a moment to gulp down my sobs before crawling through. *Stop crying, you stupid bitch. Stop it.* Thanks to the rain, no one else is out and about, and I'm able to slip inside Mather without anyone noticing.

Fortunately, no one is inside Mather's hallways either. Back in my room, I strip off my sodden, bloodstained clothes, wrap myself in my bathrobe, and make a dash for the bathroom.

I lock myself in the farthest cubicle and turn on the hot water. I sag against the wall, letting the water stream down my face. I look down at the shower floor. Pink and brown swirls run down my legs and onto the shower floor, and I get a nasty, sudden flash of Mr. Werner gasping, the branch sticking out of his eye.

No!

Think of bunnies. Cute, fluffy bunnies. Panda cubs sneezing. Baby hippos doing somersaults.

My breathing slows down. Back to normal.

Mr. Werner's tattoo flashes through my mind.

Stop it, I beg my subconscious. *Just. Stop*. Singing parrots. Grumpy cats. Surprised ocelots.

It's not working. The cute, fuzzy animals are no match for the insane mess I made. I end up sobbing in the shower again, until my skin's all wrinkly and I run out of hot water. And then I toddle back to my room, exhausted. Defeated. Irrevocably changed.

Back in my room, I find a message on my phone.

From: Danny Wijaya

I got you something. Can we talk?

There's a picture of a takeaway box of nasi goreng from the stall we went to on our first date.

I choke back my sob. Oh my god. I bury my head in my hands. Danny doesn't deserve this. Mr. Werner, as horrible as he was, didn't deserve it. Oh god. I've killed him. I've killed another human and then tried to cover it up. I just—what's happened to me? I don't know who I am anymore. I disgust myself. I—

I can't. I can't live like this. I have to make it right. I'll come clean to Danny.

CHAPTER 16

I don't have long to wait. As soon as I send Danny the message telling him to meet me outside of the Narnia hole, he says he'll be right there.

I put on a jacket and walk out of my room. Girls are coming back from dinner, so I put my head down and walk quickly, hoping no one notices me. Someone bumps into my shoulder. Elle. She rolls her eyes at me when I look at her and then shares a knowing smile with Arjuna, who's walking next to her. I ignore them, but my heart is thumping, leaping with paranoia. Do they know? Can they sense my guilt?

Wrapping my arms around myself, I hurry across the quad toward the Eastern Gardens. For the second time that evening, I crawl through the Narnia hole. The twigs and leaves brushing against my face bring about flashbacks of running through the woods, Mr. Werner coming after me, calling my name. Bile lurches up my throat and I almost start dry heaving. I squeeze my eyes shut and push myself through.

Maybe all these awful thoughts will fade after I tell Danny the truth. Even though it'll mean that I'll go to prison straight after that, maybe it'll stop the guilt from boiling through my entire being.

There's a rustling from the hedge, and my whole body tightens like a violin string. I stand there, practically quivering. God, I hope it's not kids on their way to some off-campus party. I can't handle small talk right now. I hold my breath.

Danny's head pops out of the tunnel. My breath releases in a huge sigh, then I recall why we're here, and I go back to quivering like a squirrel on speed.

As soon as Danny climbs out and stands up, brushing twigs and leaves out of his hair, I hug him and close my eyes and inhale the scent of him on a shuddery breath. This is it.

"I need to tell you something."

I blink. We both said it at the same time.

"Wait—" I have to tell him now, before I lose my nerve. "Danny, I—"

"You were right about Uncle James's cheating ring."

All thought screams from my head, cutting me off midsentence. "What?"

Danny's face is tortured. His gaze flits guiltily from my face to the ground and back to my face again. "I'm so sorry, Lia."

What just happened? What is happening? "I don't—I'm not following."

He clears his throat. "The night I had dinner with Uncle James, I found something. I picked the lock on one of his desk drawers open and I found it. The ledger. It's, um. It's a record of everything. It has price lists of grades for every test paper and every student who's ever bought a grade from him. And it has a record of his lawyer's fees and how much of the money's going to pay the lawyer and the divorce proceedings, and—fuck. I don't know. I'm sorry. I didn't know how bad things have been financially for him, and it scared me. I don't know." He looks away.

A small voice in my head is shouting, *It's not like that, Danny! He tricked you. He tricked me too. He made it seem like he cared about his kids, but he was only fighting for custody to make everyone as miserable as he was!* But thinking about this sours my stomach. I can practically feel the acid eating me away from the inside. Because who cares what Mr. Werner's motivations were? I killed him. Nothing else matters. I'm the guilty one here.

"I felt so shitty for him," Danny continues. "I—all summer, I've been living off him, whining to him about my parents cutting me off, and there he was, struggling to pay everything off. He never told me any of this stuff. If he did, I would've talked to my parents. Apologized. Begged them to help him. But I didn't know. And he let me stay at his place rent-free and eat his food, and all this time—" His voice cracks and he looks at his feet for a while, scuffing the grass with the toe of his shoe. "I didn't know what to do. I took pictures of the documents in the ledger, and when I left the room, he told me he'd gotten a call from the school about Sophie, and it was all just a mess. I thought I'd show it to you so you could—I don't know—clear your name, but then I just—I couldn't do it."

"But." I'm trying to process this, but his words aren't computing. "That night, I asked you if you found anything, and you said you didn't."

"I know!" His face scrunches up like tissue paper. "I'm so, so sorry, Lia. I didn't know what to do. I sat on it."

He sat on it. While I went and got expelled and then killed his uncle. Danny looks like he's about to jump in the river.

"I'm so sorry," he says.

I pull my hand away, and he doesn't try to take it back.

"You can hate me all you want. I deserve it. But, um. After what happened to Sophie that night, I couldn't get over the fact that my uncle's cheating business kind of caused her death. Because she wouldn't have gotten kicked out without it, she wouldn't have gotten depressed, she wouldn't have turned to drugs, wouldn't have..." His face scrunches up and he takes in a sharp breath. "Anyway. I just thought I'd let you know that I, uh. I emailed the pictures of the ledger to Mrs.

Henderson today. She called me immediately. It took a while to convince her; she seemed really certain it's all your fault." He pinches the bridge of his nose. "But she accepted it. Can't really argue with the evidence."

My mind's a blank. No, wait, it's not. It's full. And what it's filled with is rage. Yes, I still feel intense, indescribable guilt. But surging fast, torpedoing through the blanket of guilt, is anger. Because, oh god, none of this had to happen. I could've been free. And though I had killed Mr. Werner, I'd done so out of self-defense. Because if I hadn't, he would've killed me. And all of it—every single terrifying, violating moment—was avoidable. Wouldn't have happened if Danny hadn't sat on information I so desperately needed.

I want to shriek into the night sky and rip the world apart.

"She said there will be a formal investigation into my uncle. The grades from Mr. Werner's class are going to be voided. You'll be reinstated on varsity." He gives me a hesitant smile.

Varsity. The word shatters through the turbulence, and despite everything, it grounds me. Wrenches me out of the chaos and takes me home. Already I can feel the feel the track underneath my feet. I can smell the rubber, feel the plastic ribbon straining against my chest right before it splits. The weight of gold medals dangling from my neck.

But. But I can't. I came here to tell Danny the truth. And the truth is—

The truth is I want to stay. I want to stay so badly, I would give anything for it. My soul, if I still had one.

I stare at him, and I don't say anything. What happened with Mr. Werner lies thick on my tongue, waiting to spill out, and still, I don't say a word. It was self-defense.

Danny takes my hand, and I let him. He looks into my eyes and says, "You're safe, Lia."

I burst into tears.

CHAPTER 17

I can't sleep.

Each time I close my eyes, a cacophony of images and noise assaults me. Mr. Werner screaming my name. My own ragged breath ringing in my ears. And that horrible wet sound of the branch stabbing into his eye. I put my fingers in my ears and sing-shout a Billie Eilish song until Anya thumps on the wall and shouts, "Shut up! I'm trying to sleep!"

Yes, well, Anya, some of us are trying to shake off the trauma of their first homicide. But I stop anyway, because there's nothing worse than a noisy neighbor. Except for a murderer as a neighbor. Though I'm thinking, at this point, Anya would choose a murderer for a neighbor, as long as she's quiet about it.

After a while, I put in my earbuds and find the shittiest, noisiest music on YouTube. I crank up the volume until my ears are physically cringing, and then I lie there and try to let the music drown me. At some point, despite all the noise, I actually doze off.

When I awake, it's morning. My earbuds have fallen out onto the bed. Tinny music flows out of them. I grope at my side table for my phone and turn it off. Silence. Sweet, sweet si—

"Lia," shouts Mr. Werner.

I jerk out of bed. Breathe out. And in. Out again. Don't think of Mr. Werner. Don't think of that branch, sticking out of his eye. Definitely don't think of that.

I put on my uniform carefully, making sure there are no wrinkles on my white shirt, taking the time to get my tie on just right. I wrestle my thick, black hair into a ponytail. I stand in front of the mirror and nod at myself. I look very prim and proper and not at all like someone who has just killed her teacher.

Time for class.

Except as soon as I come out of my room, I realize something's off. I try to figure out what it is as I walk down the hallway. A couple of rooms have their doors open, and I see girls in there, just chilling on their beds, listening to music, chatting with each other. Why aren't they getting ready for class? I walk past Elle's room, and she and Arjuna look up at me and burst into peals of laughter.

"What's so funny?" I snap. I really shouldn't engage the trolls, but I'm really weirded out by the fact that no one else seems to give a crap about classes.

"The fact that you're such a little kiss-ass that you wear your uniform even on weekends," Elle says.

"Say 'cheese'!" Arjuna says and takes a picture of me.

I walk off in a daze. Weekend? Huh. Yeah, of course. It's Saturday. My phone beeps. A DD notification. It's the picture Arjuna just took of me, with my face blurred out. Underneath that is the caption: When you literally have nothing good to wear, so you resort to wearing your uniform on Saturday. #sosad #parasite

Already there are replies.

Reply from @TrackQueen:

That is literally the saddest. Someone please take that thing to Goodwill already.

The post and its comments should bother me, but they don't. Not even in the least. Compared to what happened yesterday, troll posts on DD seem so trivial. *It is trivial, you teens are nothing if not trivial*, Mr. Werner's voice whispers. I run back into my room and slam the door.

I really, really need to get my shit together. I shrug off my school blazer and fling it across the room. Start pacing. Okay. Get shit together. Okay.

Except I don't know how to do that, exactly. My mind keeps swinging wildly from thinking up the most inappropriate, irreverent jokes to sudden violent images to wanting to sob uncontrollably. Everything is a mess. Everything.

Make a list. Right, okay. Yeah, doing lists helps me. I sit down at my desk and take out my notebook. Here we go.

HOW TO GET SHIT TOGETHER AFTER KILLING SOMEBODY.

1. Do not write lists where you basically admit to killing somebody.

Now I totally realize, of course, that I need to burn this piece of paper right away. I don't have a lighter, so I tear the written part out and shove it in my mouth.

And that's how I find myself literally eating paper on this fine Saturday morning.

But never mind that. Moving on. New list.

HOW TO GET SHIT TOGETHER.

Good title. Generic. Could refer to just about anything. Okay.

1. Make sure there's no

I almost write *evidence* when I realize that'll also mean I'd have to eat this piece of paper as well.

1. *...thingy.*

I sit back, biting the end of my pencil, and consider everything that might be evidence. I've cleaned up his car as best as I can. I'm going to wash yesterday's clothes as soon as possible. I've told everyone I spent yesterday in my room with stomach flu, and nobody saw me leaving and coming back to campus, so I think I'm okay. Phew.

2. Motive?

This one's a problem. Anyone with half a brain will know that I have a motive for wanting to get rid of Mr. Werner. But Mr. Werner was shady AF, and surely that means he made lots of enemies. Like Sophie, for example. I think about the way she died for the millionth time, alone and vulnerable and scared. He did that. Well, not directly, but he caused it to happen, and all for what? To earn more money so he could take his own kids away from their mother. For the first time, I get this feeling—not glad, exactly, I'm not a monster—but sort of vindication for killing Mr. Werner.

The moment I think that, I'm almost overcome by a wave of revulsion toward myself. How could I think that? What kind of monster am I? *But it was self-defense!* I mentally shriek at that horrible, guilty part of myself. Self-defense. And you know what? He was an authority figure. He was supposed to be looking out for us, his students, instead of taking advantage of us, no matter how wealthy everyone else is and how badly he needed the money. He tried to ruin my life, then he tried to kill me, all while being driven by Danny's racist parents. It. Was. Self-defense. And it was justified.

By the time I'm done mentally arguing with myself, I'm a little out of breath.

I need to get my shit together. Okay, focus on this. Point two. There are others who have motive. His ex-wife. His ex-students who couldn't afford to pay for their grades. And then there's SiliconBrains, who, for whatever reason, wanted to help me in their own way.

SiliconBrains.

Realization hits like an asteroid. My skin bursts into gooseflesh. I grab my phone, scroll through the list of registered students, and make a call.

"Meet me at the Narnia hole," I say. "Now."

Halfway to the Eastern Gardens, I get a text: What's the Narnia hole?

Argh, right. I forgot that I came up with that name and not everyone calls it that.

The hole in the hedge. In the Eastern Gardens. The one everyone uses to sneak out of campus.

There's no answer. I walk on anyway. Just keep walking, just keep walking. Act normal. By the time I crawl through the Narnia hole, I'm so sure no one would come that I half wonder what I'm still doing here. I stand under a willow tree and scroll through the posts on DD. The one that Arjuna posted of me has a whole string of replies by now. Wonder which poor sod this school used to pick on before I came along.

A rustling makes me look up. I stuff my phone in my pocket and approach slowly, cautiously. I don't know why; it's not like I'm expecting a honey badger to climb out or anything.

Stacey peers out and glowers at me. "I hate this goddamn hole."

"Thanks for coming," I say, helping her up. "SiliconBrains."

Stacey takes her time brushing leaves off her jeans. Finally, she says, "Took you long enough to figure it out."

"Yeah, well. I was somewhat distracted after finding, you know. Sophie." It still hurts to say her name out loud, like I'm betraying her somehow. But I've avenged her, in a way, haven't I?

Stacey looks down at her jeans, still refusing to meet my eyes. "Yeah," she says quietly. "That was...god, poor

Sophie." She takes a sudden, deep breath then raises her gaze to meet mine. She looks tired and sad. "Anyway, what did you want to talk to me about?"

"Um, well." I gesture vaguely. "About you being SiliconBrains, obviously!"

"What about it?"

"Why were you doing it? Why did you message me? Why did you help me? Why everything!"

Stacey frowns at me. "Isn't it obvious? Because I don't like bullies."

A mirthless laugh bursts out of me. I can't help it. "That's rich, coming from you."

The frown on Stacey's face deepens. "What're you talking about?"

"You've been bullying me since like, the first day we met!"

"No, I haven't."

"Yes, you have." My voice comes out angrier than I expected. It's all just too much. Everything that's happened, Mr. Werner, Sophie, and all the girls who submitted those false claims about me harassing them. And now she's denying it like none of it ever happened. "At least have the backbone to own up to it," I sneer.

"No I—" She stops herself. Takes a breath. "Okay, how have I been bullying you, exactly?"

I flap my arms. "Uh, let's see. When we first met, you were questioning me really aggressively."

"What?" she cries. "When we first met, I was really friendly! I even joked around with you!"

"How were you joking around with me? By saying, 'Oooh, we have a drug test every two weeks, you got anything to hide, you trashy meth head?'"

"I didn't call you a trashy meth head!"

"You might as well have!"

"I was joking around with you, you huge nong, because I thought you were cute!"

What? All the anger suddenly melts away, leaving nothing but confusion in its place. Wait. Hold up. I had one of my trademark stupid retorts ready, but now all thoughts disappear, and I just stand there, gaping at her stupidly.

"Did you just call me a nong?"

She shrugs. "My cousins in Australia say that a lot. I like it."

We're quiet for a while, both suddenly very interested in our shoes.

"So..." I mumble.

Stacey sighs. "You don't have to be so awkward about it. I'm not expecting you to like me back or whatever. I know you're straight. I'm used to having unrequited crushes. And anyway, I'm pretty much over it."

"Right. Sorry, you just—I mean, I wasn't expecting—what I'm trying to say is..." Stacey watches me warily. "You're really bad at flirting."

Stacey's eyes go wide, and then we both start laughing like crazy. It's as though a huge weight has suddenly been lifted, and I don't even try to stop my laughter. It's a shrill, brittle laugh, teetering on the edge of sobs, but for now, it feels good.

"I really am," she cries, in between laughter.

"And you kept smirking at me at like, the worst times!"

"Those are supposed to be supportive smiles, like 'hey, you got this, it's going to be okay' smiles!"

By this time, I'm laughing so hard, I double over and end up falling over onto the grass. Stacey slumps down beside me and buries her face in her hands. Slowly, our laughter dissipates, leaving us spent on the grass. I take a few deep gulps of air. For the first time in days, I feel like I can actually breathe.

"God, why am I so bad at it?" she moans.

I turn my head and crook a small smile at her. "To be fair, I'm half to blame for interpreting everything you did in the worst possible way."

"Oh yeah, totally. I mean, you know how horrible you were? I'd smile at you, and you'd just give me this bitch face and look away, like jeez, woman, sorry for trying to be nice." She rolls her eyes at me, and we both laugh again. "I even warned you about taking Mandy's place on varsity."

"What?" I sit up and stare at her. "I thought you were threatening me!"

Stacey raises her eyebrows. "If I were threatening you, I'd be like, 'Don't take Mandy's place, or ELSE.'" She pauses. "I guess I did sort of say that, huh?"

We both cackle crazily once more.

"I don't know why Mandy has such a hard-on for varsity—it's not like she needs a track scholarship to go to college," I say when we've calmed down a little.

"Her two older sisters attended Draycott before she did, and they were both on varsity. Won a crap ton of medals. Her parents put a lot of pressure on her to compete as well."

I make a face.

"I'm not telling you so you feel bad for Mandy. I'm just saying that's why she's so desperate to stay on varsity."

"How do you know all that stuff about her family?"

Stacey shrugs. "We used to be close. Then I came out to her, and things got really awkward. She tried to be tolerant or whatever, but it was never the same after that."

"Shit. I'm sorry." And I am. I'm also slightly ashamed of myself. I've been so wrapped up in my own problems that I never once thought that Stacey could be going through something like this. I'd just assumed that everyone else was cruising through, having the time of their lives.

"Meh. Anyway, I overheard her telling Elle that you're in Mr. Werner's class. Mandy was all happy about it because it meant she could get you kicked out of varsity. I wasn't sure what she meant, and then I heard the news about you being off varsity 'cause you'd failed a class, so I hacked into Mr. Werner's computer and looked up his test questions."

"You what now?"

"I'm a computer genius, what can I say?"

"Holy shit. How did you hack into his computer?"

"It's complicated."

"Don't be a snob. Pretend I'm not entirely stupid and tell me."

Stacey laughs. "I am a snob, aren't I? Okay. I used a keylogger and got his user ID and password that way. Once I got those, I could log on to his computer and all his teaching records. I could even access his local drive."

"You used a keylogger? Like, one of those USB drive thingies? How did you keep him from finding it?"

"Dude." Stacey rolls her eyes at me. "Not a physical keylogger. What is this, the nineties? I sent a virus to his computer. The virus automatically gathers all of his data and sends it back to me."

"Ah. I see." And then suddenly, I do see. And shit, it's bad. It's really, really bad. Because Mr. Werner is dead, killed, and the cops will find him, and they'll probably check Mr. Werner's belongings, which means they'll check his computer, and if they find the virus and trace it back to Stacey, she might end up as a suspect. I may have cleaned up all evidence pointing to me and tied up my loose ends, but Stacey may end up going to prison for a crime she didn't commit.

CHAPTER 18

I can't let Stacey take the fall for something I did, especially not now that I've found out how badass she is. Just to clarify, I wouldn't let her take the fall even if she were a basic bitch, but the fact that she's cool somehow makes it that little bit worse.

We walk back to Mather together. Stacey is going to show me how her virus works, but as we walk down the hallway, Beth pops her head out of her room and grins when she sees me.

"Where've you been? Why haven't you answered our texts? Oh, hey, Stace."

"Uh." I check my phone. Sure enough, I have about half

a dozen unread texts, all from Beth and Sam. "Sorry, I forgot to turn off silent mode."

"Come on, we're going out," Beth says. She opens her door to reveal that she's all dressed up—skinny jeans, an off-shoulder top, sunglasses, and a large Louis Vuitton carry-on bag.

"I'm not really in the mood," I say. The last thing I want to do now is go out and pretend to have fun.

Beth sighs. "Nobody is in the mood, especially after what happened to Sophie. We need this, okay? We deserve a break from all the bad vibes here."

I'm about to reject her again when I realize it'll make me look really suspicious. I've been saying yes to everything, going along with all of Beth's crazy escapades, and if I were to suddenly sit one out the day after Mr. Werner died, it's going to look really bad. I take a deep breath, feeling exhausted, and nod.

Beth claps and goes, "Yay!"

"I'll leave you guys to it," Stacey says.

"No," I say. "Stay."

There's a weird pause, all charged, like all of us are surprised by what I've just said. Which I guess we all are. But as soon as I said it, I realize I mean it.

Beth shrugs. "Come," she says to Stacey. "We've got plenty of space on the jet."

"Yeah, they've got plenty of space—what?" I blink. "Did you say *the jet*? Is that like a new way of saying *car*?"

It is not. Less than an hour later, I'm clutching an overnight bag on the tarmac, staring up at a small airplane.

"Isn't she a beaut?" Sam says. "I call her Bertha."

It seems somewhat weird, naming something so sleek *Bertha*, but I suppose I know nothing about naming private jets. There are eight of us here—Sam, Grace, Beth, Stacey, Danny, the two Aidens, and me. Apparently, we're off to Vegas because Grace's parents are opening a new nightclub at the Bellagio. The last thing I want to do is spend the day partying, but I need to act normal. So Vegas it is.

The inside of Bertha is beautiful. There are sleek, white couches built into the sides with faux fur blankets thrown across them. A large coffee table is laden with champagne flutes, fruits, and gorgeous little cakes. Sam clears her throat and says, "Let's make a toast to Sophie." We all take a champagne flute and Sam pours out the champagne.

"To Sophie," she says, when everyone's glasses has been filled. "We were never close, but she was always kind to me and had the best makeup tips."

"Same," Beth says. "We never really hung out, but I used to watch her makeup tutorials on TikTok. She was so bubbly."

"To Sophie," Grace says.

"To Sophie," we all say, then we drain our glasses. An air attendant appears with another bottle and starts to refill everyone's glasses.

Despite the champagne loosening up my system, the sight of all the nice things still makes me feel ill. It's so wrong that I'm able to sit in a private jet with my friends one day after the incident with Mr. Werner. I want to go back to my room, where I can pace endlessly and gnaw on my fingernails until they're nothing but ragged stumps. But if I were to suddenly leave now, that would definitely look weird.

"You okay?" Danny says, sitting next to me. His face looks tight, and I feel a sudden jolt of guilt, as painful as a stab wound. He doesn't know what I've done. He doesn't know yet that his favorite uncle is dead. I lean into him and breathe in his familiar scent. He kisses the top of my head, which is such a sweet move, it makes me all teary-eyed. I shouldn't be here. Not with Danny, not after what happened. But I want to be here. Not in the private jet heading for Vegas, but wherever Danny is. Which sounds unbelievably pathetic, I know, but I guess I'm feeling pretty pathetic.

"I'm fine. Just a bit shell-shocked, I guess. Can't believe we're actually going to Vegas," I mutter, taking a sip of champagne. "Not that I'm ungrateful. It's just surreal."

"Get used to it," Stacey says, plopping down across from me. "These kids like to travel. Last term, they were flying everywhere on Prince Danny's jet. I heard he took them to Paris at some point."

I gape at Danny. "You have a private jet?" What is this world?

He looks down at his knees. "Sort of? But it feels wrong to use it when I'm on such bad terms with my parents, since it was a present from them."

"Jeez," I mumble, taking another gulp of champagne. Just when you think you know how rich Draycott kids are, they reach into their deep, deep pockets and brandish a private plane.

"So, um." Danny pauses and glances at Stacey, who's just sitting there, looking at us.

"Sorry, did you guys want to be alone? Am I being a third wheel?" she says.

"No," I say, the same time Danny says, "Sort of?"

I frown at him.

"Sorry," he says, quickly. "It's just, I kinda want to talk to Lia alone for a bit. But I promise I'll leave her to you girls afterward. Uh, if she wants. I mean, she can make her own decisions, obviously, I didn't mean—"

"Stop talking," Stacey says.

"Okay."

"Why are men," she says, as she leaves.

Danny ruffles his hair, which is massively adorable. "Sorry about that."

"It's okay. What did you want to talk to me about?"

He takes my hand. "I just—I wanted to apologize properly for the whole thing with my uncle."

"You don't have to."

"But I jeopardized your future, and I just—"

"I don't want to talk about it right now." I don't mean to sound quite as harsh as I do, but talking about it with Danny, knowing what I've done, knowing what he'll soon find out, is unbearable.

Danny looks surprised then sheepish. "Yeah, of course. We'll forget about it and have fun."

Have fun. That should be easy, given we're off to Vegas. But I remain out of it, part of me still trapped in the woods with Mr. Werner. When we land in Vegas and are greeted with a limo, I can't summon up the energy to get all excited. More champagne is poured inside the car, and I drink deep, hoping to forget Mr. Werner and Orange Point and that branch sticking out of his eye. Even when we arrive at the hotel and are whisked into the most gorgeous lobby I've ever seen, I'm still haunted by the ghost of Mr. Werner.

The rest of the evening passes in a whirl. Maybe I've had too much champagne. I can only remember the day like snippets from a movie—walking into a huge, luxurious suite, more bottles being opened, clinks of glasses, everyone laughing and having a great time. No longer thinking of Sophie. I guess none of them were close to her, so her death isn't too hard to get over, but still.

I blink, and I'm at the nightclub, wearing yet another one of Beth's slinky dresses, holding a sticky-sweet cocktail. The music is so loud, it thuds through my entire body. I can't tell if I'm bopping along to it or if it's just the beat shaking me.

I feel sick. I don't know if it's the flying, or the alcohol, or the loud music. Or the killing. I just want to go somewhere and lie down. Someplace I don't have to pretend like I haven't just killed someone.

Someone touches the small of my back, steadying me, and I turn to see Danny there. He looks like what coming home feels like.

"Danny." Tears spring into my eyes again. I need to tell him. I thought I could keep it inside me, but I can't after all.

"You okay?" he says.

I shake my head. There's a huge lump in my throat and I can't speak.

"Come on." Danny puts a steadying hand on my back and guides me out of the club. I can't begin to describe how good his hand feels on my back.

Outside of the club, though, we run into Stacey, who's leaning against the wall, looking at her phone. She glances up when we come out, her eyes wide. "Have you guys seen DD?"

I groan. "Oh god, what are they saying about me now?"

Stacey levels her gaze at me. "My dear, sweet Lia, it may behoove you to know that the entire app does not revolve around you." She grins. "This is so much more awesome than the usual petty bullshit on there. They found a hand."

I blink. "The app found a hand?"

"No, dummy. Some hikers did. Look!" She brandishes her phone at me. DD is awash with posts about a disembodied hand found at the nearby national park, just "a ten-minute drive from campus, guys!"

Bile rushes up my throat. I push Stacey and Danny aside and lurch into the nearest bathroom, barely making it into the first cubicle before I start heaving into the toilet. My kris pendant slips out from under my top and dangles underneath my face, getting splashed by vomit, which just makes me cry because the sight of it makes me miss Ibu.

Someone knocks on the door. "Lia, you okay?" Stacey says.

Obviously not.

"Open the door. I'll give you a hand."

A hand. Like the one they found in the national park. My stomach twists again, and I go back to dry heaving into the toilet. Something nudges my foot, I turn to see Stacey pushing herself through the gap under the door into the cubicle.

"Jeez Louise," she says, gathering my hair behind my head. She tugs at a hair band on her wrist and uses it to tie my hair back. "What's going on with you?" Her eyes narrow. "Is it…morning sickness?"

"No! God." I wipe my eyes and nose and flush the toilet before pushing past Stacey and coming out of the cubicle. I find Grace there, openmouthed. Great.

"Are you okay?" Grace squeaks.

"I'm fine."

There are a couple of women at the sink area, and they both subtly edge away from me. Can't blame them. I'm a mess. My face is puffy and colored with red splotches, and there are flecks of vomit stuck to my hair. The two women finish reapplying their lipsticks and walk briskly out, their noses wrinkling. I turn on the cold tap and splash water onto my face. It's freezing cold and feels wonderful.

"When was the last time you had your period?" Stacey says.

Grace's mouth opens even wider. "Oh my god, you mean—"

"I'm not pregnant," I snap. I take a mouthful of tap water, swill it around, and spit it out. "Danny and I haven't. You know."

Stacey's brows disappear in her hairline. "Seriously? Damn, I thought Danny has more game than that."

I gargle more water.

"So what's going on?" Stacey says.

Grace raises a hand to her mouth. "I think I know."

"You do?" I say, looking at Grace. She has this horrified expression on her face. Oh my god. I think she does know. "Wait. Please, don't—"

"We need a moment alone," Grace says to Stacey and actually grabs Stacey and starts pushing her toward the door. "Give us a minute."

I've never seen Grace so decisive. She knows something. Maybe she saw me stealing inside Mr. Werner's car on Friday. Maybe—

She closes the door and rushes back to me.

"Grace—"

"Throwing up doesn't work, you know," Grace says.

I stop. "Huh?"

"Throwing up. The whole bulimic thing. You'll still get fat."

"I—what?"

She opens her purse and takes out a pen. "Give me your hand."

I'm way too dumbstruck to resist as Grace grabs my hand and writes something on it. I glance down. She's written two words: Blueseed.com and Woot1212.

"Go to this website. It's a handicraft shop, sort of like Etsy. Look for this particular seller. He sells bracelets, key chains, that kind of crap. Each item represents a different drug. Like, if you see a key chain with Mary Jane shoes, that means it's marijuana. Cuff links with the letter E is for ecstasy, and so on and so forth. You'll figure it out."

"What—" What the hell is going on, and what does this even have to do with my supposed eating disorder?

"Get the necklace with the little Coke bottle pendant. That's cocaine," Grace says. "It'll suppress your appetite. You'll lose weight in no time. Not that you need to lose weight."

I can't help myself. I look at Grace, and this time, I feel revulsion. Rage. Sophie's just died on campus from a drug overdose, and here she is, telling me to go take drugs so I can look skinny. A huge part of me wants to shriek at her, grab her by the shoulders, and shake her.

"I don't think you should be doing drugs," I manage to bite out after an eternity. The words thud out dully. "I mean, after Sophie..."

Grace's eyebrows rise, her eyes going wide. "Oh, don't worry, this seller is legit. Their drugs are so pure. They're totally safe."

"What?"

"Didn't you hear? Sophie died from taking laced drugs. Whoever sold her the drugs had cut them using some bad shit. I think they said it was like, meth or laundry detergent or whatever. Really bad street stuff. That's why if you're gonna do drugs, be smart. Only buy from sellers you can trust. This shop is run by someone in town. So it's basically a local business. You just pay for the stuff, then the seller will drop it off somewhere on campus. Totally convenient."

What the fuck? Be smart? Drug dealers you can TRUST? Grace isn't even operating on the same wavelength as I am. I blink down at my hand, wondering if I'm dreaming.

Luckily, a knock on the door jerks me out of my swirling thoughts. "There's a huge line out here," Stacey calls out.

"We're done," Grace chirps.

I close my hand into a fist and hide it behind my back as we walk out. The last thing I want to do is to continue having a conversation about freaking drugs. I think I might actually lose it then. I know Grace is only trying to help, but I can't shake off the feeling that there is something really messed up about Draycott, something that goes even deeper, beyond Mr. Werner selling grades to students. Something tells me that Draycott is rotten, all the way to the core, and nothing I do can ever fix it.

CHAPTER 19

I'm running hard, my feet pounding the track like they have a personal vendetta against it. Halfway through my third lap, someone calls out my name and I see Stacey, still dressed in her tracksuit, crouching into her stretches. She waves at me and I jog over.

"You're here early," she says.

"I only got here a few minutes ago," I lie. I can't possibly tell her that I've been here since four a.m., because when I tried to sleep, all I could think of was Mr. Werner's hand. How a wild animal must've gotten to his body and severed—

Oh god, I can't. It's been less than forty-eight hours since Vegas, and there are no words for just how much I cannot. And so, I do the only thing I can: I run. When we came back from Vegas on Sunday afternoon, I immediately headed for the track to run. And now, so early on Monday morning that it's not even light yet, I'm running again.

"You're lyiiing," Stacey says in this singsong voice. "God, you're so competitive." She straightens up and we do a couple of laps together, and she keeps nagging at me to slow down, it's "just the warm-ups, dude," and I want to yell at her that I'm not warming up, I'm trying to outrun Mr. Werner's ghost, but that's kind of hard to explain, so I don't say anything.

I shouldn't be pushing myself this hard, especially not with Mandy around. She'll think I'm showing off, and I'm not doing that at all, I just need to outrun this cursed voice in my head.

Dirty, lying, murdering bitch.

Did I mention that the voice is mean AF? But the thing is, it also has a point.

I put on a burst of speed for the final lap. Break the sound barrier. Outrun the voice.

My calf suddenly turns into a scream of pain. I thud to the ground, almost biting through my tongue, and clutch at my leg, gritting my teeth so hard, they crack against each other.

Mandy and Elle laugh as they jog near.

"This dumbass doesn't understand the concept of warm-ups," Mandy says.

"Your face doesn't understand the concept—ow, ow, ow." I roll on the ground as my leg cramps up even more. Stacey catches up and crouches by my side.

"They're assholes, but they've got a point," she says. "Why'd you push yourself so hard, anyway? We're just warming up."

"Because." Then, to my horror, I start crying.

Stacey looks surprised. I don't blame her. She starts massaging my calf, and it feels both soothing and excruciating. "Hurts that bad, huh?"

I nod, my breath hitching as she massages my leg. I wipe my face when I see Coach approaching us. They help me up and lead me toward the bench. I'm all trembly and my breath is coming out in little half wheezes, half sobs, but at least the tears have stopped for now.

"Thanks, Stacey," Coach says. "Go and join the rest of the team."

Stacey gives my shoulder one last squeeze and jogs off.

"What's going, Lia?" Coach says, lifting my leg onto the bench and helping me stretch it.

"Nothing?"

She give me a look. "I enjoy how you girls like to think that we've got our heads stuck so far up our asses that we can't tell when something's wrong. But I've been a teen before. I know when something's off. So dish. What is it?"

"It's nothing—ow!"

"You've been running your whole life. You know better than to start sprinting before a proper warm-up, and now you're sitting here with your leg cramped up and telling me nothing's wrong? I call bullshit."

"It's just. Boy trouble."

Coach sighs. "Isn't it always? Look, Lia, I don't have to remind you how much you've got riding on this. The boy thing—it's a rite of passage, I get it. Try not to let it get to you, huh? Mrs. Henderson filled me in on what happened with your English Lit teacher. She said the class will be canceled and everyone's grades will be voided, so that's good for you. You've got a second chance at this. Don't blow it. Which reminds me, there's someone who wants to meet with you. I think you're going to like this."

I doubt it. But I force a smile and go, "Yeah?"

"Her name's Mickey Gentry, and she's a recruiter. From Stanford."

Oh. Shit. I don't care—

Except I do. I really, really do care. I didn't think it's possible, after what happened with Mr. Werner, to care about much else, but it's like Coach has wrenched open a door and suddenly all these feelings are pouring out, and I care. God help me, I don't deserve anything, but I want this. So, so much.

"I'll get my shit together, Coach, I swear."

Coach grins. "Atta girl."

I will. I'm still buzzing by the time practice ends and I've showered and dressed. I just gotta focus, get my head on straight, and I'll be fine.

First period is Mr. Werner's class. I ignore the horrible sucking sensation overtaking my body and perch on my seat and keep my head down. The room fills up, Mandy shoots me her usual bitch face, Elle whispers something rude as she walks by, and then the bell rings and the class starts. Except, of course, it doesn't. It doesn't start at all, because Mr. Werner doesn't show up. Five minutes in, a woman from the admin office bursts in, looking harried, and says, "Ah, I'm so sorry, you guys, things have been so crazy at the admin office, I forgot to let you all know that Mr. Werner's class has been canceled due to—ah, unforeseen circumstances. You have a free period today. Don't worry, we'll have a sub ready for you next class." She gives us an overly bright smile before backing out of the room.

As soon as she's gone, the room explodes with hoots and claps. Aiden B. says, "Musta been a wild night for Mr. Werner," really loudly, and people laugh. Aaron Presley goes up to the blackboard, imitating Mr. Werner's walk, and says, "Okay, kids, today we'll be talking about *The Handmaid's Tale.*" He makes such a close impression of Mr. Werner that I get goose bumps all over. I feel nauseated. I want to tell him to stop, but everyone else is laughing, and I can't even watch him, because the way he moves reminds me of Mr. Werner, and Mr. Werner isn't here because I killed him, and now he's up in the woods, missing a hand, and—

"What if that hand that was found in the woods is his?" Aiden B. says, and everyone goes quiet for a second. I swear I can hear my heartbeat, a panicked thrum that everyone must be able to pick out.

"Sounds like we need to set up a—drumroll please—death pool!" Aiden B. says.

"It can't be a pool if the only candidate is Mr. Werner," Mandy says, rolling her eyes. "But whatever, I bet a hundred bucks it's Mr. Werner."

How can these kids be so heartless? He was their teacher. They were happily buying grades off him! But maybe I'm just being a massive hypocrite, given I killed the guy and everything.

Other kids pipe up, putting down bets before picking up their bags and leaving the room. I follow the stream of students out of the classroom, feeling sick. Everyone else is busy texting and chattering, making guesses as to what Mr. Werner could possibly be up to. I guess no one truly believes he's actually dead in the woods, even though almost everyone here has put money on it.

My phone rings. It's Danny. My stomach does that horrible sinking thing because I know immediately it's nothing good. People only call when it's really bad news. For a second, I consider not picking up at all. But my thumb slides across the screen and accepts the call.

"Hey, Danny—"

"Uncle James is dead."

CHAPTER 20

Heartbeat. Nothing but my heartbeat in my hearing, drown-ing out everything else as I stand outside of Westerly Hall. Danny comes out to let me in, and he's a mess. Completely destroyed. He doesn't even bother trying to hide the tears. People passing by are openly looking and I don't know what to do—what would a non-murdering, non-lying person do? I push past the guilt and fold him into a hug.

His head feels so heavy on my shoulder. I don't know what else to say. I stand there and hold him and hate myself, hate everything, go back to hating myself so hard. Eventually, he wipes his eyes, and we make it back to his room, where he slumps on the floor, his back against his bed.

"I'm the only family member he has in the area, so they

asked me to go to the station. My cousins and my aunt are on their way from Jakarta, and they'll be here tomorrow. So I had to go to identify the—" He chokes on the last word and buries his face in his hands, another sob shuddering through his frame. I put an arm around his shoulders, pulling him close. Am I really sitting here comforting him while lying to him? What kind of monster am I? And the worst part of it is that my mind keeps skittering to a single thought: Does the police suspect anything?

"His face was—god, it was a mess, Lia," he sobs. "They think he was out hiking and tripped and fell on a—there was a branch in his—fuck."

If I could only put together all the broken pieces of him. I broke him. I did this.

"It's all my fault," Danny says.

"What?" It takes a moment to register what he just said, because I was thinking the exact same thing, that it's all my fault.

"He must've been up there because Mrs. Henderson had a talk with him. She must've told him she knows about the cheating ring, and that's what he does whenever he's upset—he goes for a hike. I shouldn't have told Mrs. Henderson. I should've gone to him first, I should've—"

I wrap him in a tight hug. Can I hate myself any more than this? Not possible. Every atom in my body is seething, picking up a tiny spear and jabbing it into my being. I am officially the worst person in the history of worst people.

It was self-defense, I remind myself for the millionth time. But right now, faced with Danny's grief, the reminder that it was self-defense doesn't really help soothe me. If anything, it feels like a stupid, flimsy excuse.

But it's not. He attacked you. He tried to kill you.

"Why'd he have to go to Orange?" Danny cries, interrupting the cascade of voices in my head. "In such bad weather too. He used to tell me it was the most pathetic overlook. We used to go hiking and we never, ever bothered going there. Why now?"

"Danny—" What dirty, bald-faced lie could I possibly come up with that might make this all better? "People do weird things when they're upset. Maybe he couldn't be bothered to drive farther up." Surely, I have won the Most Awful, No-Good, Terrible Human of the Year award by now.

"Maybe," he says. He doesn't look at all convinced. "I don't know. Something's off."

"No, it makes sense. I mean, look at Sophie, why did she go to Mr. Werner's office? That's really weird, and—"

I'm jerked away as Danny suddenly explodes into motion. "Don't fucking compare the two of them!" Inside the small room, Danny's voice is a thunderclap, jarring me down to my bones.

I stare at him, wide-eyed, and his face has turned an angry red as he rants on, his arms flailing wildly. "Sophie was a fucked-up crackhead who was out to get Uncle James! She was unstable, totally fucking crazy, she didn't deserve to—" He catches himself abruptly and takes in a sharp breath, looking pained. "I—shit, I'm so sorry. God, I don't know what came over me. I'm sorry, Lia."

It takes a few moments for me to manage to nod. What was he about to say? That Sophie didn't deserve to live? Acid eats its way through my stomach. Everything inside me is twisting painfully. I can't believe what I've just witnessed. My boyfriend, ranting in such a hateful way about a dead girl. My face feels numb, like I'm wearing a mask.

"I'm so sorry," Danny says in a broken voice. "I didn't mean all those things, I'm just so messed up about my uncle. Like, I feel so, so guilty about everything that's happened to him. I was going to tell the cops about the cheating ring and everything, but. I don't know. Mrs. Henderson talked to me. Did I mention that?"

I shake my head, still unable to say anything. The fury has left Danny's face, thank god, and he's back to being nothing but remorseful. I guess his outburst was just an expression of his grief. Didn't they say that there are many stages of grief, and that anger is one of them? Yeah, that's it.

"She told me not to tell anyone about him selling grades because it would only ruin Uncle James's reputation—like she gives a shit about his reputation. But she's right. I don't want the cheating scandal to be the thing everyone remembers him for, you know?"

I nod.

"Anyway, so I didn't tell the cops anything, and the guy in charge of the case—Detective Jackson—he was a total asshole. Acted like the whole thing was a waste of his time. He was all, 'Dude came to the overlook to have a smoke, jerk off or whatever, slipped, fell on that broken branch there, and that was it.' I told him Uncle James would never have chosen Orange Point to hang out at, but he said, 'Son, you're not your uncle. Hell, I tell my wife I never go to the Pussycat Club, but come Saturday night, know where you'd find me?' and he laughed."

"Jesus." Sounds like a total douche canoe. But this horrible voice at the back of my mind whispers, *Sounds like the kind of cop you want working on this case. The kind that would let you off scot-free.* Shut up, small, horrible voice.

"He made me feel so stupid for asking more questions, like I was some CSI fanboy turning everything into a clue." The anger is back on his face, but he takes a deep breath, obviously trying to control it.

Relief courses through me, which is horrible, I know, but the realization that the cops won't be looking into it is such a huge weight off my mind that I almost start weeping then and there.

"His partner seemed more on the ball," Danny says, and just like that, the relief is replaced by crushing fear.

"What?" I blurt out, unable to stop myself in time.

"Detective Jackson has a partner. Detective Mendez. She was asking a few questions, like if I noticed anything weird about Uncle James the days leading up to his death..." Danny shakes his head. "Maybe those are just routine questions, I don't know." He lets his head fall back, and for a while, he just stares blankly at the ceiling while my mind races ahead.

Is that a routine question? I don't know. I don't know anything! Does she suspect something? Does she—

"I know why I'm so angry about everything. I know why I think it's suspicious," Danny says, and my heart stops.

This is it. He's going to say he knows it's suspicious because Mr. Werner was shady as hell, and there are way too many people with motives to kill him, like *me*, for example, sitting here sweating and squirming. I'll tell him it was painless, that he died instantly.

"Danny—"

"It's guilt."

"Say what?"

"I pretty much got him killed." Danny snorts. "Ratted him out, he got upset, got into a freak accident, and now my guilt's trying to tell me there was something more to it, so it wouldn't just be my fault."

"Stop it," I snap. I can't listen to this anymore. "You didn't get him killed. None of this is your fault." *Except, well, it kind of sort of a little bit is.* "It's not your fault," I say, louder, trying to shut the horrible little voice in my head up. *If Danny hadn't sat on the evidence, if he'd gone to Mrs. Henderson sooner, then Mr. Werner would probably be alive right now.* "NOT YOUR FAULT."

Danny looks at me weirdly. "You don't have to shout." He gives me a weak smile. "Thank you. I'm sorry I'm such a mess." He takes my hand, and I let him.

"I'm a mess too. We can be a mess together."

"Can I ask for a favor?"

"Anything."

"My aunt tells me apparently Uncle James has left some stuff for me. Can you be there when I collect the stuff? I just—I don't think I can do it alone."

No. Hell to the no. No, no, no—"Yeah, of course."

"You're the best."

I'm going to have to run miles to escape this fog of guilt, but for now, I hold Danny tight and wish I could make everything okay for both of us.

CHAPTER 21

Two days later, I help Danny haul the stuff Mr. Werner left to him into his room. There's a lot of it—two guitars, boxes of various games, tennis rackets, and of course, his laptop. The laptop is like a magnet, constantly drawing my gaze to it. Danny puts it on his desk and doesn't pay much attention to it, but I can practically feel it hum, a sickening vibration from Stacey's virus, filling up the room until all air is sucked out of it.

"Sooo." Is that the world's most obvious *so*? I believe it is. I clear my throat. "Uh, so. What are you going to do with all this stuff?"

"I don't know." Danny flops down on his bed and pats the space next to him. I fold myself into his arms and press my head into the crook of his neck. I close my eyes and try to lose myself in this. Forget about Mr. Werner and his cursed laptop. "Hey." Danny hesitates. "My parents are coming up here for the funeral, and at first I thought maybe I could introduce you to them, but um, I'm thinking it might not be the best time to do that. Um. I hope that's okay with you."

I nearly laugh out loud. In all the mess, I've forgotten that they're even here. It seems ridiculous that he would think of that. Well, ridiculous in a sweet way.

"Don't worry about it. I'd rather meet them under better circumstances."

Danny gazes at me, a crease appearing between his brows. "You sure about it? I mean, I do want you to meet them—I mean, if you don't mind them being complete dicks—"

"Really, it's fine. I'd love to meet your parents because they're your parents, and I want to meet my boyfriend's parents, but I don't think I'm ready for the whole. You know. The race thing." The mention of it poisons the moment, chilling me all the way to my core. The *race thing*. What an innocuous way of referring to something insidious that nearly got me killed. Despite myself, despite all the guilt I'm still grappling with for lying continuously to Danny, I feel a sudden stab of icy hatred toward his family.

"I'm sorry that's an issue with them." Danny kisses my forehead. "Thanks for being patient. I'll talk to them about it."

I swallow the cold rage inside me and manage a small

smile. It's all for the best that I won't be meeting his parents, because god knows what I might do or say.

The funeral service for Mr. Werner is a lavish one. Very much unlike Sophie's, which took place really far away from Draycott and was very tiny, from what I heard. I guess her parents didn't want to call more attention to her death. The school didn't even bother mentioning any of it to us. But for Mr. Werner, classes are canceled, and a school bus is provided for those of us who want to attend. I most definitely do not want to attend, but I do anyway, for Danny's sake, and also to keep up appearances and stave off any suspicion.

I sit between Beth and Sam and spend the entire service wringing my hands, watching Danny's pale face as he gives a heartfelt eulogy. I avoid looking at Mr. Werner's two kids—a boy and a girl who look about thirteen—sitting at the front row, staring dazedly at the coffin like they can't believe it's their dad in there. I get reminded of Papa, when he'd died, and I can't believe I'm putting two other kids through what I had to go through myself. Even though Mr. Werner was a monster, he was still their dad.

Stop that, I remind myself. Mr. Werner was an awful father. He'd been using his own kids as mere pawns, fighting for them just to hurt his ex-wife. If he was willing to do that, then he mustn't have been a caring father at all.

Mr. Werner's ex-wife is also there, and she looks exactly like how I imagine rich, Chinese-Indonesian aunties look. Big hair, thick, immaculate makeup, lips pursed, no tears. Next to her are—deep breath—Danny's parents. I know because the dad looks exactly like how I imagine Danny will look in thirty years' time. Handsome, with salt-and-pepper hair and sad eyes. Danny's mom looks like her sister but with less makeup, and she's at least dabbing at her eyes a little. Danny's parents look like totally normal people. Kind. Not totally racist. My insides churn, torn between guilt and anger at the sight of them.

I shoot Danny an encouraging smile and he gives me a small, tired smile in return.

"That was a good speech," Beth murmurs.

"Yeah."

The service ends and we file out. Sam wants to go to the front and give her condolences, but I'm pretty sure there's a special place in hell for killers who give their victim's family condolences, so I follow Beth out of the church instead.

"How're you doing?" Beth says, as we stroll out to the church garden.

I shrug. "It's a weird time."

"It sure is. It feels super surreal being here at a teacher's funeral. How's Danny holding up?"

"He's..." Not great, but that's probably normal, given the circumstances. "Coping. How are you doing? I'm sorry I haven't been around much for a while."

"I'm okay. Um, I feel like a total asshole saying this, but I've actually been super preoccupied by other stuff."

"Oh?" I perk up. Finally, something that doesn't have anything to do with any of this mess. "What stuff?"

"Mostly my mom. Argh, she's the worst. I got a B in my business quiz and she was *so* angry, loh! She was like, 'Girl, ah, when I was your age, right, I was selling kueh tutu after school. Each one sell only for ten cents, but by the end of my first month, I earn over one thousand dollars. End of second month, I earn three thousand.' Like that's even possible. People don't even like kueh tutu," Beth grumbles.

I laugh. "I wonder how much of what parents say is true."

"Word. I feel like every time my mom tells me the kueh tutu story, the amount of money she earned in the first month doubles. Pretty sure the first time she told me the story, she said she only earned like five bucks after a month. Anyway, it sucks, but it makes me want to prove her wrong, you know? I just want—" Her gaze flicks somewhere over my shoulder and fear flashes across her face. She stops talking immediately, her mouth clapping into a straight line.

My heart rate's tripled before I even turn around.

A burly, middle-aged white guy is standing right behind me, all up in my personal space. I take a step back. Behind him is a pretty Latina woman in her twenties. They both look very, very serious, and it's obvious as hell that they're cops.

So this is how I'm going to go down. At Mr. Werner's funeral, with everybody right here.

"Lia Set—Set-eye—well, shit, I'm not gonna get this right, am I? I mean, these names are ridiculous," the man says, with a laugh. It's not a friendly laugh.

The woman behind him steps forward, a flicker of contempt crossing her face at her partner. "Setiawan," she says, pronouncing it right. And that's when I know I'm in deep shit. She wouldn't have taken the time to learn how to pronounce my name unless she thinks I'm somehow important to their investigation.

I nod at her, forcing a polite smile.

"I'm Detective Mendez. This is Detective Jackson. Can we talk to you for a bit?"

Like I could possibly say no. I turn to Beth, and she's just standing there, looking all awkward.

"See you later?" I say. I'm not really sure what one says in these situations.

"Uh-huh. Bye," she says, hurrying away.

Questions hurl themselves through my mind as the detectives lead me to one side of the garden, away from the crowd. Is this a formal questioning? What is a formal questioning? Should I have a lawyer present? But I don't have a lawyer. Could I borrow one from somebody? Would that make me look even guiltier?

"I know this is probably really scary, but if you answer

all our questions, this will be done before you know it," she says.

But why are they even asking any questions? Danny said Detective Jackson was happy to dismiss the case as an accident.

We go to the farthest corner of the church garden, under the shade of a tree, and Detective Mendez takes out a writing pad. An actual writing pad like you see cops scribbling notes in on TV when they talk to a suspect.

"So, Lia. You were taking Mr. Werner's class?" she says, giving me an encouraging smile.

I almost deny it as a knee-jerk reaction then realize that would be futile. They'd have access to class records. I nod.

"Notice anything out of the ordinary the day before he died?"

"What day was that?" I squeak out. My limbs have turned to water and I'm this close to crumpling to the floor.

"We think he died sometime on Friday afternoon. Did you have a class with him that day?"

"No. Last class we had was Thursday."

"And nothing struck you as odd on Thursday? Anything at all, like maybe he was late to class, or maybe he was a bit moody..."

"Well, uh, Sophie—" I have to clear my throat, as my voice is threatening to break. "I um, I found Sophie's body in Mr. Werner's office on Thursday night."

Detective Jackson gives this sort of gruff snort, shifting

his weight from one foot to the other. He reminds me of a horse shaking its head and snorting. I don't know what the snort means. He doesn't look happy. Does that mean he thinks I'm guilty? Detective Mendez doesn't give any indication of having heard the snort. She continues staring at me hard. I feel naked under her gaze.

"Yes, we've reviewed the report from that night," she says. "It's very strange, isn't it, having two members of the school pass away within such a short time?"

I jerk my head down and back up. "Yeah. I mean. Yeah." God, I am barely coherent.

"Do you have any ideas why Sophie Tanaka was in James Werner's office that night?"

"No. Well, I heard that she'd been having problems with him? I don't know," I babble.

"What sort of problems?"

What sort of problems? My mind whizzes ahead. Should I tell them about Mr. Werner selling grades? But what would that do? Would it make them even more suspicious? I decide to play dumb. "I don't know. I'm just the new kid. By the time I got here, Sophie had already been expelled."

"Right," Detective Mendez says.

Detective Jackson shifts his weight from one foot to the other, looking at his watch pointedly. "I think we're done—"

"Do you know an app called"—she pauses to refer to her

notes—"Draycott Dirt?" Detective Jackson gives her a sour look.

This is a segue I was not expecting. Is it a good tangent or a bad one? Either way, it's good we're moving on from Mr. Werner. Yes? Yes.

"Yeah, I know about it, sure," I say with a shrug.

"What can you tell us about Draycott Dirt?"

"Uh. It's an app…where kids post stuff? Sort of like Twitter."

Detective Mendez gives me this look, like I'm a dog that's refusing to play ball. Which is true, I am refusing, but only because the ball is a spiky iron ball at the end of a chain.

"You've left out a pretty important detail, Lia," Detective Mendez says. "Like the fact the app is rife with bullying."

"Is it?" I say, weakly. Obviously, it is. Anyone with half a brain would take one look at it and go, "Wow, this app has a ton of bullying."

"Do you post often?"

"No." Finally, a question I can answer with absolute honesty.

"How come?" Mendez says. "There must be lots of 'dirt' you'd love to spill about some people here. I mean, some of the kids I've talked to…man."

Sorry, Detective, not gonna fall for it. "Nope, not really. I mostly keep to myself. When I'm not doing my homework,

I'm on the track, so I don't have much time to talk bad about anyone."

"Sure, sure. I get you. So. Nothing to say. Right. Not even about Mandy Kim?"

What has Mandy told them?! My mind screams. I force a laugh. "Mandy. Heh, I'm not surprised. She's been trash-talking me ever since I took her place on varsity. She lies a lot, so I tend to just ignore whatever she has to say." With superhuman effort, I manage to keep myself from asking, "What did she say about me, huh? Huh? HUH?"

"That's interesting, because according to Mandy and a couple other girls…let's see, ah, Arjuna Singh and Elle Brown, you've been harassing them ever since you got here. They said they even filed a report against you. Sounds pretty serious, Lia."

I actually feel the skin on my face tighten into a frozen mask. Mandy goddamn Kim and her gremlins. Of course. There it is, the real trap.

"I have never said or done anything to them. Those reports—they were more of a prank than anything." Did that come out convincing?

"Pretty crazy prank to play, don't you think?"

I shrug again.

She nods but doesn't look at all convinced.

"What does this have to do with Mr. Werner's accident?"

She smiles grimly. "Yeah, thing is, we're not so sure it was an accident. Coupled with Sophie dying on campus, things are looking mighty strange. And we've got a witness who said she saw Mr. Werner out with someone the day he went missing."

It's like the world's just crumbled under my feet. Not an accident. Danny was wrong. And a witness. Someone who saw Mr. Werner with me—oh.

The passerby. The woman, pushing a stroller, who had side-eyed us when we were arguing on the street.

"Just one last question, Lia." I barely hear her. She taps on her phone and shows me a picture. "Have you seen these before?"

Time. Stops.

Because right there, on her phone, bright as anything, is a picture of tattered red-and-black shoelaces, knotted into a neat ribbon. I can see the frayed edges and the familiar spots where they'd gotten stained.

My lucky laces.

How. HOW? How. The. Hell?

This is what hell feels like. This is it. The laces must have fallen out of my bag in the—oh god, where? In Mr. Werner's car? Later? In the woods? Where in the woods?

I feel myself shaking my head. "No. I don't recognize them."

"Are you sure? Look again." She pushes the phone nearer to my face.

I can't help it. I cringe, as if she's showing a picture of a dismembered body. I recover quickly and plaster a smile on my face, but it's too late. She's caught the flinch, knows that the scent of guilt is on me. Her eyes are fixed on mine, a slight crease on her forehead. She doesn't like me.

"C'mon, Mendez, the kid doesn't know shit. No offense, kid," Detective Jackson says. He doesn't even bother looking at me. Why can't HE be in charge of this investigation?

I should strive to sound like a clueless teen. "Oh, totally none taken, like, not even a little bit." Was that convincing? "I mean, like. Like. You know." Wow, speaking like this is a lot harder than it looks. Detective Jackson is convinced I'm a total moron, at least. He snorts and turns away from me, shaking his head a little.

Detective Mendez sighs. *She* doesn't buy the clueless airhead bit. "If you hear or remember something, call me, okay?" She hands me a card. "Anytime at all. I mean it, Lia. In the meantime, don't leave town."

I watch them walk off and approach Danny's family. What are they telling them? Danny meets my eye for a second, but his dad says something and his gaze flicks away. The world is slipping from my grasp, and I can't let it. Not now that I have so much to live for. I can't lose it all. I need a way out of this. I need a—

I need a fall guy. Mandy keeps coming at me, the cops are closing in, and I need someone to take the heat off me.

Someone who's already doing all sorts of illegal stuff.

Someone the cops would be happy to catch. Someone who deserves to be put away.

Someone like Draycott's drug dealer.

The thought is a fire lit under me. On top of Mr. Werner's cheating business, there's also a drug dealer on campus, and they basically caused Sophie's death. I know Grace said the stuff the Draycott drug dealer sells are clean, but who can tell for sure? And also, Sophie probably wouldn't have gotten into drugs in the first place if they weren't so readily available on campus. I'm going to hunt down the dealer, and I'm going to serve them on a platter to the police.

CHAPTER 22

I think most clearly when I'm running, so after I leave the funeral, I head straight for the track, where my mind competes with my legs to see which one can sprint faster.

Okay. So there might be a murder investigation. Which is bad. Really bad.

But there is conveniently also a drug ring. I'm going to find out who's involved in the drug ring and hand them over to the cops. Drug dealers are known to often kill people, so it would be easy to believe that the dealer probably killed Mr. Werner as well. Right? Right. That way, the cops will stop sniffing around the school; plus, they'll see me as a good, helpful kid. Maybe.

Only problem is: How? If the cops aren't able to find

out who's involved in the drug ring, how am I supposed to do it?

Okay, think. Think.

Thiiiink.

Hmm.

This Shakespeare-worthy inner monologue goes on for a while. In fact, it goes on for the rest of my run. I finish on surprisingly wobbly legs and stagger back to Mather for a hot shower. I'm just drying myself when it comes back in bits and pieces, the drunken, horrible memory of Grace telling me about an online shop in a Vegas toilet, music pulsing all around us.

My hair still dripping, I hurry back to my room. Inside, I pace a bit with closed eyes, trying to remember the words Grace had written on my hand that night. There was an online shop. Blue-something. Blueberry—nope. Blueseed. Yes, that's it. I've heard of it, though I've never checked out the site.

I open my laptop and type in the address. It's basically Etsy 2.0, a place where individual sellers can sell their handiwork. And it's huge, boasting over half a million sellers. Okay. Now the seller's name. God, what was it? It was something incredibly dumb, like Whee, or Yahoo. I try both and get nothing. Wat? No. Woo-hoo? I've typed in *woo* when the search box auto-completes it to *Woot*. That's it. I hit Enter, and I find Woot1212's shop.

The shop is—well, to be perfectly honest, it's a bit crap. Only five items on sale, and they look like the kind of cheap trinket you can get for two cents in China. And yet, Woot1212 has made—wow—over a thousand sales. Gee, I wonder why. I click on the first item. A necklace with a tiny Coke bottle pendant. Right, that would be cocaine. And the Mary Jane key chain is weed, and the healing crystal's got to be crystal meth, and—

Healing crystal.

No. No, no, it can't be. Many people have healing crystals. You see them all the time on TV. This is a coincidence. They're literally as common as like, cell phones, literally. Literally can't think of anyone who literally doesn't have a healing crystal. *Stop saying* literally. *Stop saying what I think you're saying.* I squeeze my eyes shut, but I can't unsee it.

I can't unsee those crystals all over Beth's room. And how she's mentioned a part-time job and being desperate to earn some money to prove her parents wrong. And I keep remembering that time at Mr. Werner's funeral, when the cops came to speak to me and Beth looked absolutely terrified, and I can't forget it. My insides are curling up tight, my cheeks are hot, and I want to scream at someone. At everyone. At the entire world. Why? Why the shit, Beth? Why, why, why—

I barely register walking out of my room, making my way

down the hallway. A couple of girls walking by say hello, and I blink in a daze. And then, quite suddenly, I'm at Beth's room. My hand lifts. Knocks.

"'Sup, Li? This is a nice surprise," Beth says, grinning at me, dimples on full assault.

I follow her in. Then I say it. I just drop it like some atomic bomb. "You're the drug dealer."

It's like someone's hit the pause button. I'm pretty sure we both stop breathing, the air around us crystallizing into sharp-edged shards.

And then Beth opens her mouth and laughs. "Very funny, Lia."

"I know you're the drug dealer."

"Hey, please, lah, auntie." Beth throws her hands up. "What drugs? You hit your head, is it?" She laughs again, and I need her to stop because it's the worst laugh in the history of laughs, a laugh that's brittle with fear.

I pick up a purple healing crystal from her makeup table. "I saw your online shop, Woot1212."

"Wait, what? Put that down okay, that one is for my chi, very important one, your chi." Beth jumps and snatches the crystal from me.

I look around her room, at the constant mess it's in, all these expensive clothes and purses strewn everywhere, the Miu Miu sunglasses and Prada bags, and—

Something clicks into place. Before Beth can stop me, I

fling open her wardrobe. It's only got a few items of clothing, but behind the dresses and shirts are stacks of handbags and shoeboxes.

"Hey!" Beth yells.

I reach out just as Beth tackles me from behind. I slam into the soft mountain of clothes. I flail blindly, slinky silk in my eyes and cotton in my mouth. Beth's got her arms around my waist and, tiny as she is, Beth's shockingly strong, like WTF is going on, I can't believe she is literally tackling me—holy shit, OUCH—I scream as pain bursts in my shoulder—did she stab—no, she BIT, she really just honest-to-god bit me—I flail wildly, knock into the tower of handbags and shoeboxes. The boxes tumble down, and suddenly it's raining little plastic baggies.

And we stop, we stop because we're both sobbing and Beth's nose is bleeding, and somehow I did that, but I don't know how, and my shoulder's on fire and bags of cocaine or whatever the hell are all around us, and how did it come to this, really?

I stand there, panting, and look at Beth. My first friend at Draycott, the girl who took me under her wing. Sweet, studious Beth. She's kneeling on the floor, crying, grabbing as many of the bags as she can and stuffing them back into a Prada handbag. I was right about her being the drug dealer, but this doesn't feel at all like victory.

"Beth—"

"You don't understand!" she cries, swiping at her nose savagely, leaving a streak of bloody snot on her sleeve.

"What don't I understand?" I gesture around me. "Why you're selling drugs? Why *are* you?" I wipe my face, take a deep breath.

"You don't know what it's like to be me. To grow up with all these overachievers. You don't know how hard that is. And me, always the disappointing one. You know what my mom says to me whenever I go home for the holidays?"

"Something mean, I'm guessing?" I sneer, completely bereft of any sympathy. I can't believe she's trying to make me feel bad for her.

"Nothing. She says nothing. She just goes, 'Oh, Ah Ling is back.' And then she just goes back to doing whatever she was doing. But when my older brother comes home, she throws a party. A literal party, where she tells everyone his accomplishments. 'My Kwang Li is a surgeon, you know. Brain surgeon, that is the hardest part of the body to be a surgeon for, you know.'"

"Okay, that sucks, but you're selling literal drugs."

"I know!" Beth wails. "I just wanted to prove them wrong so bad."

"How would you being a drug dealer prove them wrong?"

"I was going to save up enough money to put myself through college, and I was going to tell them I got a full scholarship."

"That is just so wrong, I don't even know where to begin."

And suddenly, I'm furious. I want to shake Beth so hard that her teeth rattle in her skull. She's selling *drugs*. Illegal drugs, drugs that hurt people, and all because she wants to play the role of a dutiful Asian daughter. My skin is on fire at the thought of it.

"Yeah, I know!" Beth snaps. "You don't think I know how wrong it is?"

"No, I don't think you do, because you're still doing it!" I shout. "How could you? After what happened to Sophie? What the fuck, Beth!"

She blanches. "Sophie—that wasn't me. That wasn't my fault."

"How the hell would you know? She died of an overdose, and you're the campus dealer! Put two and two together, for god's sake."

"No, you don't understand. I'm really careful about who I sell to. When she was still—before she got expelled, when it became obvious she wasn't doing well, I stopped selling to her. I blocked her from buying any of my stuff."

I shake my head with a snort. "Oh wow, look at you, a drug dealer with a conscience. Woo bloody hoo. Am I supposed to be impressed by that? She could've easily gotten your drugs from somebody else."

"It wasn't my stuff!" she cries. "She didn't overdose, she got laced drugs!"

"How do you know?"

She drops her gaze, her face red. "I—when I heard about what happened, I was so guilty. I had to know if she'd OD'ed on my stuff. I got my parents to ask her parents. They're friends. Her parents said the coroner's report says it wasn't an overdose. She'd taken some MDMA cut with really bad shit. Methamphetamines, laundry detergent. The combination sent her into toxic shock."

Grace had said as much in Vegas. I guess Beth had told Grace what happened. The thought of it is sickening. Beth is so desperate to distance herself from Sophie's death. "Okay, so maybe she didn't get those particular drugs from you, but still, she got into drugs while she was enrolled in Draycott, right? So she started out with your drugs."

She glares at me for a moment, all fiery rage, then her face crumples, and she starts sobbing again. "I know. You think I haven't thought of that? You think I'm sitting here feeling fine? I've felt like shit ever since Sophie died! Are you gonna turn me in? Shit." She covers her face with both hands and sobs like a little kid.

I look around at the mess, the small mountain of drug-filled baggies, and my friend Beth, looking so fragile and broken. No more than an hour ago, I'd been so fired up. I had a plan. Find out who the drug dealer is and turn her in to get the cops off my back. Get justice for Sophie.

"No," I say, and once I say it, I know it's true. I can't. Not Beth.

Beth lifts her streaming face, looks at me with naked anticipation.

"I won't turn you in."

"Thank you, thank—"

"But I'm taking these." I take a handful of the little baggies.

Beth's mouth drops open. "Hang on—"

"All of them. I'm confiscating them."

"Wait, no, you can't do that!"

"Why not?"

"I'll be in such deep shit with my supplier, I'll get cut from the business—"

"Much deeper shit than if I reported this?"

Beth's mouth shuts tight.

"I can't just walk away and let you keep doing this. You know that."

She looks balefully at me. "What're you gonna do with them? You can't snort them all, you'll die."

"I don't do drugs. Sorry, I didn't mean for that to come out so judgy." I pause. "Wait, actually, I did mean for that to come out judgy."

Beth rolls her eyes. "I don't do them either."

"No, you just sell them. It's not that much better. In fact, it's worse. Do you have a bag I can take all these in?"

I end up taking them in shoeboxes. There's so much, they fill up three shoeboxes, which seems crazy. I mean, I don't know much about drugs, but this seems like a lot.

"I can't believe you're doing this to me," Beth says, as I head for the door with the shoeboxes.

"One day, you'll thank me."

She doesn't say anything, just slams the door behind me.

CHAPTER 23

It turns out it's a really bad idea taking all of Beth's stash, because now who's the dumb shit stuck with three shoeboxes full of drugs?

I need to get rid of the pills, fast. Especially with the cops looking into Mr. Werner's death. But I have no idea how I'm going to get rid of them. The pills I can probably just flush down the toilet. Or can I? Would they clog up the toilet? Because the last thing I want is for the school to find a wad of ecstasy plugging up their drains. I very nearly do a Google search about it before I realize I can't, because the second last thing I want is for the cops to look up my search history and find *how to get rid of drugs*.

So I put them in my wardrobe, and I stare at the wardrobe

and wonder what I'm going to do with them—bury them, throw them in trash cans all over the city, dump them in the river—and then suddenly it's morning, and I'm late for track. I go through the motions of the day, pretending not to notice when Beth ignores me at breakfast and lunch. When classes end, I go to Stacey's room.

Stacey's room is on the other end of Mather. Like Beth's, it's stuffed to the gills, but instead of clothes and knickknacks, hers is filled with what looks like the latest tech that the CIA would have in their lab.

There are three huge monitors crowding her desk, each one showing rows of numbers and code. Cans of opened Monster drink are littered around the desk. Her hard drive looks like it's mutated—its casing is left open, innards of rainbow-colored wires and complicated hardware all in a tangle, spilling out in a knot of electronic intestines. A portable fan aimed at the hard drive is whirring at full speed. The place smells of stale dust and the sticky, artificially sweet stink of Monster. It's all a bit overwhelming. I reach out without thinking and pick up a bright-orange pill bottle on the corner of her desk. Xanax. Oops. I didn't mean to be a meddlesome auntie. I put it back quickly, hoping that Stacey didn't notice me being nosy.

"Make yourself at home. Mi casa is your casa." Stacey swings herself onto the bed and gestures at me to sit in her chair. I do so after checking to make sure there are no loose wires or gadgets or cans of Monster I might accidentally crush with my butt. Next to me is another computer tower, but this one is dead, no glimmering lights. It's lying open, wires sticking out, and a small toolbox sits next to it on the floor, filled with pliers, wires, and other components I can't identify.

"That's my final project for comp sci," Stacey says. She grabs an open bag of gummy bears from her side table and pops three in her mouth. "Want one?"

"No, thanks. Um, so." I'm here for a different reason: the keylogger. But how do I bring it up? Last night, I wore down the carpet in my room pacing around, my mind racing, trying to come up with a plan to thwart the cops' investigation. Now that I know the dealer is Beth, I can't possibly hand her to the cops. Maybe I should, but I can't. I still don't know what to do yet, but one thing's clear: I need to tie up all possible loose ends, starting with Stacey's keylogger. "Danny inherited Mr. Werner's laptop."

There is a marked lack of reaction. Then Stacey says, "Uh-huh. And?"

And? I flap my arms. "And? That's bad! He's going to find the keylogger you planted."

Stacey throws her head back and laughs. "And how's he going to do that?"

"I don't know! I don't know any of this computer sorcery stuff."

"Wow, computer sorcery stuff. Aren't we tech-savvy?" She pops more gummy bears into her mouth.

Why is she so blasé about this? I want to grab her by the shoulders and shake her until her head flops back and forth. But then it strikes me: she doesn't care because she doesn't know there was foul play involved in Mr. Werner's death. She doesn't know the stakes. How do I make her see that this is a Very Important Thing without making her suspicious?

Okay. Think. "I just—um, you and I are friends now, and I don't want things to get weird if Danny finds out you've been spying on his uncle."

"Sure, I guess it'll be a bit weird if he finds out. But he won't, because there's nothing linking me to the keylogger. Don't tell anyone, but I used April's ID to hack into Mr. Werner's system."

"April? As in our in-house IT support?"

"Yep. She has access to all the school's computers. The teachers' computers are technically school property, so she has access to all of them. If you received a computer from school, she has access to it as well, just by the way."

My head spins. "Okay…but how did you get her to hack into Mr. Werner's computer?"

Stacey laughs. "I didn't get her to do shit." She raises her hands and shrugs. "I may have sort of planted a keylogger into her computer."

"Stacey!" I cry. This sounds bad. This sounds really bad.

"What? Hey, if she didn't want people hacking into her computer, she should have better firewalls. I did it my first week here."

"WTF, Stacey? What is this, like something you just do for fun? You go around hacking into people's computers?"

"Sort of." She laughs at my expression. "I mean, not just anyone's computer. I'm not like that. I respect people's privacy. Most of the time. I prefer hacking into systems. I even hacked into the school's security system. Fun fact: I installed a motion detector at the entrances to Mather so in case someone ever tries to break in at night, I'd know. Or if someone sneaks out at night to hook up with somebody—"

"Okay, TMI. Go back to Mr. Werner's computer." I rub my face and try to work out this new piece of information. "You were telling me about using April's computer to hack into Mr. Werner's system, which means..."

"It means even if Danny were to somehow trace the hacks on Mr. Werner's computer, it'll just lead him to April, and he'll just think it's April doing her regular sweep across all computers for viruses or whatever. It won't come back to me. Satisfied?"

"But." I try to sort out my thoughts. "Didn't you download files off Mr. Werner's computer? Test papers and stuff? Won't it look suspicious? There's no reason why April would do that."

Stacey bites the head off a gummy bear. "I guess," she says, after a while.

Shit. My stomach sinks. I cover my face and moan.

"Oh my god, you are being so paranoid right now. So what if Danny finds out I snooped around in his uncle's computer? What's the big deal? I mean, I know the guy's dead, but let's face it, he was shady as hell."

God, how do I make her understand how important this is? I'm so frustrated right now, I'm this close to reaching out and shaking her. "Look, can you please get rid of the virus on Mr. Werner's computer?"

"Despite being a genius, I'm not a wizard, Lia. I can't just snap my fingers and make the virus disappear."

"What do you need to do to erase it?"

Another sigh. "I'll have to write a program to do it. And I'm lazy."

"Stacey!"

She laughs at me. "That look on your face. I'll do it, you nong. I'll have the program ready by tomorrow."

I exhale in a rush. "Thank you."

"Sure." There's a pause, and then Stacey drops her gaze. "I'm glad you dropped by, actually. I've been meaning to ask you something."

"Oh?"

"Yeah. What's going on with you?"

Immediately, my heart does that thing again where it beats so hard, it makes me want to throw up. Is my guilt that obvious? "What do you mean?"

Stacey purses her lips. "Don't take this the wrong way, but you look really bad, like something my cat chewed and then played with and then puked up."

"How am I not supposed to take that the wrong way? What's the right way of taking that?"

"Okay, you know what I mean. How much have you been running? Are you eating okay? You look so pale and like, I dunno. Kind of scrawny."

Oh. That. I sag with relief. She doesn't know after all. Then I look down at myself and frown.

It's true that I've barely eaten since Mr. Werner's death, because every time I put food to my lips, I feel the warmth of his legs as I try to drag him up the hill, and then bile rushes up my throat, and I just. I can't. I need a bit more time before I can feel normal again. Until Stacey pointed it out, I haven't realized just how much weight I've lost, but now I see it's true, the way my jeans are hanging off me, the way my legs feel so brittle, like they can hardly hold up the rest of me.

"I'm just tired," I say. "Between my boyfriend's uncle dying and, you know, said boyfriend grieving, I haven't been able to get much sleep."

"Oookay. As long as you're taking care of yourself."

Tears prickle my eyes. I want to tell her so badly.

I look away. "I am."

Stacey exhales. "Okay." Obviously not okay, but she's fine with letting it go for now, and I want to hug her and thank her for not pushing. She reaches into a drawer and throws a protein bar at me. "Eat," she orders.

"Fine," I grumble, but I smile as I open the packet. It feels good to have someone nag me into taking care of myself. It feels like home. I take a bite of the protein bar and grimace when my shriveled taste buds burst into life. When was the last time I ate something?

"Anyway, let's go. We're late." She stands up and grabs a brown paper bag from her desk.

"Where are we going?"

"To the river. I've got stale bread for the ducks. Those fuckers get vicious if I don't feed them for over a day."

Welp. That's...unexpected. I follow in a bit of a daze. Going from talking about computer hacking to feeding vicious ducks is quite the jump, but the more I find out about Stacey, the more I like her. We walk in silence, but it's a comfortable silence, kind of like slipping into your favorite coat. For a while, I feel almost at peace. Then guilt comes hurrying behind me and catches up, sinks its little claws into my flesh.

"What if Danny hires a hacker to help him? Would they find traces of the virus? Are you able to remove absolutely one hundred percent of the virus?"

"Dude, where's he going to find another hacker? 1–800-HACKERS? We're rare creatures who like to hide from the sun."

"You've just described vampires."

"And you know how hard it is to find those. Relax, okay?

It's going to be fine. No one here knows how to do what I do, and I'll create a nice little cleanup program tonight. Danny won't find out a thing."

I could practically kiss her.

CHAPTER 24

Danny is obviously tired, but he looks glad to see me. His whole face, pale and thin, breaks into the kind of smile little kids get when you surprise them with a cookie. I always forget just how good he looks, not just because he's so handsome, which he is, but because seeing him makes me feel…I don't know. Like I'm whole again. Wow, that's cheesy. But it feels like all the holes ripped out of me from the past few months are being filled out, and I'm okay. I'm okay.

Except I'm not, because I've come here to betray him even more than I already have. Guilt squirms its way through my stomach, and I have to remind myself that the cops are on the case and I need to do this now.

"You have no idea how good it is to see you," Danny

says. We kiss, our lips moving, searing hot against each other's, then he takes my hand and leads me into his room, and suddenly I'm so nervous, my legs forget how to walk. I know how stupid it sounds, especially when I think about the reason I'm here in the first place, but I can't ignore the feeling of this moment. It feels official somehow, like we've crossed something, some chasm, and we're on the other side, and suddenly I'm acutely aware of the fact that I'm in my gorgeous boyfriend's room. And god, I wish so hard that we were just two normal teenagers with nothing to hide from each other. When I look at Danny, all I see in this moment is a boy. A boy I'm pretty sure I'm falling in love with. And it hurts so bad. I reach out toward him, drawing him close to me.

Calm down please, hormones. Focus on the task.

My phone rings, and the moment breaks. We jump away from each other, and I can't decide whether I'm disappointed or relieved. Maybe both. I clear my throat and answer.

"I'm freezing my ass off out here. Are we doing this or not?" Stacey says.

Heat bursts in my cheeks, and not the pleasant kind that just happened, but the fire-ants-biting-with-tiny-sharp-incisors kind. I jump to my feet, every muscle taut. "Yeah," I say hurriedly and hang up. My gut churns. I can't believe now I'm about to con Danny into leaving his room, moments after we were about to—uh. Whatever we were about to do. What *were* we about to do? I can't meet his eye.

"You okay?" Danny says, sitting up and pushing his hair out of his face.

"Yeah. I just—um, I'm really hungry." The lie flops out of my mouth like a live snake. Surely he can sense that I'm not being honest. "Can we go get some food?"

"Now?" He frowns, chews his bottom lip. "You don't wanna—um. Stay?"

My face is burning. Literally burning. "Maybe next time. Let's go grab something to eat. Maybe off campus?"

When I had talked about the plan with Stacey this morning, it had seemed so simple: I distract Danny while Stacey slips inside his room and installs the cleaner in Mr. Werner's computer. To do this, I'll have to make sure: 1. He leaves his door unlocked, and 2. He stays outside of his room for at least fifteen minutes.

But now that I'm actually doing it, every part of me is fighting against it.

"Yeah, okay. That's a great idea, actually," Danny says, and I have to stop myself from sagging with relief. He gets up and grabs a jacket, then pauses. "Hey, I just wanna say…I'm sorry if we were going too fast. I just—um—I got carried away, and—"

"No!" I can't let him think he scared me away. Not like this. I catch his hand, pull him close, so close, I can see each stupidly long eyelash. "I loved it. And I want to. With you. One day. Soon?" Who knew how hard stringing words into a complete sentence is?

"One day soon," he says, kissing me on the forehead so gently that tears rush into my eyes.

I feel that sharp-edged guilt digging, biting into my insides until everything feels shredded and bleeding. Despite this, I still need to go through with it. I can't go to prison. Not now. I get a flash of Detective Mendez saying they're looking into Mr. Werner's death. I can't not do this.

As we leave the room, I stuff a small wad of paper into the door lock so the latch won't catch properly, and then we walk out of the building, my heart heavy as an iron fist as I lead my boyfriend away so my new friend can break into his room.

Hand in hand, we walk through the campus, past the old chapel with its steepled, faded-blue roof and stained glass windows, past the more modern Dewey Building and the huge, rambling Meyers Library. It feels like everyone's hanging out on the grass, even though summer has well and truly slipped into fall and it's way too cold to be sitting out here. Or maybe I feel this way because every time someone looks our way or says hi to us, I feel exposed, like they must know the kind of shady person I really am.

People keep coming by to us and asking Danny how he's doing, which is really sweet but also really awkward. He deals with it all graciously, though, a lot more graciously than I would've.

"Hey, Danny," Mandy calls out.

I'm immediately on my guard, every muscle inside me tensing as Mandy and Elle approach.

"How's it going, Mandy?" Danny says.

There's that familiar smirk on Mandy's face that makes my chest tighten. I know, even before she opens her mouth, that nothing good is going to come out of it.

"So Elle and I have a bet. Do you think they'll ever find the wolf or bear or whatever that ate your uncle?" Next to her, Elle is smiling and sort of frowning at the same time, like she was prepared for Mandy to say some mean shit to me but not like, *this* mean.

I'd been expecting something bad, but holy shit. The anger ignites deep in my belly and rages up and out. "What the hell is wrong with you?" I snap.

The acidity in my voice catches Mandy off guard, and she turns the full heat of her attention on me, bearing down on me like a beast of prey. "Oh, look, the little worm's talking back." She steps toward me and shoves me back.

"Hey!" Danny says. "Stop that."

Instead of stopping, Mandy shoves me again, this time with all her might. It's so shockingly strong that suddenly, I'm snatched back to that cursed day in the woods. Mr. Werner's breath hot in my ear, my hands slick with blood and sweat, grasping at something, anything. That moment where everything civilized stopped existing and we were shaved down to the bone, nothing but teeth and claws.

"Lia," Danny says, but his voice comes from afar.

All thought has come to a screaming mess in my head, and I taste the metallic tang of fear in my mouth as I swing my hands up to cover my face, to protect myself from Mr. Werner, and I only realize what I've done when my flailing hands smack into Mandy's face.

It wasn't a hard smack, but Mandy stumbles back with a shriek like I've just punched her in the face.

"You slapped me!" she screams.

"I—what? No, I didn't, I wasn't—"

"You pushed her first," Danny says.

"Oh, your little girlfriend assaulted Mandy. I saw that very clearly," Elle says with a smirk.

Kids are crowding around Mandy and Elle, who are shouting, and my blood is pounding in my head and everything is swimming. Tears spring to my eyes and dimly, I realize that Danny's leading me away.

As soon as we turn a corner, Danny swings around to face me. "Are you okay? Holy shit, that was messed up. God, I'm so sorry I didn't hold her back or something, I just froze."

"It's not your fault. I shouldn't freaked out like that. When she pushed me, it just—" I stop myself in time. I can't tell him that when Mandy shoved me, it snatched me back to the woods with Mr. Werner.

"Shit, shit," Danny mutters.

"What is it? I'm okay, don't worry about me."

"Draycott has a zero-tolerance policy on physical violence." Danny sags against the wall. "And knowing Mandy, she's going to spin this into something worse than it really was, and Elle would back her up. I'll speak up on your behalf, obviously I will, but Mandy always has a knack for getting people to believe her version of events."

Oh god. Draycott has a zero-tolerance policy on violence. It does. Of course it does. Most schools do. Oh my god, how could I have been so stupid? I've fallen right into Mandy's trap. I want to bury my face in my hands and shriek until my throat is ragged and bleeding.

"I—"

Whatever I'm about to say dies away when my phone starts ringing. Danny and I stare at each other in horror. The caller ID says *Draycott Administration Office*. You've got to give it to them. They're efficient. I barely realize that I've answered the call until I hear the receptionist's voice.

"Hello, Lia Set—Set-eye-ay-wen?"

I don't bother correcting her. "Yeah?"

"This is Margot from the admin office. Please report to Mrs. Henderson's office right away."

Oh my god. My stomach turns to stone. My arms are lead. I can't breathe. I can't—

"Hello, are you still there?"

I manage a squeak, which Margot takes as a *yes*. She tells me they're expecting me soon and hangs up.

This is it, then. This is how I get myself kicked out of Draycott. Not by killing Mr. Werner, but by accidentally hitting Mandy. I stare at my phone. I stare at Danny.

"Lia." His voice comes out hoarse.

I open my mouth, but no words come out. There is a lump too big for words to slip around.

"We'll fight it together. I'll tell Mrs. Henderson what really happened," Danny says.

I nod numbly and let him lead me toward Castor, which is good, because I'm in a daze and barely know which direction to face. I can't believe I'm about to get kicked out of Draycott after all.

At the admin office, Margot says to Danny, "I'm sorry, you can't wait here unless you've got an appointment."

Danny steps forward. "But—"

"Trust me, she's in enough trouble without you making it worse," Margot says.

Danny and I gape at each other for a second, then he says, "I'll get my phone. I'll make calls. I'll—"

"I'll be fine," I say, and I barely recognize my own voice. "Don't worry about me."

Danny smiles, and it hurts to see how fake it is. How he's so obviously doing it for my sake. "I'll get my phone from my room real quick and call my family lawyer. It'll all be okay." He pulls me in for a second, his familiar scent filling my senses. I close my eyes and breathe him in.

And then I walk into the principal's office, and just as the door closes behind me, I realize Stacey's still in Danny's room.

CHAPTER 25

I turn around, practically pouncing on the doorknob, but Mrs. Henderson says, "Lia. Sit down." And it's clear she's not messing around. Her mouth is a tight, pinched line. I don't have a choice.

With every step I take, my heart slams against my rib cage guiltily. Stacey. Stacey. Stacey. I have to warn Stacey.

I reach for my phone as surreptitiously as I can. When I get to the chair in front of Mrs. Henderson's ginormous desk, I sit and glance down on my lap. Thank god for the desk; Mrs. Henderson can't possibly see that I'm holding it.

"I've just received a phone call from—"

Key in the unlock code.

"It is with the utmost importance—"

Tap on my texts. Tap on the message chain with Stacey. Type. Danny com—

"Young lady, are you listening to me?" She's standing up, shitshit—

Hit Send. I look up, stuffing the phone under my thigh. "Yeah. Utmost importance."

Her eyes narrow. For a second, I think she's going to leap across the table and grab my phone, but instead, she takes a deep breath.

"I suppose you know why you're here," she says.

I cock my head to one side and try to look as innocent as I can.

"Mandy Kim is at the health center. She says you assaulted her."

"That wasn't what happened. Mandy pushed me and I got scared. I was trying to cover my face and I accidentally swiped at her a little, but it was an accident—"

"There are many, many witnesses who saw you assaulting her."

What the hell? "Many" witnesses? As far as I know, only Elle and Danny saw what happened. With a sinking feeling, I realize that Mandy must have rounded up the rest of her gang to support her story.

From afar, I hear Mrs. Henderson say, "We have a zero-tolerance policy on violence. I'm afraid there's nothing I can do."

It is these words, *there's nothing I can do*, that slice through the fog of fear. And suddenly, there it is again, my old friend—rage. When I look up and finally meet Mrs. Henderson's eye, I see her for what she is: a coward. A greedy, selfish coward who doesn't give a shit about her students. And I realize, again, how disappointing it is to realize that the adults who are supposed to be looking out for you are only looking out for themselves. This time, I'm not going to let her flick me away like I'm a piece of lint. This bitch is coming down with me.

"There's nothing you can do?" I say, softly.

Mrs. Henderson gives a rueful sigh and shakes her head. "I'm afraid not, Lia."

"You mean like the time I came to you for help and told you about Mr. Werner's cheating ring, and you told me there was nothing you could do, even after Sophie's death?"

Her mouth snaps shut. She turns white. And I don't know what it is, maybe it's adrenaline, maybe it's the cops treating Mr. Werner's death as murder, maybe it's acceptance that I'm not just straddling two sides, but I'm full-on barreling down the dark side. I've gone full Sith, and I know it's the only way I'm surviving all of this.

"Or did you mean *nothing* like how you asked Danny to tell the cops nothing about his uncle's side business? Was that the nothing you meant?"

Luckily for Mrs. Henderson, she's already sitting down,

because she looks like she's about to do one of those dramatic swoons and drape herself over a chaise lounge. She blinks several times, like she's trying to clear her vision.

To be perfectly honest, I'm feeling kind of woozy myself. All the blood has rushed to my head, and I'm pretty sure the slightest bit more pressure will make it explode and spatter my brains all over the walls. I was raised to be a good, obedient kid. I have never talked back like this to authority. Somehow, I manage to remain sitting, biting hard on my lip and watching Mrs. Henderson go from Stepford white to Trump orange.

When she finally regains her voice, it comes out in a hiss. "Listen, you little—"

"No," I say, and my voice is so loud, I surprise myself. "No, I'm done listening. There's a murder investigation going on right now, and you asked Danny to withhold information from the cops. You knew about Mr. Werner's cheating ring and you didn't tell the cops about it. That's obstruction of justice. Do you know how much shit you'd be in if the cops found out about it?"

Her mouth opens and closes. She looks like a fish gasping on land. "I chose to omit that information because it would merely obfuscate their investigation," she sputters. "It has absolutely nothing to do with his horrible accident."

I almost shout, "IT HAS EVERYTHING TO DO WITH IT," but I stop myself in time. Instead, I say, "Shouldn't you let the cops decide that for themselves?" Do I want Mrs. Henderson to tell the cops about the cheating ring? Would that be good for me? Actually, it might be. Or it might be bad, I don't know. But at least it would throw them off-balance, probably. And in this moment, it's certainly throwing Mrs. Henderson off-balance, which is exactly what I need.

Mrs. Henderson catches hold of herself, and there's a terrifying moment where she wrestles with herself internally—she looks like she might explode—and then she snaps, "What do you want, Lia?"

"I want to stay at Draycott. I want my scholarship intact. I want all of you to leave me the hell alone so I can continue my education in peace and graduate with a chance of going to a good college. That's all I want."

"I *was* leaving you alone, until you went and assaulted another student!"

"I didn't assault her, she pushed me, and I stumbled back and accidentally hit her!" Mrs. Henderson massages her forehead.

"Just get out," she sighs after a while.

"Am I—"

"No, you're not expelled, but I swear to god, I see you here one more time and you are done here. Now go."

I don't need to be told twice.

CHAPTER 26

I've never seen Stacey this mad. Her cheeks are blazing red, her hands are shaky, and it's awful. It takes everything to not shrink away from her.

"I was counting on you. You were supposed to have my back. I mean, I was only in there because you begged me to clean up the virus!"

I clutch my kris pendant and grimace, my insides twisting guiltily. "I know, I'm so sorry, but I got called to Mrs. Henderson's office, and I thought I was going to be expelled, and I just—I panicked. I'm sorry."

Stacey stops pacing and stares at me. "Why did you think they were going to kick you out?"

I can't meet her eye. "I accidentally hit Mandy."

"How do you 'accidentally hit' Mandy?"

The words won't come. How do I explain to her that I'd freaked the hell out because of trauma from what happened in the woods with Mr. Werner? From everyone else's point of view, none of what I did made any sense. If Mandy had pushed anyone else, they'd probably have shaken it off and moved on instead of flailing like I did.

Stacey shakes her head at my silence. "So instead of looking out for me like you were supposed to, you get in a fight." She whistles. "Unbelievable."

"I'm sorry, it really wasn't much of a fight. I just—I don't know how to explain it. I'm sorry," I groan. "I did send you a message."

"No, you didn't."

"But I—" I scramble for my phone, look at my message history. I must've not tapped the Send button properly, because Stacey's right. My warning didn't get delivered. God, can I feel any shittier? "Did you get caught?"

"Almost. Someone stopped Danny and talked to him outside the room, so I realized he was about to come in and I practically jumped out of his window." She showed me her arms, scratched and bruised. "I don't think he saw me. I ran and didn't look back."

"God, I'm so, so sorry." I look down and wince. The cuts don't look too bad, thankfully.

"'S fine. You owe me, though. Like a huge favor. Huge. The biggest."

"Anything."

"That's unwise," she says, and there's a small smile tugging the corners of her lips. The sight of it lifts the weight off my chest, if only for a bit.

"Um, I feel like a huge asshole for asking, but did you manage to clean the computer?"

"I don't know. I was at ninety percent when I heard Danny's voice. We just gotta hope for the best."

Hope for the best. It feels like all I've been doing ever since I moved to Draycott is hope for the best and get slammed in the face with the worst possible thing. But maybe this time will be different.

Mr. Werner's substitute is nothing like him, by which I mean she's not running a cheating ring. I know because Mandy looks absolutely ill when the sub tells us we're going to have a pop quiz. I get a B minus, which is great considering how little time I've devoted to my studies, and is even better considering how many of my classmates flunked it. That's right, dipshits, no more paying for As in English Lit. Now you actually gotta do the work like the rest of us peasants.

Honestly, I could probably survive the rest of the semester like this. Over time, I'll stop thinking of Mr. Werner as much, and then my stomach will stop seizing as much, and I'll get my appetite back and be 100 percent fine. Everything will be okay.

On the third morning, I join Sam and Grace for breakfast as usual.

Sam gives me a once-over as I put my tray down, and she and Grace exchange a look.

"What?" I say, sitting on the bench.

"You're like, really skinny," Sam says.

I sigh. I've got a banana and a bowl of granola, and I'm going to give eating a proper meal a good go this morning. My stomach's even growling at the sight of the food. "I've had a lot of things on my mind lately."

"Just as long as you're okay," Sam says. "Anyway, what's going on with Beth?"

I can't meet anyone's eye. "I don't know."

"We went to her room last night," Grace says. "She said she's got beef with you."

Did I detect a hint of accusation in Grace's voice? My hackles rise. "Why don't you ask her what the beef is?"

"Whoa, hey, chill," Sam says. "We're not taking sides here."

"We just want you guys to stop being such brats," Grace says. "Both of you."

"It's her fault," I mumble, peeling my banana. My phone buzzes. It's a message from Danny.

Can u come to my room? Need to show u something. It's urgent.

Another buzz.

It's about my uncle.

What little appetite I have shrivels up and dies. Another buzz.

Something's wrong.

I stand up so fast, I end up knocking over my carton of milk.

"Everything okay?" Grace says, looking up from her fruit salad.

"I gotta go." I grab my bag, sling it over my shoulder.

"What? You haven't even touched your food!"

My stomach's doing that thing again, wringing itself like a wet towel. Eating's out of the question, but just to appease them, I take my banana and wave it at them before I rush out of the cafeteria. I sprint all the way to Mansfield, and though I'm practically flying, it takes forever to get there—why is this stupid campus so huge, what are these other buildings even for, nobody ever has classes at Burton or Johnson House, why is the dining hall so far from the dorms, why—

And then, quite suddenly, I see the L-shaped building of Mansfield, and now I wish there was even more distance to go, because I'm not ready for this. I don't want to face Danny, I don't know what to say, I don't know what lies will fall out of my mouth, I don't know what he knows and I don't want to know.

I push through the front doors and walk down the hallway, my ragged breath loud in the closed silence. The place is deserted, probably because everyone else is having breakfast. I'm not used to this silence, not in the dorms. It's unnatural, like the whole place is holding its breath and watching. When I finally knock on Danny's door, it's like a gunshot. I make myself jump.

He looks bad. Awful. Like he's aged overnight. Pale, so pale, skin like paper. Like I'd tear it if I'm not careful, and I'm careful, I really am, but I'm shaking, because I know whatever he's about to say is going to be the end of everything.

He closes the door behind me. I can't stand it; I can't bear this heavy silence, so complete, I can hear our heartbeats, both of them rapid, both broken, out of rhythm.

"Someone hacked into his computer."

Boom. Just like that. My world spins. I have to sit down. I'm sitting down. When did I sit? Danny's pacing. A wild animal, prowling, heat radiating off him. Scent of a predator. Caught the scent of blood? I shake my head, try to clear it. Do I ask *whose computer*? Play it dumb? So dumb. No. Sit here, gaping silently. A goldfish. I'm harmless, Danny, see?

"Yesterday morning, I turned on Uncle James's computer to get our old pictures and stuff off it. But there was something weird going on with it. It kept freezing, and I kept getting these Error messages, so I ran a virus scan, and then the computer just sort of seized up and died. I thought I did something wrong, so I took it in to a computer repair shop in town, and guess what they found?"

I give a little shake of the head. My chest is a fist, clenching. I can hardly breathe.

"A keylogger." Danny looks at me for the first time, and his gaze is a sword, stabbing all the way to the other side, through all the darkness and the tangle of lies. I hear the lies' dying screech, and I have to look away. I can't meet that feverish gaze. He'll see the truth, wriggling like a worm on my face. "Someone hacked into his computer, Lia."

"It's probably the school looking into his cheating ring." Amazing how fast that lie slipped out.

Danny looks unconvinced. "Really? But the school wants to shut that down, so why would they dig it up? I should turn it in to the cops. Yeah, I should—I don't know why I haven't, I should call them now—"

"You shouldn't!"

Danny stares at me. "Why not?"

"Because." They might link it back to me, the real killer? "Because...then they'd know about him selling grades to students?" Oh shit, that actually makes sense. I launch fully into it. "He probably has like, incriminating stuff on his laptop, and you don't want to ruin his reputation like that, do you?" Great, I'm actually gaslighting him. "The media will be all over this. Plus, I'm sure it was just some virus he accidentally downloaded when he was torrenting TV shows or whatever."

Danny rubs his eyes. "You're right. I don't want

everyone to know him as the shady teacher who sold grades to his students. But this is so—I feel like I'm losing it. There's something else, but—I don't know, you'll think I'm crazy. I don't know."

"What is it? Tell me," I plead. I need to know everything, even though my stomach is clenching and going, *No, I don't want to know.*

Danny hesitates for another moment before he finally says, "The other day, when you got called to Henderson's office and I came back to get my phone, I—uh. This is going to sound so crazy, but I saw something. A shadow moving under my door, like someone was in my room."

Oh my god. Oh god, shit, oh shit. He saw her.

"But someone in the hall asked me something, and by the time I opened the door, there was no one there."

My breath is coming in and out in little gasps. It's a struggle to pretend like I'm totally calm. Did he see her or not?

As though he read my mind, he says, "I think it was Stacey."

My heart explodes in my chest. I feel like I'm about to pass out. Before I can reply, he says, "It makes sense if she was the one who hacked into Uncle James's computer. We all know she's a computer geek. She does shit like this."

No, I want to yell. She has nothing against him, it's all me, all my fault, I shouldn't have asked her to clean up the virus, she was right, Danny probably wouldn't have found the virus in the first place, and now, because of me, it's all blowing up and I've roped her into this mess.

"That's just crazy," I say and try for a laugh.

"No, it's not!" His fist shoots out and slams down on the desk so hard that the wood cracks.

I squeak—an actual, frightened squeak that a small, furry animal might make a split second before some large predator descends upon it.

Danny looks down at his fist with wide eyes, as though surprised at his own outburst. But then he shakes his head and glares at me, anger radiating from him. "Stop fucking defending her. You're only doing it because you guys are friends," he growls.

My stomach turns to water. I've never seen Danny like this. Flashes of Mr. Werner stab through my mind. Mr. Werner chasing me in the woods. Mr. Werner on top of me, snarling—

No. Stop that. But now, I can see the relation between them, even though it's not genetic. That same focused rage burning in their eyes. I recall too, how Danny had grabbed Henry's wrist that night we all went clubbing. It had happened months ago, but now the memory comes to me with such clarity. I can remember every detail as though it happened yesterday—the look of pure terror on Henry's face, how panicky Danny looked afterward, like he hadn't meant to lose control like that. Without meaning to, I stagger back a step.

"Danny, please. I'm just pointing out to you that Stacey has nothing to do with your uncle. She's not even in his class. I mean, she's the type of person who'd put keyloggers on everyone's computer for a laugh. I don't think she had it out for Mr. Werner."

Every muscle inside me is knotted painfully, ready to spring up and run like a frightened rabbit. Because, holy crap, Danny is scaring the shit out of me. So much so that my eyes are actually pricking with tears and my hands are shaking.

The silence stretches on for a painfully long time. Deep and suffocating. Would I have time to scream if he were to—

To what?

This is Danny I'm with. My sweet, perfect, loving boyfriend.

And as though he could hear my thoughts, Danny exhales, his shoulders sagging.

"You're right," he says quietly. The boiling anger dissipates, and the hunter's mask falls away, leaving the old Danny behind.

The relief is so overwhelming, I nearly burst into tears.

"I'm so sorry," he says. "Lia, god, I just—I'm sorry, I'm losing it, I know. I'll get some help. Are you okay?" He reaches out and puts a gentle hand on my arm. I manage not to flinch.

"It's okay," I say. "You're under so much pressure." And so much of it is my fault.

"Yeah, well. How crazy is it to think someone was in my room, right?" He snorts. "The shoelaces are probably a bigger clue, anyway."

"Shoelaces?" Why did I choose to say that out loud? It's like a gavel, slamming down on everything, and the silence is painful.

"They found a pair of shoelaces in Uncle James's car. Um. Everyone says it's from someone on the track team."

I think I laugh, though it doesn't sound much like one. "How would anyone know that? People outside of the track team wears shoes with laces. It's not like, an exclusive track thing." Wow, stop babbling.

Danny makes a noncommittal sound. Still not looking at me. Whywhywh—

"So Mandy talked to me."

That's why. Apparently, I should've punched her even harder.

"She wanted to apologize for what she said to me about Uncle James."

"As she should." I can't quite keep the quiet rage from my voice.

"She also said—um." Danny looks up at the ceiling. Sighs. Turns away. "Never mind."

"Tell me."

He says it to his feet. "She said she's seen you wearing those laces."

My laughter is harsh, like a bark. "She's lying." And she is. I've never worn those laces, because they're so old, I wasn't sure I could wear them without them snapping in half. But Mandy, with her stupid, vindictive lies, is getting way too close to the truth, and to her, this is all just a game, and I could kill her, I really—shit, did I really just think that? I couldn't. I couldn't kill another person. But the rage inside me is boiling hot, and this is it. I keep turtling, keep running into dead ends and hoping things will be okay, but I can't anymore. If I continue down this path I'm on, I'm going to end up depressed, out of my mind like Sophie was. I don't want to end up like Sophie. I see her pale face again and I clench my fists. I am not going to end up like her. I was right before about needing a fall guy. I was wrong about wanting the fall guy to be the drug dealer. Now I know better. Mandy is going to be my fall guy.

CHAPTER 27

Know what's turning out to be really useful to have around? Three shoeboxes filled with drugs. Do I feel great about doing what I'm about to do? No, no, I don't. But a girl's gotta do what a girl's gotta do, even if it means framing her asshole classmate for murder. Does that sentence even make sense? It's hard knowing what makes actual sense.

When Mather is asleep, I sneak out, scurry through the Narnia hole, and walk all the way to town, where I find a twenty-four-hour internet café. I buy a cup of surprisingly decent coffee and use a VPN just in case. Then I look up how to unlock a combination lock. According to the internet, there are several ways of doing this. I jot them all down before scrubbing the browser's history and going back to Draycott.

I stop by my room, take out the shoeboxes of drugs, and slip out again. It's one in the morning, and I'm very nearly delirious from exhaustion, but I have to keep going. It's harder sneaking this time round. I'm painfully, excruciatingly aware that I'm carrying three shoeboxes full of DRUGS, and if I got caught now, there would be no saving me.

Luckily, the gym's locks are so old and rusty that all I have to do is insert a bobby pin and jiggle a little before they give. I guess there's not much you could take from the gym, so they don't really care about the security. Still, the tiniest clicks and clacks I make sound awfully loud in the silence, and by the time I get to the girls' changing room, I'm sweating a river and jumping at the slightest breeze. My hands are so sweaty by now, I keep almost dropping the boxes. I wish I could say I'm keeping my cool, but nope. If I hear a sound right now, any sound, I'll literally die.

The girls' changing room is eerily dark and silent. I knew, obviously, that it would be, but knowing and actually being here are two different things. My footsteps echo in the silence. I swear there are eyes in the darkness, watching me. There's a sense of a breath being held. I can barely see where I'm going, but I'm too scared to turn on the lights. Finally, I compromise by using my phone screen to create a bit of light, just enough for me to locate Mandy's locker. I set down the boxes and get to work. My sweaty hands keep slipping from the lock, and I botch my first few tries. I take a few deep breaths. They come out all shaky. I don't want to do this. To my surprise, I'm sort of crying a little. Mandy is awful, but this is—god, am I really going down this road?

A flash of Danny's fist slamming down onto his desk. That animal anger on his face. His insistence that Stacey has something to do with it. Or that it's whoever owns those shoelaces.

I can't afford not to do this.

Somehow, I manage to will my trembling fingers into fiddling with the lock again, following the instructions I got online. It's not going to happen. They've made it sound too easy, but in reality, it's too—

With a defeated click, the lock opens.

For a few moments, I just sit there and stare stupidly. It worked. I can't believe it actually worked. Something, some strange instinct, makes me turn around sharply. I swing my hand round, the glare off my phone bouncing wildly in the room, but there's nothing. Just empty benches and lockers.

Still, I can't shake that feeling of being watched. Quickly, I wipe down the shoeboxes before putting them carefully in the very back of Mandy's locker. I rearrange her stuff so it covers the boxes. Then I step back and look at my handiwork.

No. Too obvious. With shaking hands, I remove two of the shoeboxes. Just one lonely box sits in the far corner. Okay, that'll do. It'll have to. I pile her clothes on top of it. That looks okay. Shut the door and lock it, give it another wipe down, and take a step back, trying to get my breathing under control. I've done it.

I should feel glad, victorious. I only feel sick.

I take the other two boxes, briskly walk into the bathroom, and rip the baggies open one by one, watching as the pills rain down into the toilet. So slow. I need to move faster. Five bags' worth of pills per toilet. Flush. More pills. Flush again. I feel soiled and I'm never going to get through the entire stash.

Ages pass, and when I reach into the shoebox for more bags, I find that they're all empty. A grateful sob wobbles out of me. I hurry out of the stuffy gym and gasp in the cool night air. God, the breeze feels so good against my skin. But I don't have time to stop and savor it. I tuck the shoeboxes under my arms and make my way across campus toward the Narnia hole. The entire time, I can feel eyes crawling over me. But whenever I look over my shoulder, there's nothing but a deathly quiet school. Everyone is sleeping by now.

By the time I make it through the Narnia hole, I'm exhausted. I make myself keep going until I get to a nearby gas station, where there's a huge trash bin at the back. I dump the shoeboxes in there, trudge to the pay phone up front, pull my shirt up over the receiver, and dial the local police department's number.

An automated voice says, "You've reached Draycott Police's Nonemergency line. For emergencies, please hang up and dial nine-one-one. Please leave your name and contact number and we'll get back to you."

The sound of it makes fireworks go off in my head. This is not a dream. I'm actually doing this. I'm making the call. Oh god, oh g—

"Um." I clear my throat and try again, making my voice as gruff as I can. "I—uh, I'm calling about, um, a suspicious activity. At Draycott Academy's athletics department. I think, um, one of the track girls has drugs in her locker." Does that sound too obvious? I've never made one of these calls before. What do people even say? Snitching is a lot harder than it seems. "Um. Okay, that's all. Thanks." I hang up hurriedly before I say something idiotic that would no doubt give me away. Then I rush back to school.

By the time I get back to the dorms, I'm running on fumes. I practically crawl into my bed, not even bothering to brush my teeth or anything. I fall asleep as soon as my head hits the pillow.

Later that morning, track practice is a total and utter nightmare. I'm completely exhausted, for one. I can't remember the last time I felt this tired. But maybe it's a blessing, being this tired, because I have no energy to be nervous. I watch blearily in the changing room as Mandy, chatting to Elle, opens her locker. My heart rate blips up a bit, but Mandy doesn't even bother looking inside her locker when she grabs her shirt. She catches me looking and snaps, "What're you looking at, bitch?" There's still bruising around her nose. I look away, my insides crawling guiltily.

"You okay?" Stacey says, plopping down next to me.

I nod. I don't trust myself to say anything.

"Do anything fun last night?"

I stare at her. That's a weird question to ask. Is it a weird question to ask? I don't know, my brain is running on fumes. "No," I mumble thickly. "You?"

"Well, I—"

But she doesn't get to finish her sentence before the door bursts open and Coach marches in, followed by Detective Mendez. Coach looks like she's about ready to choke a deer. Her hands clench and unclench by her side. Mendez, on the other hand, looks like the cat that swallowed the expensive can of tuna. Or the salmon. I dunno, something more delicious than a stupid canary.

"Alright girls, line up!" Coach calls out. "Random locker check."

"What the hell?" Mandy says. "Why?"

My cheeks go hot. She's going to look even guiltier than I expected. Which is good. But wow, does it ever feel shitty. I stand up and follow the other girls to form a line. My legs tremble a little.

Mandy stays where she is, arms folded across her chest. "I don't think you have the right—"

"Mandy, shut up and fall in," Coach says with a sigh.

Someone telling her to shut up? That shut her up. She stomps over to the line and says, "I'm telling my mom about this. You're violating our privacy."

"Yeah, yeah," Coach says. She turns her head and glares at Mendez. "You wanna take over from here?"

"With pleasure." Mendez steps forward. "When I call your name, please lead me to your locker and open it."

"Jesus," Mandy says.

Detective Mendez's head snaps to face Mandy. "Let's start with you," Mendez says.

Oh god. This is it. It's happening now. I watch, frozen, as Mandy leads the detective to her locker. Half of me is screaming to stop them, to call it off. The other half is rubbing its dirty, red hands with glee. Once they open the locker, there's no going back. I step forward.

"Wait—" I say.

The locker swings open and Detective Mendez plunges her hands inside.

I step closer, but Stacey catches hold of my arm. "What are you doing?" she whispers. "Stay here, dumbass."

"But—" I turn back and—this can't be right—Detective Mendez is straightening back up, empty-handed.

"Alright, you're clear," she says to Mandy.

What?

I look at Mandy and back to her locker. Could she have found it beforehand and gotten rid of it? No, she doesn't look relieved or smug or anything. She just looks pissed off as she kicks her locker shut, still grumbling about the cops not respecting boundaries. Have I put the drugs in the wrong locker?

I scan the rows of lockers frantically, retracing my steps. I'd been half-delirious from lack of sleep. It's possible. Did I stop at the correct row last night?

The second girl—Arjuna—leads Mendez to her locker. My heart stutters again. Would it be in there?

Clear.

Then Yoshi has her turn, and then Elle, and then three other girls, and they're all clear. And now a dark feeling is worming its way through my stomach. Something's gone very, very wrong. And when Mendez makes eye contact with me, I know now, where the drugs will be found.

I lead her, my throat dry, each step taking me closer to my doom. I stop in front of my locker and stare at the lock for a moment. Does it look like it's been broken? I take it in my hand, trying to squeeze an answer out of it.

"Everything okay, Lia?" Detective Mendez says.

I nod and turn the lock, its little clicks reverberating through my hand, each one a bullet being loaded. One final click, and it snaps open. I pull it off and—one final breath—I open my locker. Nothing looks moved. I'm about to reach in when Detective Mendez grabs my arm.

"I'll do that," she says and pushes me gently but firmly to

the side. She ransacks my locker as I watch, helpless, but as the seconds go by, it's clear there's no shoebox to be found.

I practically melt into a puddle. I just. What's happening right now? Did I imagine it all? The world takes on a dreamlike quality, and I watch wordlessly as Detective Mendez goes through the rest of the lockers and finds nothing. Maybe I'm so sleep-deprived, I dreamt the whole thing. Maybe instead of putting a box in Mandy's locker, I actually threw it all away. Maybe there are three empty shoeboxes in Safeway's trash bin and not two.

Whatever it was that just happened, Mendez is not happy. Down to the last two girls, and she ransacks their lockers like she's got a personal vendetta against them, then she whirls around and snaps, "Okay, which one of you kids made the call?"

We all look at her blankly. Well, I try to look as blank as I can, which is easy because I still have no clue what just went down.

"You guys think this is funny?" she says, her eyes hard as flints. "You prank call the police department, make us waste our fucking time—" She slams the last locker shut as she says the word *time*, making everyone jump. "I don't know what you kids are playing at here, especially when we've got a murder investigation going on, but this isn't a fucking joke, you hear me?"

Coach goes ballistic. "Hey!" she thunders, and when

Coach thunders, she goes full-on Zeus. "We're done here," she bellows. "Girls, haul your asses to the track now. Warm-ups. Go, go!" As we hurry out, I turn and catch one last glimpse of Coach and Detective Mendez having some kind of staring showdown, and I hear Coach saying something about lodging a formal complaint and Mendez saying something along the lines of *bite me*, and then the door swings shut and I can't hear anything else, and I stagger to the track, wondering what the heck just happened.

CHAPTER 28

After that day in the changing room, I keep expecting the sky to crumble down on me. Whenever anyone raises their voice, I jump, thinking the SWAT team's finally here to—I dunno, swat me. I keep wondering how the murder investigation is going, how close they are to finding the real killer. The thought of Mendez digging and digging sickens me until I see her in my nightmares.

But weirdly enough, the next couple of weeks pass by and nothing happens. I guess Coach must've lodged a complaint about Mendez, because I don't see her around anywhere, and the drugs don't make an appearance either, and weirdly, gradually, we kind of move on from all the crazy shit. Midterms are upon us, and we're all wound a bit tighter, sleeping less and studying more, and the atmosphere settles into an anxious hush, everyone's head buried in books.

Danny still stays away during mealtimes. Once or twice, his friends approach me to ask what's going on with him, and I tell the weak version of the truth: he's really stressed out.

Stressed out. I don't know what to call it, really. Every afternoon, once classes end, I drop by his room with a sandwich and check on him. He takes the sandwich and gives me one-word answers.

Have you showered/eaten/drank water? Yes, yes, yes.

And still that deep, dark rage lurks underneath his skin. I can sense it, even though he never raises his voice around me. I can practically hear it ripping him up from the inside, scrabbling to come tearing out, and every time I leave his room, I feel spent. All my insides, carved out and empty.

I know it's not healthy, but it's penance. I killed his uncle—yes, it's self-defense, yes, yes, but the knowing and the accepting are two very different things. The least I can do is stick around for him.

Unfortunately, we're unable to focus on much else outside of our studies.

Then there's the matter of English Lit, and for once, when I say that, I'm referring to good news. Mr. Werner's sub, Ms. Oyongo, hands back our midterms results, and I actually get an A minus, which is incredible. I can't stop the grin from taking over my entire face, and I don't even try. I sit there, beaming, and then I look over at Mandy. Mandy, who's leaning back in her seat, looking like she's about to cry.

I want to say I feel glad to see Mandy struggling, but it really only brings a hollow satisfaction, like getting full of junk food. After class, I head over to Stacey's before going to Danny's. Ever since I discovered Beth's drug business, I haven't really hung out much with her. Not for lack of trying. I've texted a half dozen times, but she's been ignoring everything, so there you have it. Not sure what else I can do about that.

I still have meals with Sam and Grace, but it's somewhat strained because I can't tell them what's happened between me and Beth. Grace is in a foul mood because she hasn't been able to get any "goodies." I don't know how much of a drug habit she has and what kind of drugs she takes, and I feel absolutely helpless, sitting there, listening to her bitch about Woot1212 suddenly closing up shop.

When I try to talk to Sam about it, she stops me and tells me she knows. She keeps a close eye on Grace and once or twice, I see them walking on campus with Sam's arm around Grace, her head tilted down toward Grace's protectively. I'm glad Grace has someone looking out for her.

My appetite has returned, but I'm still running way too much, a fact Stacey makes apparent when we're hanging out in her room one day. My exams are over, but she still has one test left.

"How do you expect me to focus on American history—which is bullshit, as our textbook very conveniently omits the genocide of Native people and our long history of slavery, by the way—when you keep fidgeting?" she says, shutting her textbook.

"My legs are really hurting," I grumble, shifting again to find a position that doesn't make my legs feel like they're eating themselves. Which is impossible, as it turns out.

"Yeah, you know why that is? Because you insist on running like a mad woman on speed." She reaches to her bedside table and flings a granola bar at me. "Eat this."

I have to laugh. "You'd make a good Asian mom. You've got the nagging part down, and you're always telling people to eat more."

"Only when they do need to eat more." She tosses her history textbook on the floor and stretches.

"Uh-oh, are we giving up on American history?"

"I'm going to write a whole thing about how I refuse to partake in any history class that insists on lying to its students. It'll be titled Teach Us the Real History, You Whitewashing Assholes!"

I laugh again, flopping on her bed and gazing at the posters she's hung up. There's a whole bunch of them, mostly games I don't know, but there's one of two girls holding hands, and I vaguely recognize them as characters from *Overwatch*. It makes me grin. Stacey's turned out to be such a likable dork, it's hard to remember how much I hated her when I first came to Draycott.

"—Mendez the other day."

"What?" That snaps me back to the present. The pleasant haze I've been feeling cocooned up in Stacey's room disappears.

"I said I saw Mendez the other day. She came out of Henderson's office looking pissed as hell."

My heart tattoos a painful rhythm in my chest. "What do you think—why—what—" Wow, I can't even English anymore.

"My guess?" Stacey says, propping her chin on her hand, "Henderson got the investigation shut down."

I could cry, I really could. I look at her and almost go, "Really? You promise?" as if I were five years old and she were Santa. I manage to catch myself in time. Come on, get a grip. It's not like Stacey would know. I tear my gaze from hers and force myself to take a deep breath. "Cool," I mumble, as though I didn't care, as though I weren't mentally jumping up and down and screaming to the universe for a break.

"Hey," she says.

Something in her tone of voice makes the back of my neck prickle, and I look back at her. "Yeah?"

Stacey gives me a long, slow look, and I sense something large behind her eyes, some dark things she badly wants to share, and my shoulders tighten. My smile freezes.

Maybe she catches it, the lake of fear stirring inside me, because she breaks eye contact, says, "Eat more," and flings another granola bar at me.

I chew slowly, itching to know what she was going to ask me, but not quite daring to ask. Some secrets are best left buried.

CHAPTER 29

The crushing weight of midterms is suddenly lifted as soon as the last exam is done. When the last bell rings, we hand in our papers with a flourish, and I swear it's as though my bones have turned from lead to pure oxygen. I'm made of starlight and moonbeams. I fly out of the classroom and what do you know, I immediately spot Danny in the crowd. My sweet Danny.

He catches my eye and smiles, and the past few weeks of awfulness immediately melt away. We scythe through the crowd of students milling about in the hallway and meet each other in the middle.

Is he back to his sweet, old self? I search his eyes for any traces of anger or mistrust and find nothing. He's just Danny.

My disarmingly charming, cheerful boyfriend. I crush him with my hug.

"I'm so sorry," he whispers, kissing the top of my head. "I've been such an asshole."

"No, you haven't. You had a lot on your plate."

He gives a slightly shuddery laugh. "It was all too much—Uncle James and exams coming up and everything. But I'm here now. I'm okay."

I grin up at him, unable to speak because of the huge lump in my throat. When we finally kiss, it's just as good as I remember it.

The parties start being thrown that same night. The next morning, I hear of Elle Brown throwing one at the rooftop of the Randolph, and Anya Scott having a bash at her family's country club. I'm not invited to either of these, but Sam and Grace are, and when they show me pictures over breakfast, and I would be lying if I said I'm not just the tiniest, teensiest bit jealous.

"I'm not even the tiniest, teensiest bit jealous," I say, through a gritted smile.

"Reeeally?" Sam says. "'Cause you seem jealous."

"Pfft, jealous over some stupid party at some stupid, swanky country club? That is the saddest venue I can think of." Maybe. I don't know, having never been to a country club. I wasn't even aware that teens could hold parties in one.

Sam laughs. "Don't be jealous, because you're invited to my party. On my yacht."

"What!" I yell. A yacht party? YES!

Danny glances up from his dude table, sees me grinning like a loon, and shoots me a quizzical smile. I grin even wider, and he laughs before heading over. "What's up, Cheshire cat?"

"Not much, just *a freaking yacht party*."

"Ah, you told her, then," Danny says to Sam.

"You knew?" I say. "He knew?"

"He helped me plan everything."

"What?" Okay, now I'm really surprised. I get that he's no longer in that same bad place as he has been the past few weeks, but going from that to helping plan a party seems rather drastic. Or is it? Maybe he's just making more of an effort to go back to normalcy.

I must look really confused, because Danny shrugs and says, "I think I kind of spiraled a little back there. But I'm feeling a lot better now. More optimistic. I just want to end the semester on a high. Feels like good luck or something."

Wanting to end the semester on a high—well, can't argue with that.

I spend the rest of the afternoon digging through my closet for something to wear, which reminds me of Beth and makes me feel terrible. If I hadn't fallen out with her, I would be in her room right now, getting ready together. I miss her.

I go to her room, and, with a deep breath, I knock on the door.

"Come in," she calls out.

Beth's putting on mascara. When she sees me, she goes, "Ugh," and rolls her eyes, and then goes, "Ouch! Motherfu—" She blinks furiously, her eyes tearing up, and snaps, "What do you want, Lia?"

I grab her tissue box and hold it out to her, but she ignores it.

"Well?" she says.

I hug the tissue box to my chest like a shield. "I, um. I just wanted to know if you're going to Sam's party."

She gestures to herself. "Hel-lo, do you not see how fabulous I look? Obviously, I'm going to Sam's party." She glances at the mirror and groans. "Except now I'm going to have to redo my eye makeup, thanks to you. You know how long it took to get the gold leaf on?"

It's true, she looks like some Roman goddess, if Roman goddesses wore minidresses and gold leaf on their eyelids. And were Asian. The effect is striking, and seriously, only Beth could carry off something this wild, and before I know it, I stride forward and catch her in a tight hug.

"Ew, get off me—"

"I hate us fighting," I say, and she stops struggling.

"You're an asshole," she says.

"I know, I am, and I'm sorry," I babble, "But you being a literal drug dealer kind of caught me off guard, I didn't know what to do, I—"

"I was. Past tense."

"What?" I release her.

"When I told my supplier that I lost my entire stash, she fired me. I had to pay her off, obviously. Sold most of my jewelry and half of my closet to do that." She sighs. "You were right. I shouldn't have been doing that. I don't know what I was thinking. And I feel truly shitty about everything, especially after what happened with Sophie. I'll never be able to make up for everything I've done, but I'll try."

"I—wow." I haven't dared to think of the logistics of Beth's business, but it seems like the best end she could've hoped for.

"What did you do with the stash?"

There's a momentary pause as I recall how I lost a third of the stash. "I flushed them down different toilets."

"Methodical," Beth says, nodding approvingly.

"Very." I look at her. "So. Are we good?"

"No."

My heart sinks.

"We're not 'good,' not with you wearing that thing." She

starts rummaging around her closet, which is just as well, as I need a bit of time to will away my tears.

We arrive at the dock fifteen minutes late, looking totally amazing. I gasp out loud when I see Sam's yacht. It's amazing. The size of a house. Even from the dock, the music from the yacht's so loud, I can practically see it vibrating with the noise. The entire thing is strung with lights that change color in time with the music.

Beth and I strut across the plank because we're fab like that. Okay, we try to strut, but I totally fail because the plank's moving ever so slightly, and it's enough to throw me off. Once we get onto the yacht, we're greeted by a server who puts a champagne flute in each of our hands. The place is heaving with kids. Many of them must've arrived early because some are already visibly drunk, moving haphazardly in the swaying crowd.

"This is crazy," I say.

"What?" Beth yells.

"Nothing," I yell back.

"What?"

I take out my phone and type out, I want to find Danny.

Beth nods and gestures for us to make a round. We make our way across the sun deck, where kids are dancing and shouting and laughing, and down to the main deck.

Inside, the music's slightly less loud, and the atmosphere is more laid-back. Everything in here is swanky, shiny furniture and leather seats. Instead of jumping up and down and dancing, the students here are playing card games and/or making out. I see a flash of boob and avert my eyes.

"You guys made it!"

I turn to see Sam and Grace. Sam looks incredible, dressed in a silver dress that shows off her long legs. Grace is in a gold dress with a plunging neckline, and together they look like the sun and the moon. "Wow, you guys look amazing."

"You do too!" Grace squeals. She seems…high. Or maybe I'm just imagining it?

"There you are," someone says behind me, and I turn and see Danny, looking way too handsome. It's really not fair, how gorgeous this boy looks. I immediately put my arms around him and kiss him, because honestly, you can't not.

"You're beautiful," he says, and I melt.

Groans all around us.

"Get a room," someone says.

"Yeah, there are plenty of rooms in here," Sam says.

I grin sheepishly. "Sorry."

Then, from behind Danny, I see Stacey. My mouth drops open. "You came!" I didn't think parties were her jam.

She scowls. "Danny made me come."

"Really?" I look at Danny.

He shrugs. "I thought it might be nice for you to have all your friends here. And"—he turns to Stacey—"you shouldn't spend the end of the semester all alone in your room."

She sighs and gives him a reluctant smile. Wow.

I can't believe Danny invited her, especially after all that paranoia he had about her and the keylogger. If that isn't the sweetest thing a boy has ever done for his girlfriend, I don't know what is. "Thank you," I say to him, squeezing his hand. He shrugs again.

I hug Stacey. "I'm so glad you came!"

"Where's the waiter for this deck?" Sam says. "We need drinks here."

"I'll go get some," Danny says. "You guys sit tight."

We claim one of the sofas, and soon we're chatting and shrieking with laughter, and it's incredible and overwhelming, and what is my life right now? I can't believe I'm on a giant boat atop the Pacific Ocean, surrounded by the nation's richest kids, and despite everything, I've somehow made it through the semester.

Danny returns with two icy bottles of Dom and we cheer. He's already opened them, and he hands out glasses and pours for everyone. We toast to the end of "the most batshit semester," and the drink feels like magic sliding down my throat. Danny pours more for everyone, and then we all head up to the sun deck to join the heaving crowd on the dance floor. I don't know if it's the movement of the boat, but everything is spinning crazily in the best possible way, and I feel like my veins are filled with music and light. We jump to the beat and I kiss Danny and dance with Beth and Stacey, and at some point, we empty our glasses, and Danny gets us another round and everybody goes, "You've got the best boyfriend," and all I can do is grin stupidly.

The next hour is a whirl of more dancing, jumping up and down, screaming with laughter, spinning, and making out. Everything is swirling lights and hot, slick bodies, and I'm so glad to be alive, to be surrounded by my friends. I'm a butterfly. A bird. A molecule bouncing free in the atmosphere.

At some point, the thirst hits me. It hits hard, and fast, and I'm suddenly panting. All the cells in my body are crumbling to ash. I'm no longer a butterfly but a lead ball. I grab hold of Stacey and manage to pant out, "Water."

She's busy dancing with a sophomore, their hips swaying close to each other's. She ignores me. Dammit, Stacey. Beth and Sam and Grace are still jumping like little grasshoppers. I look around for the bar, but when I turn my head, the entire world turns dizzyingly, and I almost fall. Danny's arm shoots out, seemingly from nowhere, and catches me.

"You okay?" he says.

"Water."

He nods and swings an arm around my shoulders, holding me tight, and I cling to the reassuring warmth of him. We make our way to the side, where he helps me onto a seat and then heads for the bar. He returns with bottles of water.

I snatch one out of his hands and gulp the whole thing in one go. Grab another one and finish half before I feel like I can finally slow down. I sit there, blinking, tapping my feet, unable to stay still. Wanting to keep dancing, wanting to scream and laugh and have sex and jump overboard. Which doesn't seem all that normal. I've gotten drunk before, and this isn't it. This is more. But then fireworks go off—real fireworks, not just ones in my mind, and I lose all train of thought.

Danny comes back carrying even more bottles of water. I haven't even realized that he'd gone for more.

"Come on," he says, "the others are probably thirsty too."

Still clutching my half-finished bottle of water, I plunge back into the dance floor. Danny's right, as soon as Sam and the rest spot the bottles of water, they stagger toward us and chug the bottles gratefully. Danny walks over to Stacey, still dancing with the sophomore, and hands her a bottle. She grabs it and waves the sophomore away before taking huge gulps.

"Wow, this water tastes like asshole," she shouts, but she drinks it anyway. "Sam, you need to stop skimping on the water, man. This tastes like tap."

Grace and Beth do a mock gasp, and Sam flips Stacey the bird. "It's Fiji, you spoiled brat."

I laugh, and a sudden surge of mirth pushes me, and I pull Stacey toward me and hug her. "I love you, you big goof."

"Love you too, dumbass."

God, I feel like I could run a freakin' marathon.

Why not?

I tug Stacey's hand and we run through the crowd, the boat teetering up and down in the waves, and I have no idea where we're going, but I'm glad I'm running with Stacey. The sky is showered with stars so bright, and we throw our heads back and spin and spin until our legs give out and we tumble in a heap onto a couch, laughing and gasping hard.

We stay there for a while, lying down, our hands linked. A minute. An hour. I can't tell. The stars are dancing for us and this is the best night ever.

"Definitely," Stacey says. I didn't even realize I've spoken out loud.

"You're still speaking out loud right now, you doofus."

What about now?

"Yep," she laughs. "Oh my god, you're such a nong, I swear. Hey, Lia." Her voice is suddenly serious.

"Yeah?"

"Did you know you're the first person to hang out in my room?"

"Really?" What am I saying *really* to? I've already forgotten what she just said.

"I said, you're the first person to hang out in my room."

Wow, okay. I mean, that's pretty huge.

"You're sort of. My best friend." Her voice slurs. "I gotchu. Just so you know. No matter what you've done."

"I gotchu too. You're seriously like, the best friend ever," I babble. "Like, the freakin' best."

"That's why I couldn't let you like. Do that thing to Mandy, man."

"Wha?"

"That night. You snuck out of Mather. You tripped my alarm."

"What?" The sky is spinning way too crazily for me to keep up, but a jumble of memories assault my senses. Stacey telling me she's rigged Mather with motion sensors so she knows who's sneaking out at night. Oh. "You took the shoebox from Mandy's locker."

"You wouldn't have been able to live with yourself," Stacey says. "So, yeah, I took 'em. You're too good to go down that route. Or whatever."

I laugh. So that's what happened. No wonder there was nothing in Mandy's locker. "You're amazing," I tell her. "I mean, you're literally the best person ever." No answer. "Stace?"

She's closed her eyes, her chest rising and falling slowly. I turn back to watch the peppered sky, marveling at how clear the stars look out here, how incandescently beautiful it all is.

My eyelids become heavier. Everything's wonderful. I'm going to be okay. I'm going home soon, and when I come back next semester, I won't be a new student anymore. I have a good group of friends, I've got an amazing boyfriend, and everything's cool. My eyes drift shut and I sink into a deep sleep.

When I wake up, Stacey's in a coma.

CHAPTER 30

Red and blue lights flash against the bright morning sky, blinding. All of it so bright and so painful. I need to run after Stacey's ambulance and climb into her hospital bed and hug her and tell her everything will be okay. I need to crawl into a cave and curl up tight and forget the world. I need to vomit. I need to do so many things, and yet I'm stuck here at the dock, barely able to stand on my feet as detectives Mendez and Jackson question everyone.

"I wasn't expecting to be back here so soon," Detective Mendez says. Her face is grim. A few feet away, Detective Jackson is talking to Sam and Grace. They're both sobbing. My heart cracks open. I would cry too, except I feel utterly empty, all my insides carved out like a watermelon.

"Here," Detective Mendez says, giving me a bottle of water.

I'm so dehydrated that twisting open the cap makes the joints in my hands ache. My entire arm shakes as I lift the bottle to my mouth and gulp. How much did we drink last night, exactly? We've gone out drinking plenty of times before. How did it go so out of control last night?

As though she reads my mind, Detective Mendez says, "It's a bit early to say for sure, but the team thinks there might be traces of ecstasy and cocaine on the boat. It looks like some of the bottles of champagne have been tampered with."

My mind is heaving. Or maybe that's my stomach. Too much water, too fast. I lean over to one side and dry heave. Stacey. Ecstasy and coke. I don't get it. The tears come, finally, and now I can't stop them. I don't understand. *But I took care of the drug problem*, I want to wail. *I solved it. I confiscated Beth's entire stash, threw it away. Stace threw the rest away*. Something slices through the anguish. Anger. Beth. She must've been behind this somehow. She must've lied to me about being cut off by her supplier. She must still be selling.

I look around and don't see her.

"Are you sure you don't know anything about this?"

"I don't. I have to go." I have to go strangle Beth.

"Don't do anything stupid, Lia," Detective Mendez says,

and there's a weird note in her voice that makes me pause. I look at her for the first time, really look. She seems worried for me, but that can't be right.

"Don't know what you're talking about," I mumble.

"Lia," she sighs. She steps closer, lowers her voice. "I'm on your side, can't you see that? I see so much of myself in you. This isn't your natural environment, and I'm not saying that because it's a fancy school for rich kids, but because there's something truly wrong here, and you're sitting there neck-deep in shit and telling me it smells just fine. Who are you trying to protect? This isn't your world, child. Give any of these kids here a chance and they'll throw you under the bus, just to make sure this place keeps going, you know what I'm saying?"

If she'd told me that a week ago, I would've told her with all the confidence in the world that she's wrong, that I have true friends here, that we're not like what she thinks. But now I see that she's right. Everything she said is true. Everything, that is, except for the fact that I'm the biggest snake in this nest of vipers. Sure, Beth's a drug dealer, and sure, everyone else here seems to be involved in something shady, but the only killer around is me.

Except...

Maybe I'm not. Mendez said some of the bottles of champagne were tampered with. What if whoever did it didn't just do it for fun? What if it was a deliberate attack?

"I gotta go."

"Remember what I said, Lia," Mendez says, and I'm sure I'm not imagining the sadness in her voice.

"Beth! Open up. BETH." I slam my fists against the door, not caring how much it hurts.

Footsteps. Wild, hurried. The door swings open. She's been crying. Is still crying. It catches me off guard.

"Was it you? Just tell me that. Were the drugs in the drinks from you?"

She lifts her small, streaming face to me and shakes her head. "I don't know. I don't think—I mean, I don't—"

"What do you mean you don't know?" I shouldn't shout. The door's closed, but these walls are thin, and we don't know who might be listening. I know that, and yet it's so very hard to keep my voice down. "You're either still selling, or you're not. Which is it?"

"I'm not!" she cries. "I swear I'm not, but you don't get it. There's only ever one seller around at any given time. And as far as I know, my supplier hasn't found a replacement for me. I saw her the other week, and she complained to me about how good, reliable sellers are hard to come by, and she wouldn't risk her entire business on some kid unless she's a hundred sure they're legit, and she was trying to get me to come back, but I didn't, I swear."

Maybe she's telling the truth, or maybe she's one hell of a liar.

"Okay, if you're not selling anymore, why aren't you sure if the drugs came from you?"

"I've been the only seller around for a whole year. It means the drugs must've come from me. Maybe one of my customers saved up for months and then dosed the drinks. When I heard that Stacey OD'ed, I just—I don't know, I freaked out and came back here, and I still haven't figured out yet what I'm gonna do. My supplier's not picking up my calls—I think she knows I'm in deep shit and she's cut off all communications with me, she's ruthless like that, I guess they all have to be like that in this business—"

I tune out her babbling. I'm trying to think, but everything's a snarled-up mess, and I can't make heads or tails of anything. At the back of my mind, an insistent voice keeps whispering, Sophie. The same thing happened to Sophie.

But what does that even mean? Sophie took her own life. She was depressed. She wanted to end it all. It doesn't have anything to do with this. Does it? I squeeze my eyes shut, trying to clear my head.

Beth's still yammering away when I abruptly tell her I'm going.

I catch the bus to Draycott Medical, which is a lot larger than I thought it would be. Once I go through the sliding doors, I'm suddenly unsure. What am I even doing here? I haven't really thought about what I'm coming here for. I'd thought—I don't know, that I really wanted, *needed*, to see Stacey. But now that I'm here, with nurses and patients and doctors walking briskly around me, I'm suddenly hesitant. Is she even here? I'd just assumed—

I make my way to the information desk and ask the receptionist for Stacey's name. She glances up at me, takes in my disheveled, ruined dress from the party, my rat's nest hair, and her eyes narrow.

"Please," I say, hoarsely. "I really need to see her."

She sighs, shaking her head slightly. "Room 203. Down the hall and to your left."

I hurry down the hall as directed, my heart torn between jumping and singing and squeezing at the thought of seeing Stacey. But when I get there, I hear voices from her room. Adult voices. I creep closer, wondering for a crazed half second if Detective Mendez's here too. But through a small gap in the door, I see a blond woman.

"—what you get for sending her to that goddamn school," a man's saying.

"I did not 'send' her anywhere, she applied and got a robotics scholarship," the woman snaps.

"And much good it did her, look at her—" The man's voice breaks, and the woman moves out of sight, probably to hold him as he sobs.

I can't go in there. I crane my neck, hoping to catch a

glimpse of Stacey, but I can't see much. I don't want Stacey's parents to see me. Not now, not like this. But before I leave the hospital, I go to the gift shop and buy a small teddy bear, which I leave outside of Stacey's door.

Five laps. Six. Seven. At some point, I lose count. A day has passed since the party, and I'm no longer nauseated nor dehydrated, but I still haven't figured anything out, which is why it's back to the track for me. DD is rife with posts about the party—about Sam's dad's yacht being held for investigations, about Stacey's overdose, about the cops. It hurts, and I want to shut it out, but I also can't stop myself from reading everything, just in case I've missed a clue somewhere. Still, all I've found so far is crap like:

> *Posted by @TrackQueen:*
> Booze: $15,000. Yacht: $1.7 mil. Having a party so wild that somebody ODs: priceless.

My classmates, always full of sympathy. The thought of DD spurs me on and I push myself to run faster. Harder. Instead, my legs give out and I crash onto the track. It feels like I just got run over by a semi. As if to add insult to injury, my calf muscles seize up, knitting themselves in agony, and I roll around, gasping, hissing curses, clutching my legs.

No need for the team doctor to tell me I'm not practicing right. I know the kind of ache that means I'm pushing myself well, and this is not it. This is splintering stabs, nails being dug into deep tissue, my body begging me to stop. But whenever I stop, Stacey speaks to me.

You're the first person to hang out in my room.

I squeeze my eyes shut. I want to go to the hospital again, but I can't, not before I figure out who did this to her. And I'm no closer to an answer.

The next few days melt into one another. I wake up. Scroll through DD for clues. Go to the track. Shower. Breakfast where none of us say anything much to each other. Classes. Go back to the track. Go back to room and doom-scroll through DD again, obsessing over every post, every picture from the party.

Every photo could be a clue. I scrutinize them all, memorizing each detail until they all swim in my head without meaning, all the smiling faces melting into one another. The answer is in here somewhere, I can feel it, just out of reach, and it's driving me insane.

Danny's the only thing that wakes me from the haze. In the evenings, we crawl through the Narnia hole and walk, hand in hand, to town. He doesn't mention the party and neither do I. We go back to our first date, under the strung lights, and make our way through each stall without saying much to each other. One night, we go to the hospital but find

Stacey's mom still in the room, dozing next to Stacey's bed, her blond hair strewn across the blanket covering Stacey's legs. Asleep, she looks so much like Stacey that I burst into tears and hurry off, and Danny follows without comment. He just wraps an arm around me and pulls me in close, kisses the top of my head, tells me it'll be okay.

By the time regionals come, I can barely walk without my legs trembling. Despite everything, I find myself getting excited about the match. Does that make me a shitty person, an awful friend? But this is the thing I've been looking forward to all semester, the reason I'm here at Draycott. The meet that would secure me a spot in Stanford. Putting on my official track outfit that morning feels like waking up from a dream. I get a flash to the first day of school, when I'd worn my Draycott track outfit and looked in the mirror. I look at myself in the mirror now. My cheeks are hollow, my limbs a lot thinner. I've lost way too much muscle mass. I look away. Over Thanksgiving break, I will pig out massively, get my weight back up to optimal sprinters' weight. For now, regionals.

I've never seen the stadium this full before. The bleachers aren't actually full, but they're about as full as they're ever going to be for a sport that isn't football. Friends and relatives pepper the rows, waving down to us and cheering. I don't bother looking for a familiar face. I haven't told Ibu about today's match because she'd take time off work to come, which would make me feel guilty, and plus, I'm not ready to face her yet. Not after everything that's happened. I need to get my shit together for that. I told Danny not to come either, since it would just make me nervous, and I'm already enough of a wreck without all the added nerves.

A wreck. Yeah, that describes my current state perfectly, swinging back and forth from "OMG, REGIONALS!" to "omg, Mr. Werner-Stacey-drugs-what." I guess the latter will continue to be a low-key fear thrumming at the back of my head no matter what I do. I go into my stretches and still the world feels all weird and wonky, my thoughts super loud inside my head. Shut up, I tell my mind. Focus on this. Nothing else matters for now. *OMG, how could you think that? What about Stacey, huh?* Okay, Stacey obviously matters, but for now, focus on this.

When I'm done with my stretches, Coach, calls me over. She's just as nervous as I am.

"Lia, how you feeling? You okay? Everything good? Yes?" Her smile is weighed down with concern as she gives me a once-over. "You're too skinny. This isn't good. You don't got enough muscle mass."

"I'm fine," I say hurriedly. "Really. I've just been studying a bit too hard." I bounce up and down to show her I'm totally fine.

"Okay..." She doesn't look entirely convinced, but she smiles at me again. "So, exciting news: see that woman in the red shirt over there?" She points at the bleachers, where a woman in a bright-red shirt and red hat's standing. The woman waves at us when she sees us looking over. We wave back. "That's the Stanford recruiter." Coach grins at me. "You ready to show her you deserve an all-expenses-paid ride at Stanford?"

My left leg chooses that moment to give a particularly hard tremor. I clench my fists and force a teeth-gritting smile. "Always."

"Awesome. Go get ready for your event." She swings her arm to give me the usual shoulder slap but holds back at the last moment so she won't hit me as hard. Do I really seem that fragile? By the time I'm finished with my warm-up jog, I'm breathing hard. A jog's made me winded. A jog. Note to self: Get your crap together, please.

I sit down on the bench and try to get my breath back.

"Uh-oh, don't tell me you're out of breath just from warm-ups?" Mandy says. Ugh. I've forgotten that she's replaced Stacey in the roster. I ignore her and focus on breathing deep.

My event is announced and I walk into position. I'm still somewhat out of breath, but stepping onto my lane fills my body with fizzy energy. I kneel into position, revel in the feel of the rubber underneath my fingers. The noise of the crowd melts away. My world shrinks, narrows to just the lane in front of me.

"Set."

Raise my hips, muscles taut, my whole being quivering with energy.

The gun pops and we're off.

Wind whizzes past my cheeks, cold, refreshing. I'm flying, zipping past everyone else, breaking the sound barrier. I'm one with the track. No one can deny that I was so clearly made for this.

Why am I not at the finish yet? My legs aren't pushing me as fast as I'm used to. I will myself to go faster. Run harder. Then, from my peripheral vision, I see something that's never once happened to me, not ever. A girl's catching up. And another, on my left. Eating into my high, poisoning my victory. My chest squeezes tight. They can't do this, they're not allowed. This is my moment. Go faster!

But I can't stop glancing over, and then I see something else, at the bench. A flash of black. The cops. They're looking straight at me—

The world tips sideways. I don't understand what's happening—

Everything is knocked out of me. My thoughts. The air in my lungs. Time crashes to a stop and I don't. I—

What. Just. Happened.

I blink, and it's like I've plunged underwater, everything unfolding in slow motion. I see my competitors running ahead, their movements so slow, their footsteps dull. Someone gets through the finish, and noise floods everything.

Hands shake my shoulders. I'm rolled over, yanked up, a rag doll. Coach on one side, the team doctor on the other. They're both talking, but their voices sound weird and hollow, and it doesn't matter anyway, I need to know what the cops want. I push them aside, look around, and there they are, heading straight toward me, their faces steel. Mendez reaches into her pocket and comes out with—my world ends—a pair of handcuffs.

I can't speak. Can't breathe. Can't do anything but watch as my fate claims me.

Coach follows my gaze and turns around. Her mouth drops open, her expression morphing into angry mama bear mode, and then she spots the cuffs, and that catches her off guard. She falters. "Detectives—"

They push past her. To me.

I hang my head, lift my hands, and—

They walk past.

Straight to Mandy Kim, who's grinning and waving to the crowds. She frowns when they get to her, and then her frown melts into confusion.

"Mandy Kim, you're under arrest for possession and assault with class one narcotics. You have the right to remain silent," Detective Jackson says, while Detective Mendez puts the cuffs on Mandy.

Mandy's so confused, she doesn't even protest at first. Then it hits her, and she snaps, "Get your hands off me! What the hell is going on? This isn't funny! Coach, help me. Stop them. Coach!"

Coach takes one step, but the look on Detective Mendez's face stops her, and we stand there, rooted, and watch as Mandy is hauled away by the cops.

CHAPTER 31

The school is on fire. Not a literal fire, but everyone's running about like ants that just sensed rain, and nothing makes any sense. Mandy's arrested, which should make me happy, but only adds to the sense of WTF-ness of everything. The problem is it feels wrong. Sure, Mandy's a big ole asshole, but she's never been overtly mean to Stacey. Plus, Stacey said they'd been close before, and Mandy tried to "tolerate" her or whatever. Something's not adding up. I go back to Mather, my thoughts going a hundred miles an hour, and have a good cry in the shower for the millionth time—honestly, do I do anything BUT cry while I shower?

But it's impossible to try to stop the tears, because in addition to everything—Stacey, and Mandy's arrest, and the general mess the entire school's swept into—there's also the tiny matter of my athletics scholarship.

Gone, just like that.

And it feels awful to care so much about it, but god, I do. And the realization that everything I had worked so hard to achieve had been for nothing is a lot to bear. Coach had told me it's fine, that I'll have other chances, but it feels like my career is over before it even began, and it's too much.

The cry does me good, at least. By the time I'm done, I'm all cried out, all my insides scooped out, leaving me with just one thing—a burning need to find out what the hell happened out there on the track. And the only person who's got any hope of knowing anything is Mrs. Henderson. As soon as I'm dressed, I march straight to Castor.

Her receptionist tells me she's on a call, so I wait outside her office. Her door's cracked open, and snatches of Mrs. Henderson's voice float out. I inch closer, keeping one eye on the receptionist so she doesn't notice me practically pressed up against the wall right next to Mrs. Henderson's doorway.

"—very helpful, thank you, sir." Wow, I've never heard Mrs. Henderson grovel before. "And ma'am. Such wonderful news. Thank you, yes. The board will be so grateful to hear this. We're all so relieved those police officers won't be—yes, oh god, especially that awful Detective Mendez, good grief, like a dog with a bone—oh, yes, thank you." She gives the world's fakest polite laugh. "You too. What time is it in

Jakarta? Goodness, so late. I won't take any more of your time. Good night, and thank you again."

The door swings open, and we both startle as I come face-to-face with her. She frowns when she sees me. "How long have you been skulking there, Lia?"

"I wasn't skulking," I say and try my best to look less skulky.

"Mm-hmm. Why are you here? If it's not urgent, it'll have to wait. There are about a million fires for me to put out—"

"Mandy Kim was arrested today."

She doesn't even pause. "Yes, I'm fully aware of that. Margot, how many times has Mrs. Kim called today?"

The receptionist consults her notes. "Seven."

Mrs. Henderson sighs. "If you'll excuse me, Lia..." She goes back inside her office and looks surprised when I follow. "What do you want?" Her tone is a lot less friendly.

Something is bothering me, calling to me for attention, but I can't quite put my finger on it. I shake it off and get to why I'm here. "I need to know why Mandy was arrested. The cops said something about possession of narcotics—"

"The cops have evidence of Mandy being in possession of drugs, yes. Anything else?"

"What evidence?"

"Really, Lia, it's none of your business."

"Please! I need to know." I don't know why I need to know, but something's taken hold and it's like a rabid dog, refusing to let go. "If you tell me, I'll—uh, I promise I won't breathe a word about Mr. Werner's cheating ring to anyone."

Mrs. Henderson sighs again. She sighs a lot when she's around me. "And I'm supposed to just take your word on this?"

"No," I say, hurriedly. "I'll sign a contract or whatever."

"A nondisclosure agreement? I'm quite sure any hastily drawn up makeshift agreement won't be recognized in a court of law." She shakes her head and shrugs a little. "But there's no reason for me not to tell you. It'll get out sooner or later."

I lean forward, mouth slightly open.

"The cops did a swab of the girls' changing room at the gym and found traces of narcotics in Mandy's locker."

I blink. Oh. Shit. So that's why. They must've done another search after the incident at Sam's party, and this time, they did swabs, and…

My plan worked.

I have never felt so incredibly awful in my entire life. In a daze, I leave Mrs. Henderson's office and walk back to Mather. I'd thought—I don't know. I don't actually know what I was thinking. That framing Mandy would make my life a lot easier? That it was just tit for tat? I mean, she was technically trying to place the blame for Mr. Werner's death on me. I was just trying to protect myself.

But wow. I did not foresee feeling this sick, like my insides have rotted, and if a surgeon were to open me up right now, they'd see that everything's black and decomposing. And that sense that I'm missing something important is still burrowing its way through my guts. When I get to my room, I bury my face in my pillow and scream everything out. That look on Mandy's face when the cops led her away. And the crime they charged her with—assault with narcotics. They're charging her for Stacey's overdose. Everything inside me twists painfully at the thought. This is not what I planned. This is—I know my whole plan was awful, but now that it's come true—god, I feel sick. I need to tell someone. The truth is escaping, wriggling out of me like some fat worm.

I need to make this right. I'll go to the cops, I'll tell them every—okay, maybe not everything, not about Mr. Werner, but I'll tell them about the drugs. And before that, I'll tell Danny—

Danny.

My stomach twists painfully. That dark, sharp sensation, the one that whispers of something wrong, something rotten, resurfaces. And I can't hide from it anymore.

Because the past few nights, as I doom-scrolled through DD, there was one picture that had caught my attention. One photo that I kept coming back to without quite understanding why. It was an innocuous photo of the two Aidens midcheer, brandishing their cocktails. Nothing suspicious about that. But my hand ignores the rest of my brain and I watch as my thumb scrolls through DD and locates that photo. I tap on it—nothing weird, nothing to see—and expand it. And there, in the background, standing in front of the drinks table, his back to the camera—

All the breath is wrenched out of me.

It didn't sink in before, probably because my consciousness wouldn't let it, but I'm letting it out now, in its raw, ugly form.

When I'd overheard Mrs. Henderson talking to someone on the phone, groveling, she'd asked what time it was in Jakarta. Jakarta, Indonesia. Where Danny's family still lives. His powerful, wealthy family.

It all crashes into place with horrible finality. Danny's anger. How pale and cold and angry he had been the past few weeks, how he had isolated himself. And how he'd come out of that so quickly as though by magic. Or maybe it was because he had formulated a plan and was carrying it out. Danny, who's never been that into parties, nudging Sam into throwing one on her yacht. Danny, always ready with drinks and bottled water at the party. So helpful, I'd thought then. So sweet and considerate. I was so lucky to have him. And then Stacey ended up in a coma, and Danny's parents got the cops to close the case.

I need to call the cops. Call Mendez. And say what?

I'm missing the why. Why would Danny have done all that? Why would he want to do that to Stacey? What's she ever done to him?

I'm breathing so hard, I feel like I might pass out. Why would he—

Stacey's voice whispers in my head. *You know I'll always have your back, right? No matter what you've done.* My vision swims as tears spill out. I—did she know? Did Stacey know all along that I killed Mr. Werner? Did Danny do something to her because of it? But it made no sense why he would.

I don't have a choice. I'm on my own now. I have to do this. For Stacey. For Mandy. For myself. I need to find out what exactly Danny's done.

CHAPTER 32

My stomach continues wringing itself like a towel as I crawl through the Narnia hole. I try to calm myself down, reminding myself to breathe, taking a long inhale, but the crisp, cold air feels like knives in my lungs, and I cough it out.

My phone rings, shattering the silence and nearly giving me a heart attack, but it's only Beth. Weird that she's calling instead of texting. I hit Accept, and Beth's face fills the screen. She's laughing and babbling incoherently.

"What's going on?"

"—awake!" Beth cries, flapping.

"What?"

"She's awake!" Beth aims her phone from her face toward

a bed. A hospital bed. With Stacey in it. And Stacey is indeed awake, blinking at me.

Her mouth quirks up into the sardonic smile I know so well, and she says, weakly, "'Sup, loser."

I gasp. "Stacey. Oh my god. Do you—should I come over?"

"Nah, don't bother," Stacey says. "I'm pooped, and visiting hours are over in five. Um." She turns to look at Beth. "Not that I'm saying you should leave, Beth. But like, why are you here again?"

"Oh!" Beth says. "I just came to, um. Um. To see you?"

"Is it because you wanted to make sure your drugs didn't kill me?"

Beth and I both gasp. "You knew?" we say at the same time.

Stacey rolls her eyes. "That Beth's a drug lord? I know everything about everyone, when will you people learn this?"

"But how come you never told—" Beth says.

"I don't know. Because it's none of my business. Because you always seemed so stressed out. Maybe I should've. Stop doing it, okay?"

I don't see Beth's reaction, but Stacey gives a small smile. "Okay, talk to you two kids tomorrow. Turn off the lights when you go, will you?"

"I'll see you tomorrow!" I call out, and Beth waves at me and disconnects the call.

Wow.

I mean.

Just.

My breath comes out in a shaky *whoosh*. My best friend's okay. She's fine, she's as sassy as ever, and I can see her tomorrow. She's okay. Tears sting my eyes.

Footsteps crunch close and I look up to see Danny, cheeks red from the cold and hair all tousled, and my breath catches. The sight of him. It's like a punch straight to my solar plexus. It reminds me of all those times when I saw him and thought he was the most beautiful person I'd ever seen. And now he's still making me catch my breath, but for all the wrong reasons.

"You okay? You're kind of staring," he says.

"Oh, sorry." I break eye contact and stare down at my feet. But then I realize this will probably weird him out and make him realize something's off, so I look back up at him, except I can't look him in the eye, I just can't. I settle for his chin instead.

"How did the meet go?"

"I fell flat on my face and came dead last."

He laughs, then he sees my expression and stops abruptly. "You're kidding, right?"

I shake my head.

"Jesus, Lia. Are you okay?"

The concern in his voice stabs through my heart. Surely

he can't be faking that. It's so convincing. He really does care about me. Which makes this even worse somehow, that he's not just a monster, that there is a part of him that's true. "Yeah, listen, I don't really want to talk about it right now. I just—" I falter. Now that I'm right here, standing right in front of Danny, everything I thought I could just say falls apart. Every word I come up with sounds ridiculous.

"What's up?" Danny says, moving closer to me, reaching out to hold my hand. I flinch away, and he frowns.

How do I broach the subject?

Stacey. Yeah. I lift my face and look him in the eye and say, "Stacey's awake."

And there it is. I thought I was prepared for it, but in the beat of silence that follows, the glimpse of rage that I catch in Danny's eyes breaks me in two. I want to beat him, punch that beautiful face of his and shriek at him until he tells me everything.

He smiles and says, "That's great. I'm happy to hear that."

I stare at him. How does he manage to look so innocent? What's truly lurking underneath that warm smile? "Did you hear about Mandy?"

He shakes his head. "I've just been playing *Fortnite*."

"No one's messaged you?"

"Maybe? I don't know. I put my phone on silent mode."

"Then how did you get my messages?"

He suddenly looks shy. "I may have put you on my favorites list, so my phone beeps whenever you message."

Before, this would've made me melt. Now, it just makes me want to vomit all over his face.

"So, the meet?"

"It was interrupted because the cops came and arrested Mandy for drugging the drinks at Sam's party." Again, I stare hard at him, not daring to blink for fear of missing any minuscule reactions.

Danny's mouth drops open. His eyes widen. Then they narrow. He starts to say something, stops, closes his mouth. Eyes go wide again. This goes on for a while, then he finally says, "Whaaa?"

Such a great actor. It makes my skin crawl. Actually, it makes me want to rip off my skin and fling it at him. I can't back off now. I need to forge ahead. Tear that mask off. "But Mandy didn't do it, did she?"

"Huh? She didn't?"

"No, because she never even knew she had drugs in her locker."

Danny's eyebrows crash into each other. This reaction is at least genuine. "I don't get it. You just told me she did."

"No, I said she got arrested for it. But she didn't do it."

"How do you know?"

"Because I planted the drugs in her locker." Boom. There it is. My breath comes out all ragged. The truth didn't come easy; it came up clawing and ripping at my windpipe, fighting to stay inside.

"What?"

"I—she was spreading all these lies about me, making it seem like I have something to do with Mr. Werner's death, and I don't know—I got so angry, and I had to get the cops off my back, and so I looked for the drug dealer and I found them and I stole the drugs, then I thought—you know, this will shut Mandy up for a bit, so I planted the drugs in her locker and called the cops, but when they came, there were no drugs. Mandy looked so confused. She couldn't have been faking it." It's all coming out now, and there's no stopping the torrent. And now it's down to him to fill in the rest.

Danny blinks and shakes his head. Runs his fingers through his hair. "I don't understand. Wait, but. The drugs don't belong to—" He stops and shakes his head again, like he needs to clear it. "Why're you telling me all this?"

"Because I know *you* did it, Danny." The words come out as a harsh whisper. "I don't know how you got your hands on those drugs, but you did, and you drugged Stacey. Why?"

Danny laughs, a horrible, cracked sound. "You're talking crazy. You're not thinking straight. Is it 'cause you're so sad about the meet? Come on, we can talk about it."

"Stop talking about the fucking track!" I snap. "Just tell me why you did it. You drugged Stacey and then got your parents to close up the investigation, didn't you? I overheard Henderson talking to them. She was so grateful."

This time, it hits home. Danny blanches. He tries to smile, but it doesn't stick. It falls away, leaving him looking tired and broken and—

He frowns, looking at me in a different light. "Why were you so scared of what Mandy was telling the cops? I mean, sure, she spread all those rumors about you, but so what? It's not like you had anything to worry about—"

I swear I'm about to puke up my heart. "Stop trying to change the subject. Why did you do that to Stacey?"

Danny ignores the question and cocks his head to one side. I feel something shift behind his gaze, like a dark beast lurching awake. "When my uncle died, you stopped eating. You used to be all about food, and then…"

Shit. I take a step back.

"Did you have something to do with—" He chokes on the next words. Gives a weird little laugh that doesn't sound like a laugh at all.

I can't take this anymore. "Why did you do it?" I scream it so hard, the words rip us apart.

Danny laughs, and now it sounds deranged. "Why? Why do you think? Because she killed my uncle! Everyone here's out to get Uncle James. First there was Sophie, ranting about him, she had a whole freaking vendetta out against him, and I had to take care of it, and then there was Stacey, and you, and what the hell is wrong with you girls?"

"Wait." I blink, trying to sort through the jumble of

words he's just said. "Sophie?" Something dark unfurls deep in my belly. "What do you mean, you had to take care of it?"

He gives another one of those cracked laughs that sends goose bumps sprouting down my arms. "Oh, I thought you'd figured that one out too, Miss Nancy Drew." He snorts bitterly. "When my parents cut me off, I had to earn money some way, just to get by. I tried to get into the drugs business—it's so lucrative here, isn't it?—but I didn't know how to get in. The Draycott dealer didn't want any partners. I didn't even know who it was. So, in the end, I just bought a bunch of drugs from the online shop and I cut them with other stuff to bulk them up a bit, earn some money doing that."

"Cut them...what?" I whisper. No, this can't be real. I'd solved it. I'd discovered Draycott's drug dealer, and it was Beth. There wasn't supposed to be more than one dealer.

Danny shrugs. "It's not a big deal, god." He sneers at me. "Always such a suck-up, aren't you? God, can't believe I thought I was in love with you at one point. Sophie caught me dealing, and she wasn't gonna do anything about it at first, but when she got expelled because of Uncle James, she decided to take some revenge. Told me she was going to expose me as a drug dealer unless I dug some dirt up on Uncle James. You know what would've happened if she'd exposed me? That selfish bitch. Just because she'd thrown her life down the drain, she wanted to take me down with her."

I gape at him with numb horror. "How did you dose her?"

"She was such an addict by then. She never went anywhere without carrying a stash on her. I just met up with her and switched out her stash for one I'd laced. I didn't think she was gonna go nuts and break into Uncle James's office." He laughs a little. "Crazy bitch."

I feel sick, but more than everything else, I need to know what happened to Stacey. I can't not dig. I'm so close to the truth. "And what about Stacey? Why her?"

"Like I said, she was out to get my uncle. She'd done all that stuff, hacked into his computer, so I searched her room, know what I found? I found the fucking drugs, Lia." He laughs again. "I don't know how they got there after everything you've told me, but at the time, I thought *she* was the school dealer. And know what else I found? A USB drive with his name on it. She was collecting dirt on him. She wasn't hacking for fun. She was out to get him."

What? Why would she have done that? Why—

Again, those words swim through my head. *You know I'll always have your back, right? No matter what you've done.*

She knew. She knew about me killing Mr. Werner. And maybe she thought collecting dirt on him might help me somehow. Might become important evidence if I ever got caught.

"You could've killed us all," I whisper. Now that I've got the truth out of him, I feel hollowed out. This is no victory. And why is Danny so ready to spill everything? Why is he so willing to tell me every revolting act he's done? Unless maybe—

"I even came clean about Uncle James's ledger to Mrs. Henderson. All because I was in love with you. That was before I found out my girlfriend's a fucking murderer!"

I've made a mistake. I've been so wrapped up in my own heartbreak that I don't notice he's moved forward until he suddenly catches my wrist in an unforgiving grip. I cry out, but he doesn't let go.

"And all this time, while I was going nuts trying to find enough evidence to put Stacey away, it turns out it was you all along. My own fucking girlfriend." He gives a vicious yank and I stumble forward with a cry. I crash into him, his chest granite-hard and radiating a sick heat. His breath is hot in my ear. "You killed him, Lia? You killed my uncle?"

Fear slams into me. This is why. He didn't hold back, didn't bother hiding anything, because he's going to kill me. "Let me go."

His grip on my wrist tightens so hard, it makes me yelp. I swing my other arm back to hit him, but he catches it easily, as though I were a child. I can't fight him, not in this state, not when I can barely stand without my legs quivering.

"Why?" he says, his eyes bright with tears. "Why'd you do it?"

"I didn't mean to. I only wanted to—I just. I wanted to talk."

Danny shakes me and my head snaps back like a whip. "Don't lie to me."

"I was going to blackmail him!" I cry. "Okay? He was making me fail his class, and I tried to blackmail him, and he took me to Orange Point and tried to kill me. I ran away. He came after me. We struggled—" The memory of it flashes in broken, jagged pieces through my mind. The shock of Mr. Werner's weight on me. The animal struggle. "I pushed him, and he fell on that—that thing. I didn't mean to kill him. I really—" I'm still talking, but the words aren't coming out.

Danny's wrapped his hands around my throat, and there's no pain, but the words aren't coming out and I don't understand it and I can't breathe, and I ask him to let go, but nothing comes out and the edges of my vision get fuzzy, and I don't know what's going on. I claw at his hands, but they're solid steel and my hands may as well be seaweed flopping at him, and as they fall, they catch on something.

My necklace. The kris pendant. Me joking to Ibu that one day the cap will come off without me knowing it and I'll accidentally stab myself. I rip it off. Only the size of my pink finger. It won't do any good. But I don't have any other choice. Stars burst in my vision and black spills out of them. Quickly now. My fingers are sausages. Danny's face is red, his teeth gritted, his eyes that of a beast. I don't recognize the boy I love. My fingers scrabble at my necklace and rip the chain off my neck. I pull off the cap. Unsheathe the blade. He doesn't notice. I will the last dregs of energy I have and push my hand forward. Everything goes dark.

I thud to the ground. Air rushes in, sparkling, cold, electrifying. I gasp it in, cough it out, gulp more in. Light filters through my eyes, crowding out the black stars. I look up, and Danny's just standing there, staring at the tiny dagger sticking out of his midsection. It looks ridiculous, so small, too small to be of any consequence, but when Danny pulls it, a thin stream of blood pours out.

"You bitch!" he roars.

I scramble up to my feet and run. Just as I'd feared, the dagger's too small to do any real damage, but it's bought me a few more precious seconds. My windpipe still feels like it's crushed, and I can't seem to catch my breath, but I push myself to move my legs. Run as fast as I can. Run like a hunted rabbit. Behind me, I hear Danny's ragged breathing. I reach the Narnia hole and pounce, crawling through the dark space. Something closes around my ankle. I shriek and kick back frantically. My left shoe connects with something and I hear Danny's curse. I kick again, and the grip loosens. I squeeze through the hole, coming out the other side at last, and don't spare a second to look behind me before I dash toward the buildings ahead.

I don't even realize I'm screaming until doors open and people come running out toward me. Someone appears in front of me, and I collapse into their arms, and dimly, I hear them asking, "What's happening? Are you okay?"

It's over. There are enough people about now that Danny can't possibly hurt me like he meant to. I turn my head now, and I'm right. He's just standing there, holding the wound in his stomach, and he looks defeated, the furious light going from his eyes, leaving him sagging. He's no longer recognizable to me.

As I open my mouth to answer, a myriad if-onlys spin in the air, glittering with a thousand different possible outcomes.

If only he hadn't sat on evidence of Mr. Werner's cheating ring.

If only Mrs. Henderson had believed me when I told her about the cheating ring.

If only I hadn't snuck into Mr. Werner's car.

And, of course, the last one: If only I hadn't come to Draycott in the first place.

But we all made the choices we made, and every lie that slips out of our mouths brings us that much closer to this moment in time, with my boyfriend and I standing in front of the whole school, phone cameras out, every single one of them aimed toward us.

It's forever before red and blue fill the sky, and our Narnia hole swarms with cops and paramedics, and they take the boy I love away.

EPILOGUE

THREE MONTHS LATER

"Ready for the surprise?" Stacey says.

I shrug.

"Stop fiddling with your monitor."

I look up from my ankle. "Easy for you to say, you're not the one who has to wear one of these twenty-four/seven." Though I can't complain overmuch. In the end, it all worked out sort of okay for me. Well, for a given value of okay, anyway. I'm not in prison, for one. The cops still don't know much about Mr. Werner's death, and after the freakishly huge mess of a case, all the school's benefactors—Danny's parents included—have swooped down and called in all of the favors they can call in, and the case got shut down before anyone could say, "Drugs?"

I'd waited, in excruciating anxiety, for Danny to tell the

cops how I'd killed his uncle. I'd waited for them to come charging into my room and arrest me. But days passed, and nothing happened. And it became clear, then, that Danny hadn't told anyone. Probably because he realized that if he did, I would tell them that he'd killed Sophie, and he would be put away for actual murder, something which even his affluent parents wouldn't be able to wipe away.

For days after that realization, I grappled with my own conscience, wondering if I should tell the cops that Danny had killed Sophie. But in the end, my own selfish needs and sense of self-preservation overcame everything else. I don't want to battle Danny. I just want to move on from all of this.

In the end, nothing could be pinned on me, not without Danny coming clean. The cops slapped Mandy with a one-year probation and moved on to other cases. Who knows, maybe I'll get another shot at Stanford, though to be honest, the thought no longer lights the same kind of fire it used to inside me. The thought of being in a school full of rich, entitled kids has lost its appeal to me.

I sigh and shake my head. "I'm not in the mood for a surprise."

"Aw, come on, don't be such a wet rag, I worked on it all through Christmas break."

"Pretty sure it's wet blanket and not wet rag."

Stacey stares at me. "Why would a blanket be wet? That doesn't make any sense."

"Why would a rag be wet?"

"Because you wet it under the tap before you use it to wipe down the table."

I take a deep breath. "As riveting as this conversation is, what's the surprise you wanted to show me?"

Stacey's face splits into a huge smile, her eyes shining, and despite the gray haze that's blanketed me the past three months, despite the nightmares and the crying and the too much of everything, I can't help but smile back at her. Because every day, I thank the universe she's still here, alive, next to me. And Stacey's not above using that to get her way, the asshole.

"How are things going with Laura?"

"Don't change the subject," she scolds, but she can't hold back the smile from taking over her face. A month ago, she started dating someone from the robotics club, and they're painfully adorable together. They've even got matching blue streaks in their hair now. Laura's all right—she treats Stacey like the queen she is and, unlike everyone else at Draycott, doesn't ever bother asking me for details about Danny.

"Behold," she declares, brandishing her laptop at me with a flourish.

"What am I looking at?"

"God, you caveman. This is an HTML code. Now, if you'd come forward and hit the Enter key…"

I narrow my eyes at the screen, trying to make sense of the jumble of symbols and numbers, but I may as well be reading an alien language. The last line says: <Execute?> The cursor blinks expectantly at me. I'm too tired to argue with Stacey, so I hit Enter. The screen scrolls up by itself and is replaced with balloons and streamers and confetti. The words *YAY! You did it!* appear.

"Sorry, that's just a little effect I added for your benefit," Stacey says. "Laura suggested it."

"What did I just do?"

"Open Draycott Dirt."

I groan. "Do I have to?" The past few months, it's all been about Danny, excited, scandalized whispers about Danny in juvie, Danny's parents scrambling to pay the right people to get him out, Danny who apparently tried to kill his girlfriend, Danny, Danny, Danny. And, of course, about me, the evil parasite-slut-whore-witch-bitch who corrupted Danny the golden boy and pushed him into trying to kill me.

"Trust me," Stacey says, and her voice is soft, her face earnest. And I do. There's no one I trust more than her. So I take out my phone and click on the Dirt app icon. I brace myself for the onslaught of notifications of people tagging me in hateful posts, but there's only one new post, pinned to the top of the page.

Posted by: @SiliconBrains

Hiii assholes! Guess what? I broke the app. Oops!

Why did I do it? Because it's nothing but a

cesspool of—okay, you guys know exactly what the app is. Anyway, so I broke it. And I'm sorry but I'm totally one hundo percent NOT sorry, betches. Go out and enjoy the sunlight or whatever. Get a fucking LIFE. Bye!

A smile spreads across my face, slow like honey. Just as I finish reading Stacey's message, a window pops up on the screen, and I can't help but laugh.

Warning: App is unstable and might corrupt your device. Please uninstall and reboot your device.

ACKNOWLEDGMENTS

Thank you, as always, to my husband Mike, who is an unwavering source of support and encouragement. Without your help, I would have given up writing approximately ten years ago. Thank you for watching the kids so I could do anything and everything writing-related.

A big thank-you goes to Uwe Stender, for believing in me as a writer and for being one of the first people to read the early iteration of this book so many years ago. Over the next few years, the novel changed from *Sharp Edges*, to *Dirt*, to *The New Girl*, and through it all, Uwe was stoic in his belief that it was a story worth being told.

I'm so happy and grateful for the team at Sourcebooks who has made my journey with *The Obsession* and *The*

New Girl so incredible. Annie Berger, my editor, can always be relied on to give valuable, sharp, and brilliant feedback. Thank you also to Cassie Gutman and Jackie Douglass.

My menagerie family, as I call them, is my chosen family. I love each and every one of you so much: S. L. Huang, Toria Hegedus, Maddox Hahn, Tilly Latimer, Rob Livermore, Elaine Aliment, Lani Frank, Emma Maree, and Mel Melcer.

To the folks at Absolute Write, a place where I learned so much about publishing and writing: MacAllister, Lisa, Calla, and Nicole Lesperance have all made my stay at AW so wonderful and brilliant.

To my family, especially Mama and Papa, for being so proud of me, for always telling me to dream big. Thank you for showing me off to your friends; it is just so massively adorable seeing how much pride there is!

And of course, to my dear readers, thank you so much for sticking with me through my publishing journey. Thank you for reading my books and leaving reviews and posting about them. All of your messages have meant so much to me, and I will cherish all of your words.

ABOUT THE AUTHOR

Photo © Michael Hart

Jesse Q. Sutanto grew up shuttling back and forth between Indonesia, Singapore, and Oxford, and considers all three places her home. She has a master's from Oxford University but has yet to figure out how to say that without sounding obnoxious. She has forty-two first cousins and thirty aunties and uncles, many of whom live just down the road. She used to game, but with two little ones and a husband, she no longer has time for hobbies. Jesse aspires to one day have enough time for one (1) hobby. She is the author of *Dial A for Aunties*, *The Obsession*, and *The New Girl*.

DON'T MISS

ANOTHER PAGE-TURNING THRILLER
FROM BESTSELLING AUTHOR
JESSE Q. SUTANTO

Your hub for the hottest young adult books!

Visit us online and sign up for our newsletter at FIREreads.com

 @sourcebooksfire

 sourcebooksfire

 firereads.tumblr.com